78 MPH

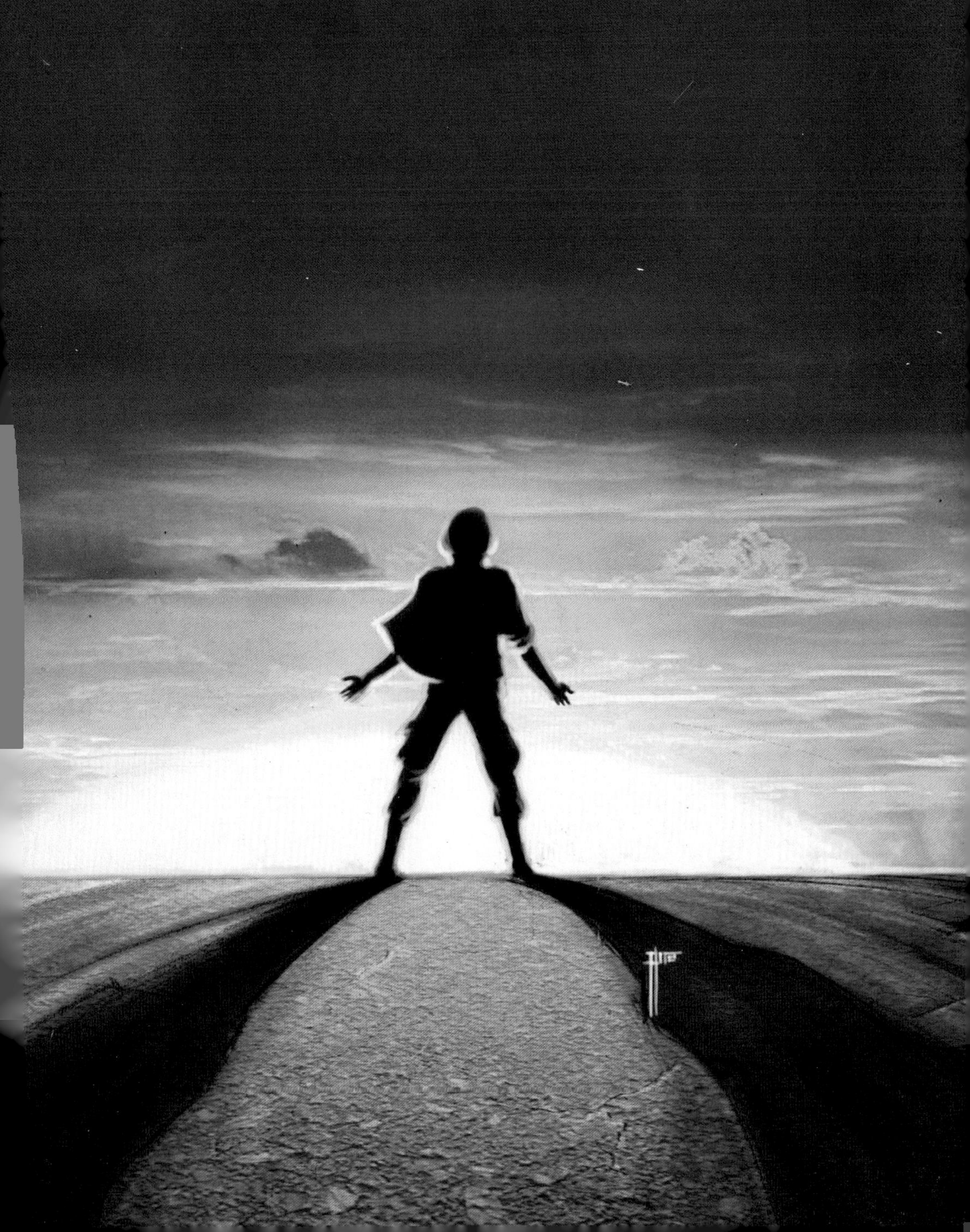

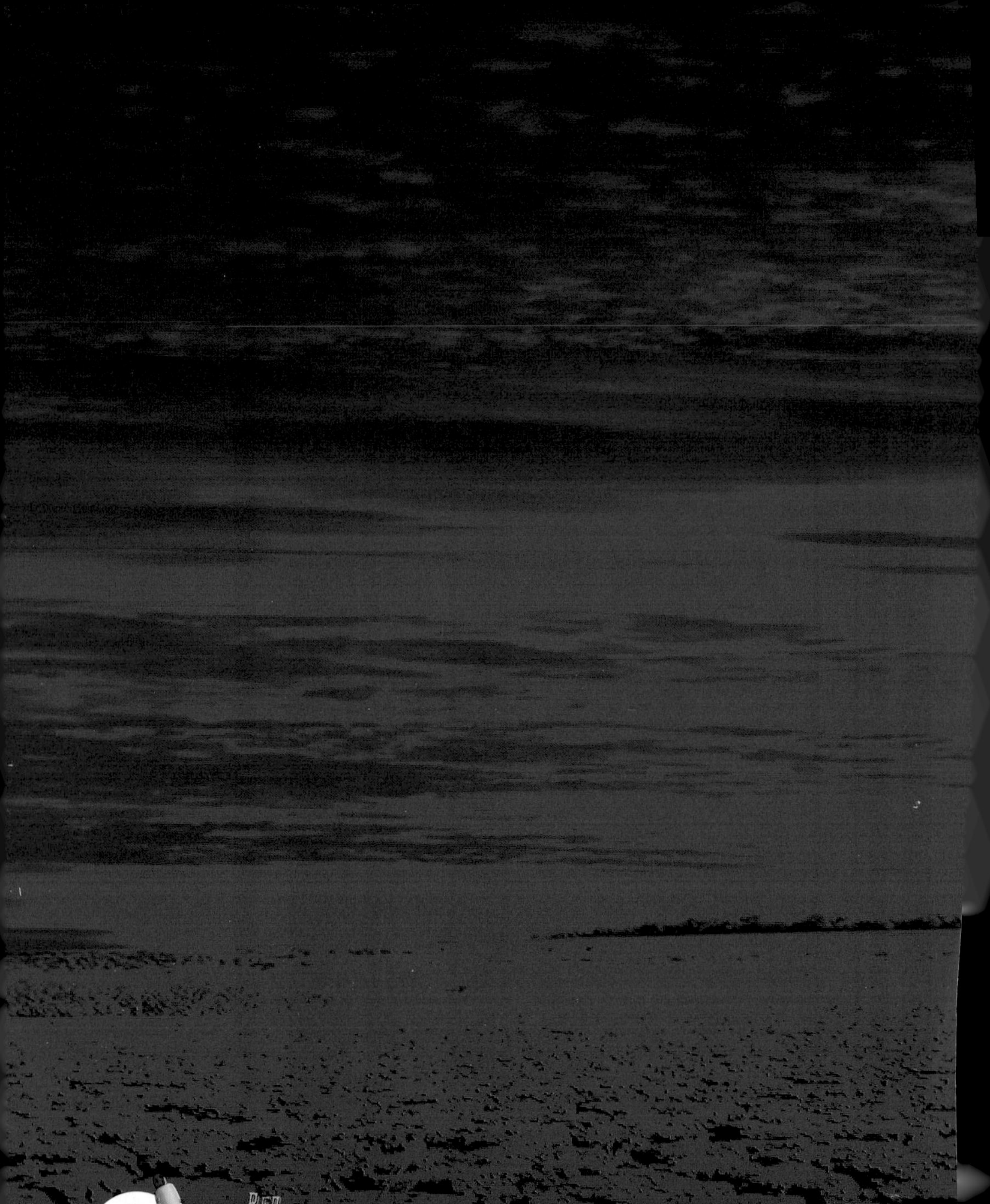

RED 5 COMICS: Paul Ens, Scott Chitwood, Joshua Starnes.
STONEBOT COMICS: Matias Timarchi, Diego Barassi, Martín Casanova, Chris Ortega, Rodrigo Molina.
Revision: Sara Lindsay, Leandro Paolini Somers & Chris Ortega
Special thanks to Germán Erramouspe

78 MPH, September 2022. First printing. Published by Red 5 Comics, Ltd., 27103 Kelsey Woods Court, Cypress, TX, 77433. Printed in Canada at Marquis.

78 MPH

MAURO MANTELLA
SCRIPT

TOMÁS AIRA
ART

GERMÁN NOBILE
COLOR

ALTERCOMICS STUDIO
LETTERING

GERMÁN PERALTA
COVERS

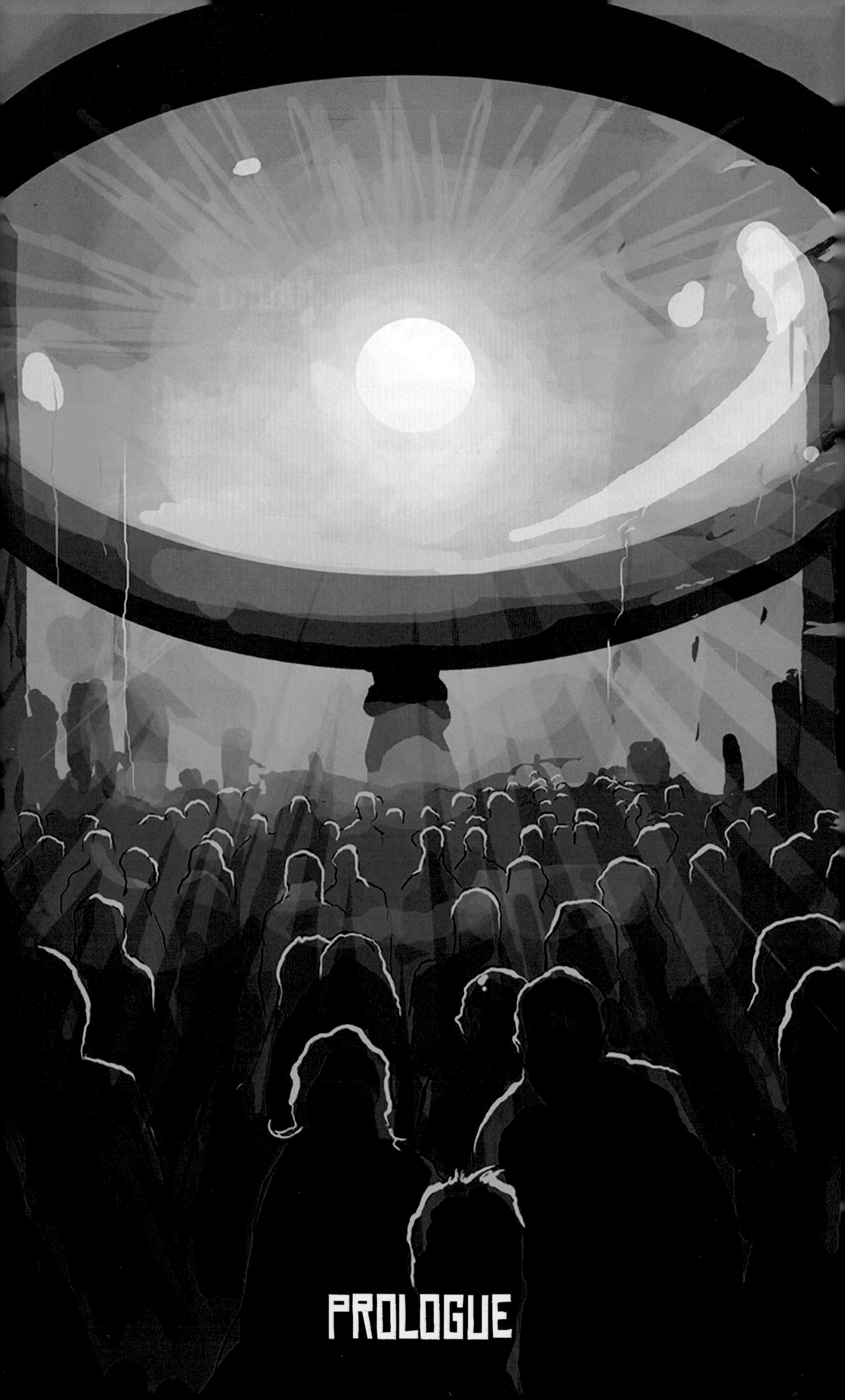

PROLOGUE

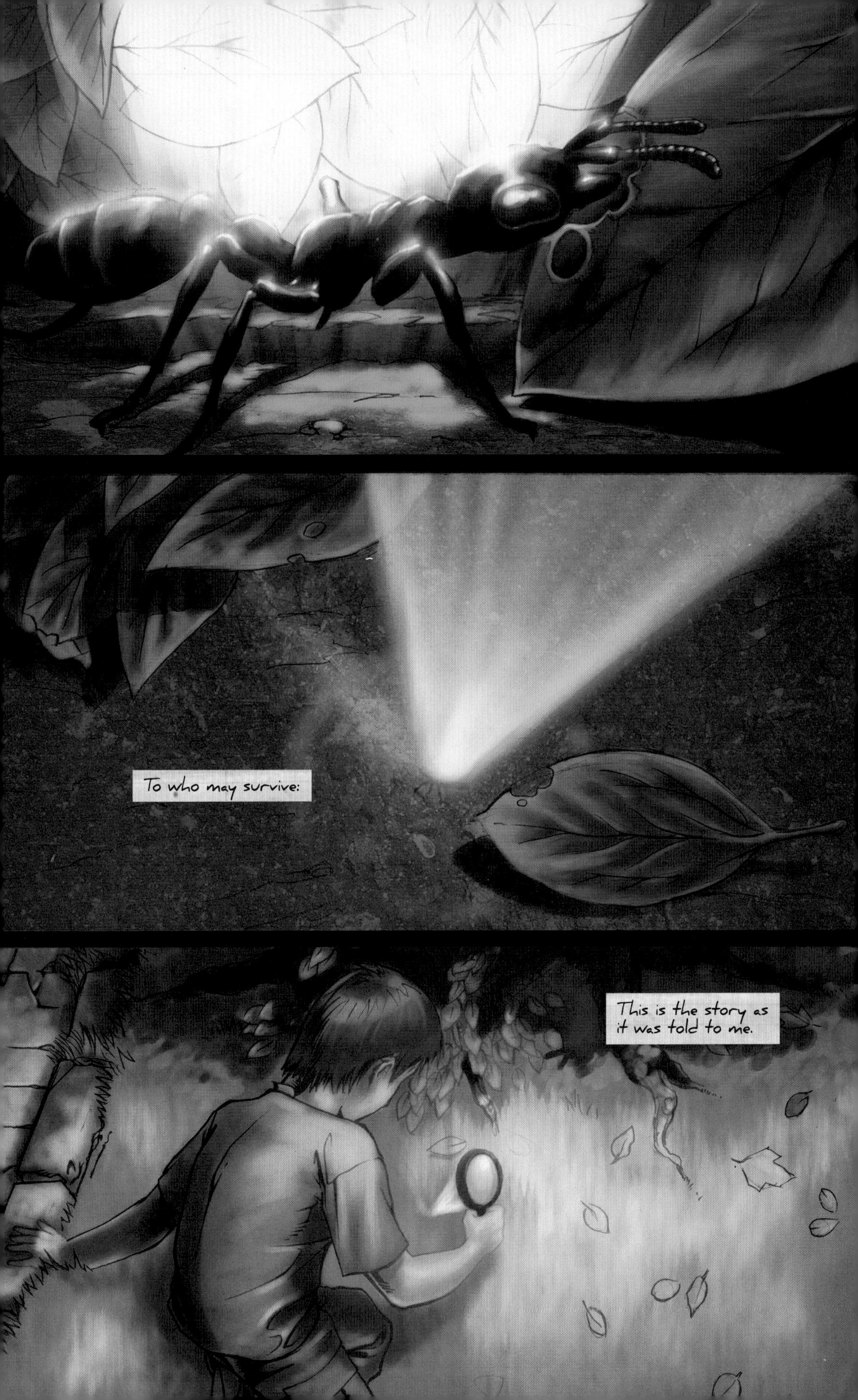
To who may survive:
This is the story as it was told to me.

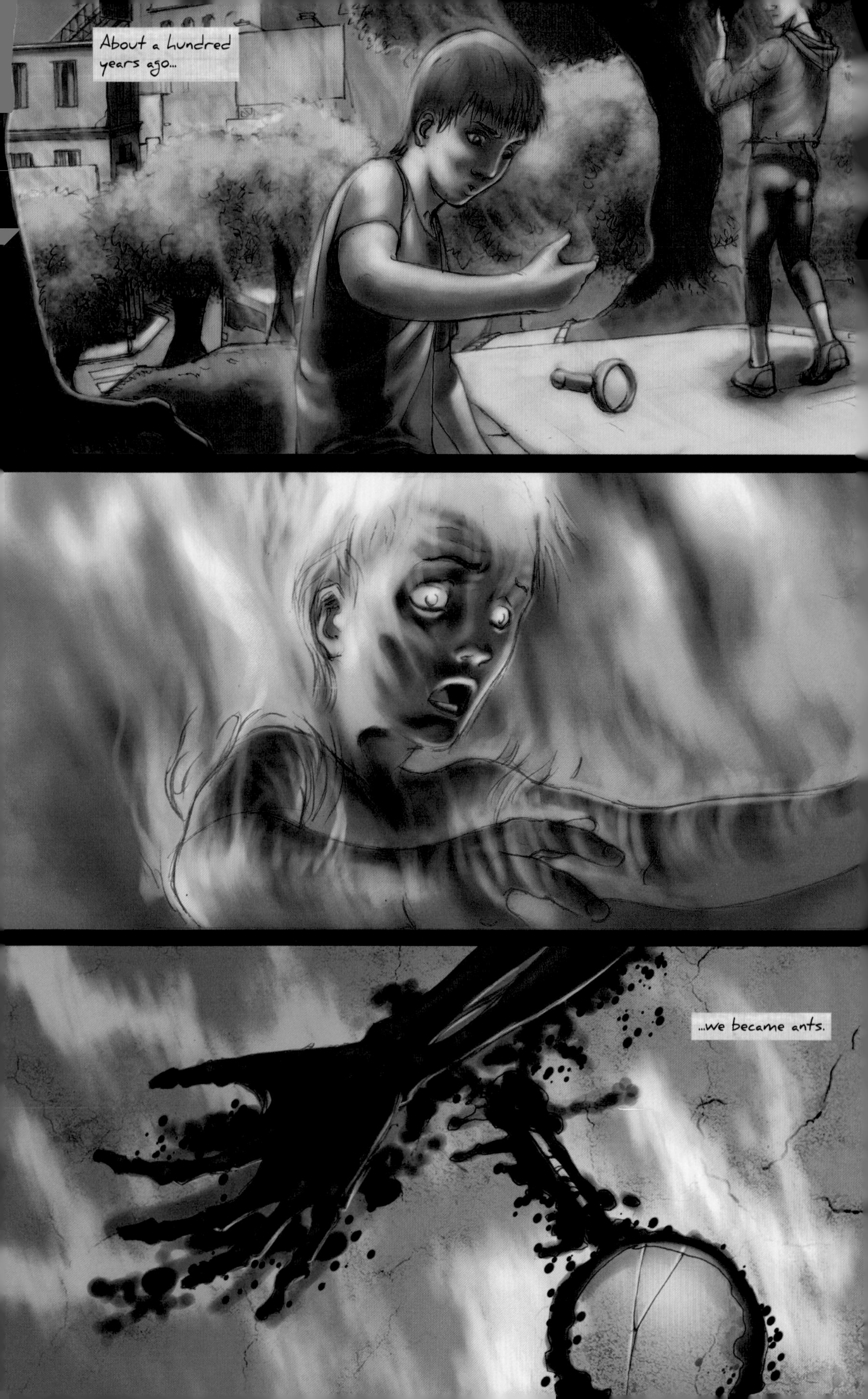
About a hundred years ago...
...we became ants.

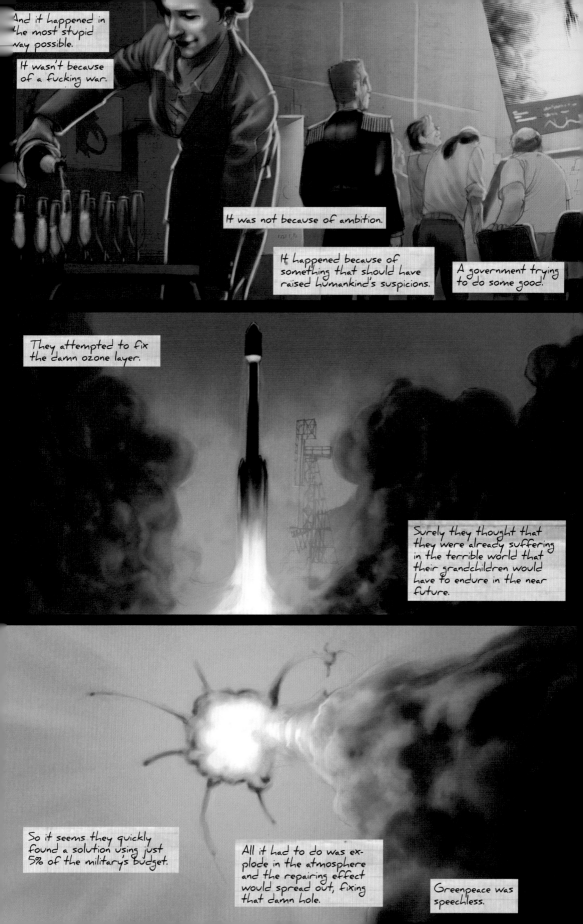

And it happened in the most stupid way possible.

It wasn't because of a fucking war.

It was not because of ambition.

It happened because of something that should have raised humankind's suspicions.

A government trying to do some good.

They attempted to fix the damn ozone layer.

Surely they thought that they were already suffering in the terrible world that their grandchildren would have to endure in the near future.

So it seems they quickly found a solution using just 5% of the military's budget.

All it had to do was explode in the atmosphere and the repairing effect would spread out, fixing that damn hole.

Greenpeace was speechless.

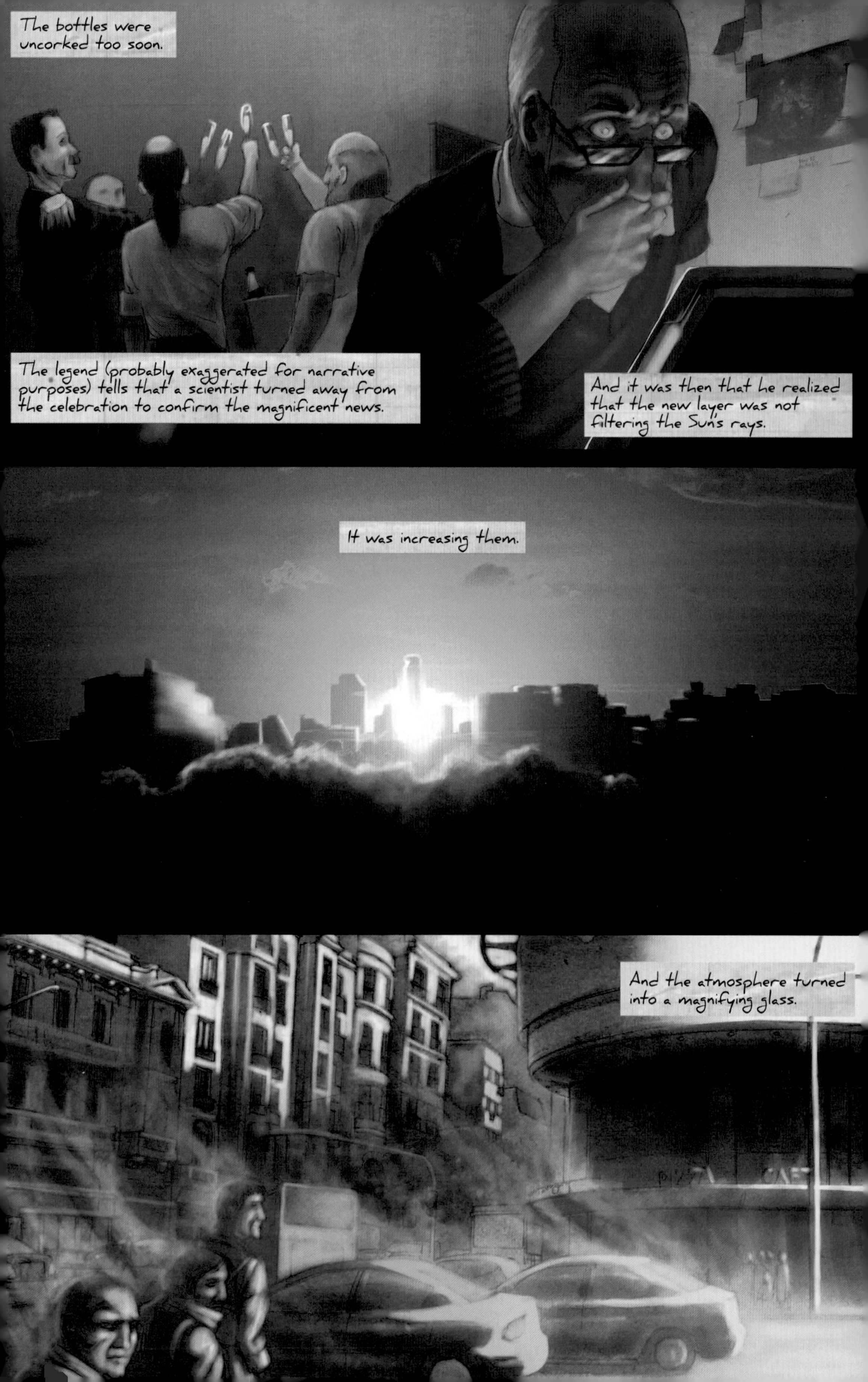
The bottles were uncorked too soon.
The legend (probably exaggerated for narrative purposes) tells that a scientist turned away from the celebration to confirm the magnificent news.
And it was then that he realized that the new layer was not filtering the Sun's rays.
It was increasing them.
And the atmosphere turned into a magnifying glass.

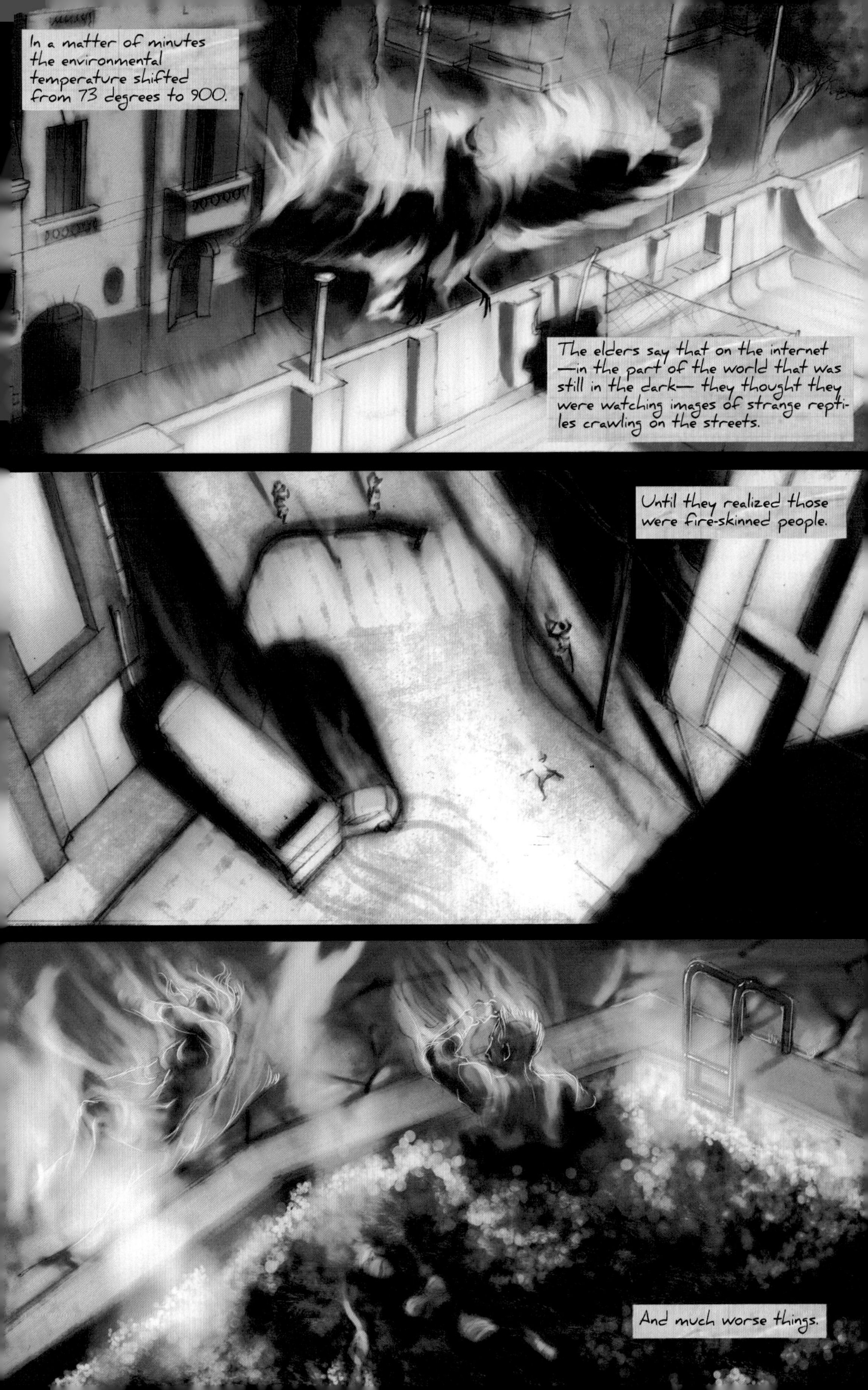
In a matter of minutes the environmental temperature shifted from 73 degrees to 900.
The elders say that on the internet —in the part of the world that was still in the dark— they thought they were watching images of strange reptiles crawling on the streets.
Until they realized those were fire-skinned people.
And much worse things.

Nobody knows which one or why, but some nation decided to launch its complete nuclear arsenal at the nation responsible for the planetary tragedy.

As if the Earth didn't have enough fire.

But the missiles did not fly.

An unthinkable mistake happened when activating those armaments— they ignited all of them at the same time in their underground base.

A thermonuclear explosion beyond imagination that almost took the planet out of its orbit.

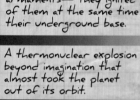

And that was what saved us.

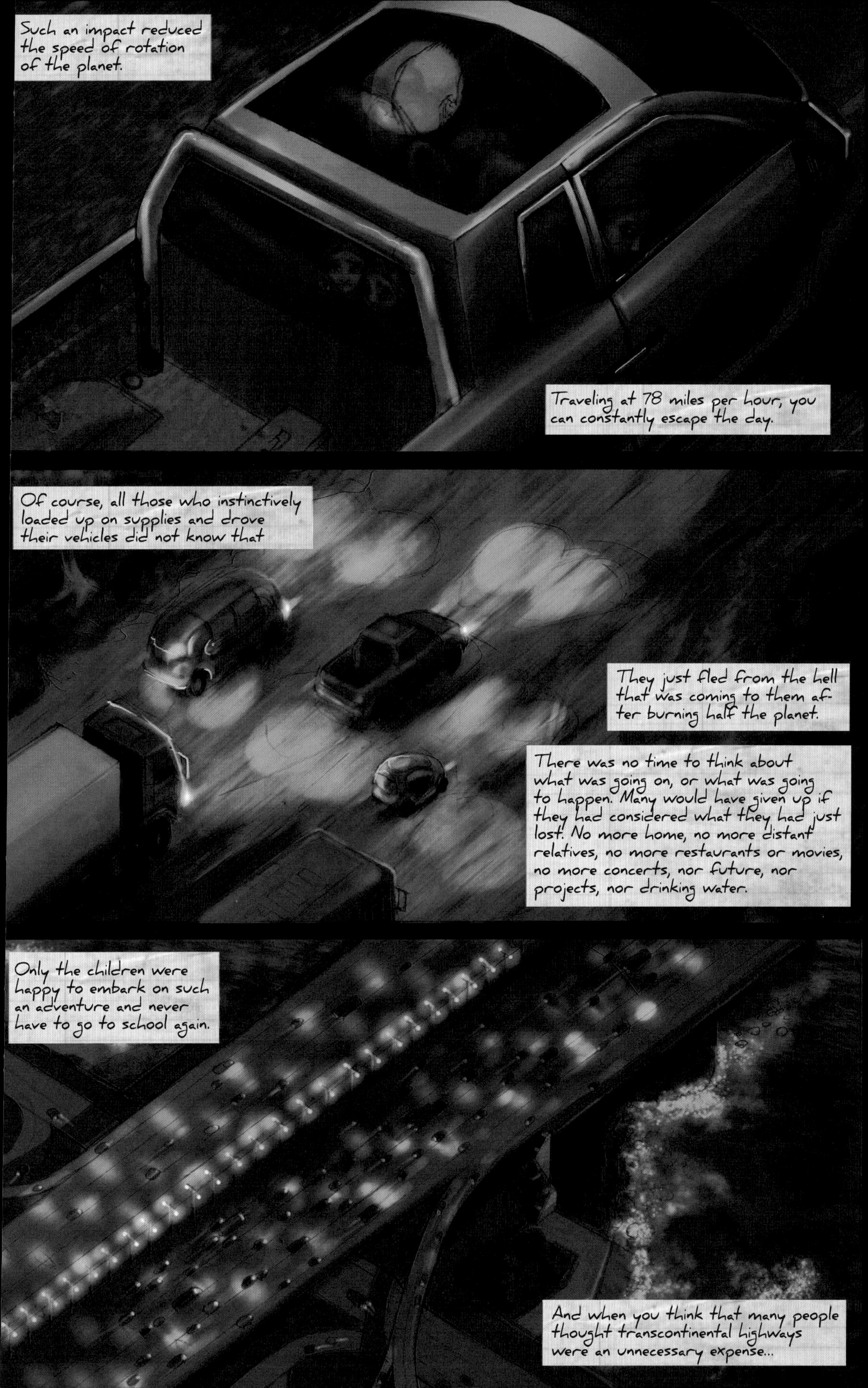
Such an impact reduced the speed of rotation of the planet.
Traveling at 78 miles per hour, you can constantly escape the day.
Of course, all those who instinctively loaded up on supplies and drove their vehicles did not know that
They just fled from the hell that was coming to them after burning half the planet.
There was no time to think about what was going on, or what was going to happen. Many would have given up if they had considered what they had just lost. No more home, no more distant relatives, no more restaurants or movies, no more concerts, nor future, nor projects, nor drinking water.
Only the children were happy to embark on such an adventure and never have to go to school again.
And when you think that many people thought transcontinental highways were an unnecessary expense...

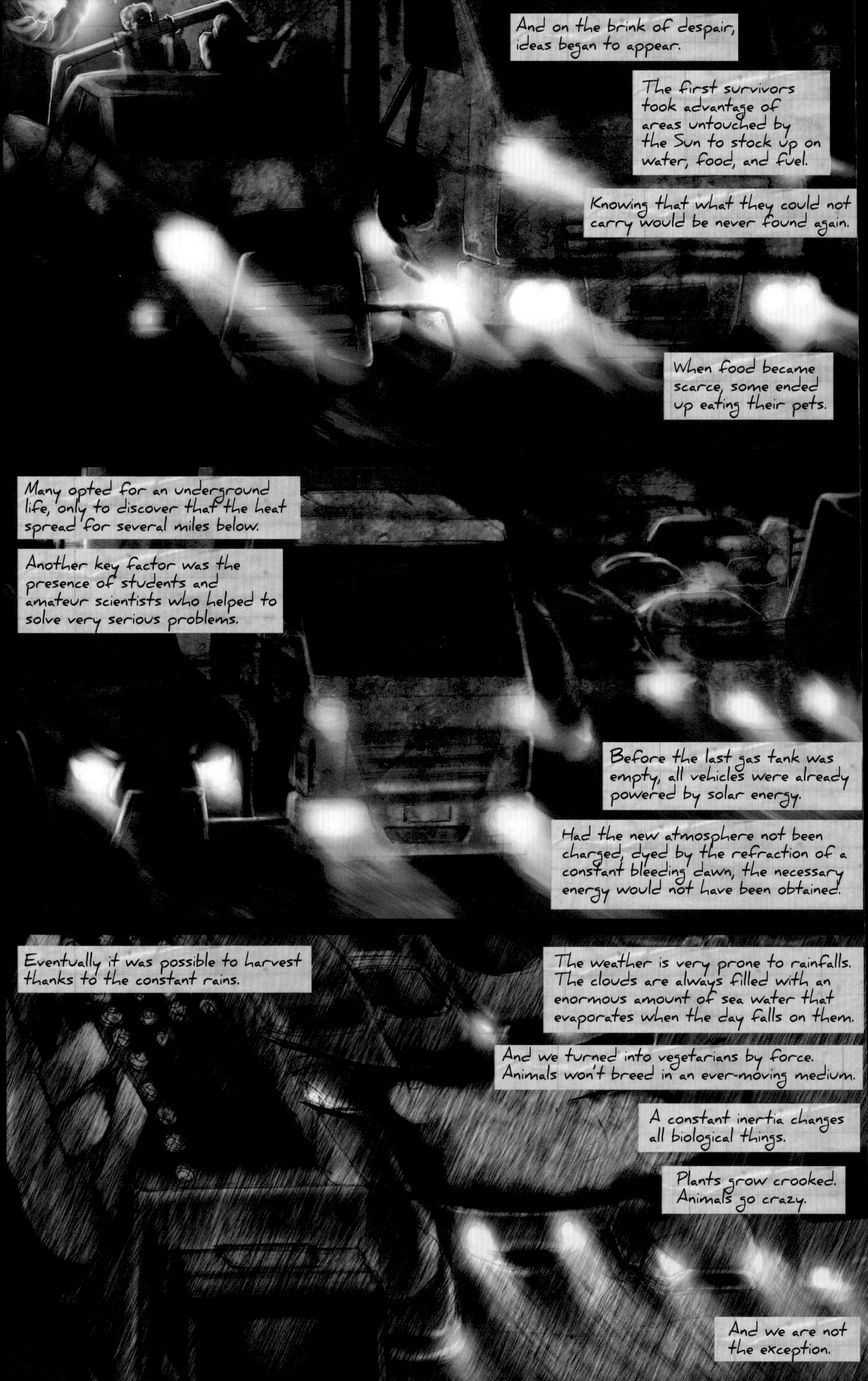
And on the brink of despair, ideas began to appear.
The first survivors took advantage of areas untouched by the Sun to stock up on water, food, and fuel.
Knowing that what they could not carry would be never found again.
When food became scarce, some ended up eating their pets.
Many opted for an underground life, only to discover that the heat spread for several miles below.
Another key factor was the presence of students and amateur scientists who helped to solve very serious problems.
Before the last gas tank was empty, all vehicles were already powered by solar energy.
Had the new atmosphere not been charged, dyed by the refraction of a constant bleeding dawn, the necessary energy would not have been obtained.
Eventually it was possible to harvest thanks to the constant rains.
The weather is very prone to rainfalls. The clouds are always filled with an enormous amount of sea water that evaporates when the day falls on them.
And we turned into vegetarians by force. Animals won't breed in an ever-moving medium.
A constant inertia changes all biological things.
Plants grow crooked. Animals go crazy.
And we are not the exception.

The children do not know what stillness is.

Some believe that we are motionless and that the road is the one moving.

I still remember the horrible dizziness that almost made me faint when the Salamander II stopped for the first time.

Except for the elders, the others had never seen the Sun.

And we cannot understand how an incandescent sphere located 93 million miles away can cook us to death.

There are those who believe that it is actually a monster or a fire-eyed demon that kills everything it sees.

I do believe that it is a sphere.

But one that rolls over the Earth annihilating everything in its path.

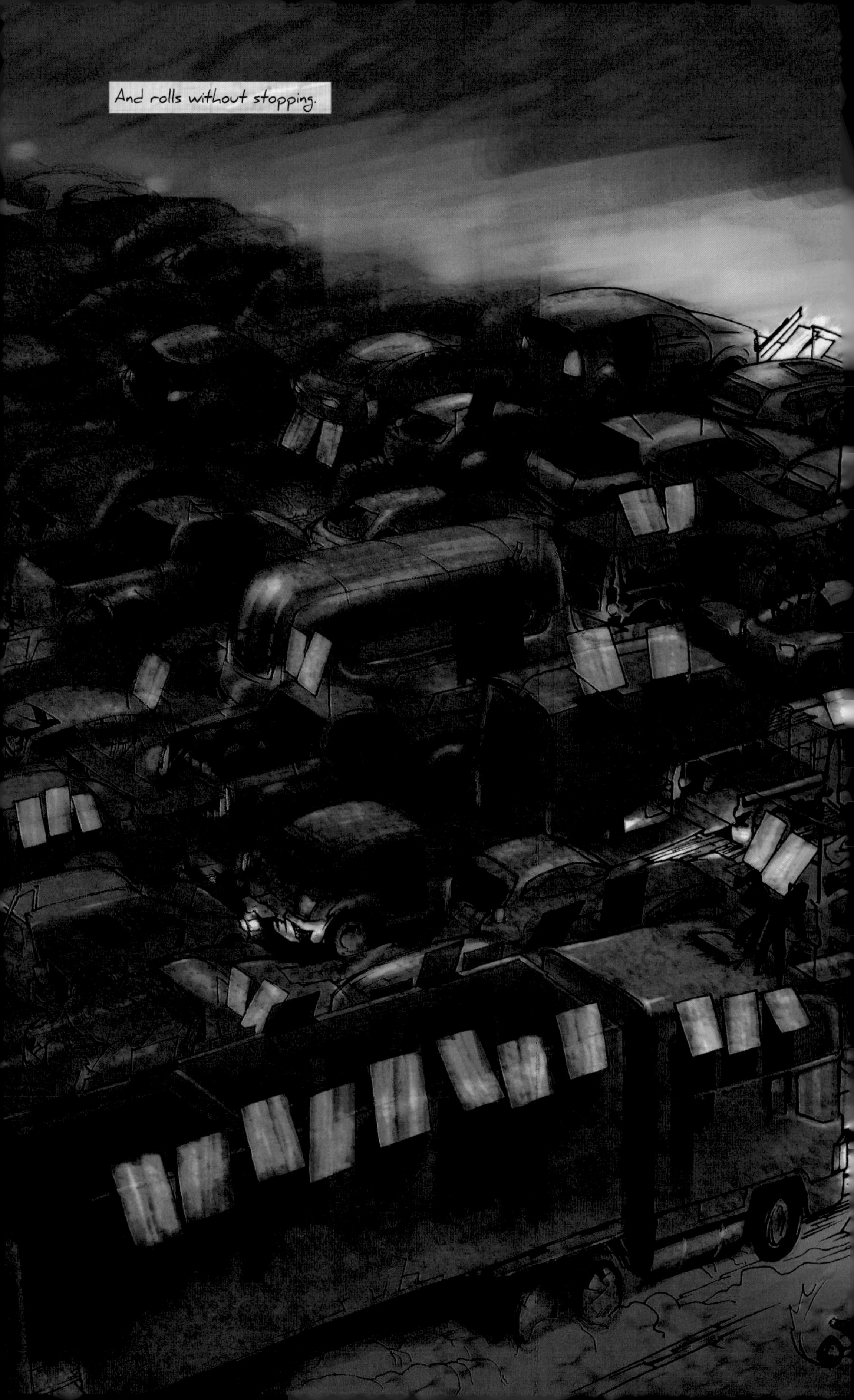
And rolls without stopping.

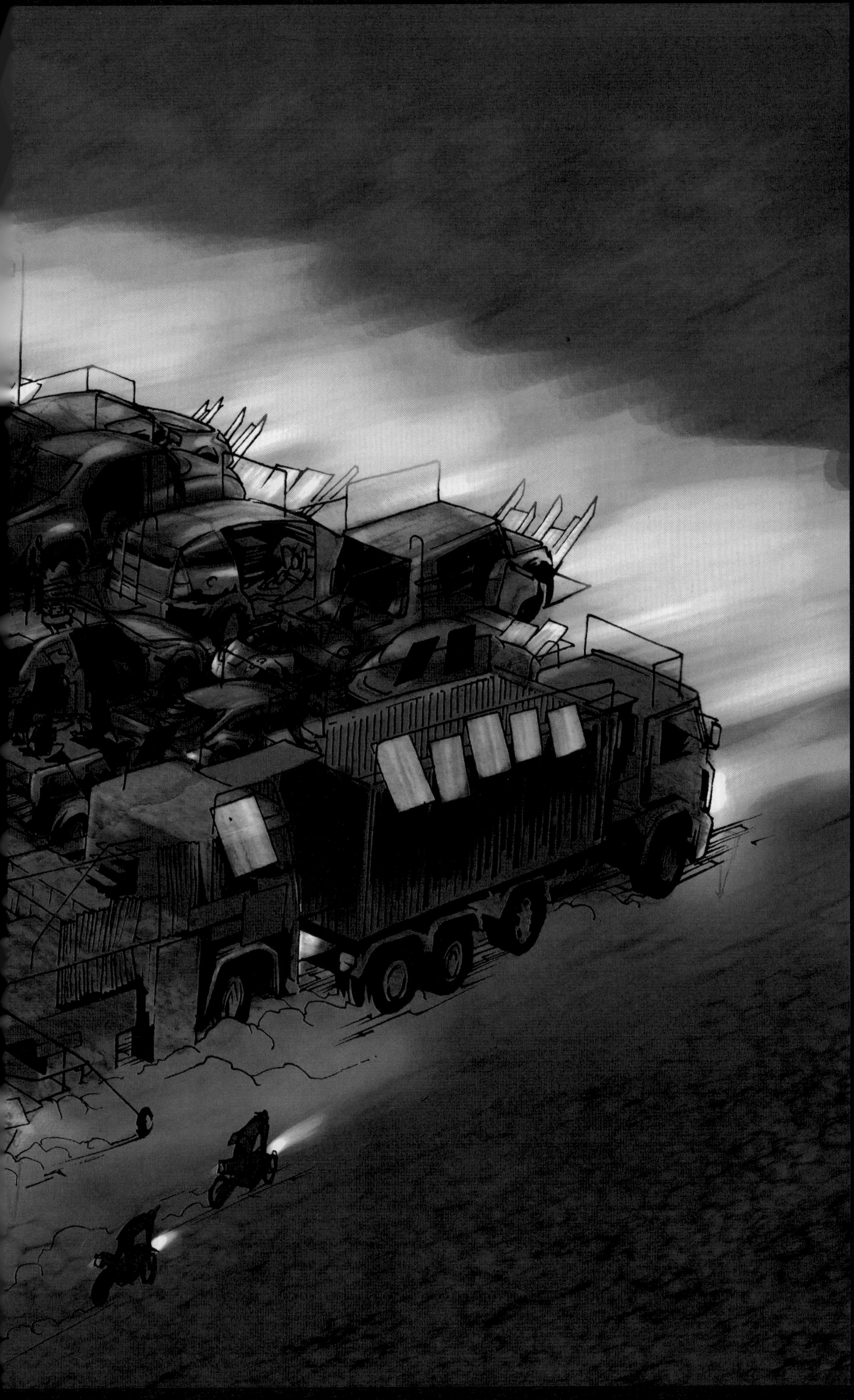

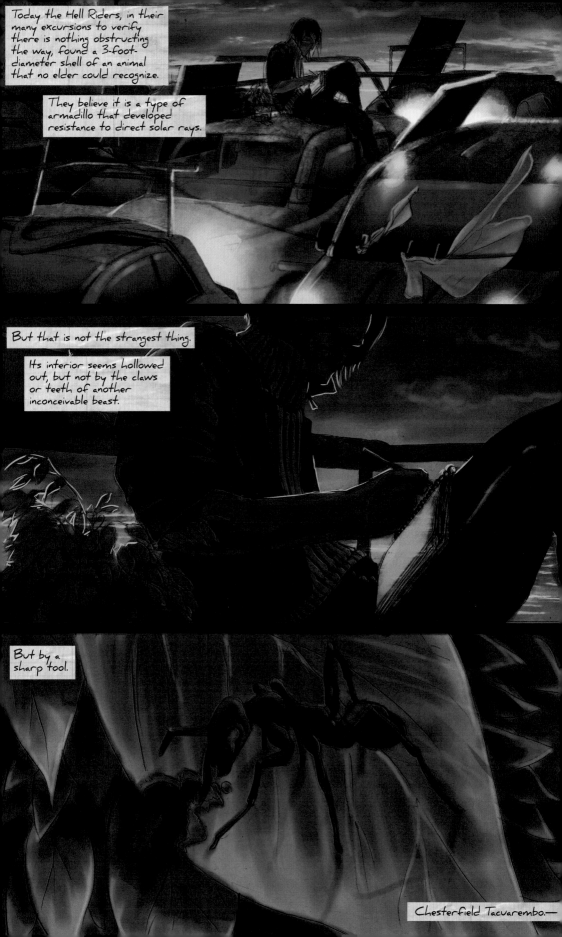

Today the Hell Riders, in their many excursions to verify there is nothing obstructing the way, found a 3-foot-diameter shell of an animal that no elder could recognize.

They believe it is a type of armadillo that developed resistance to direct solar rays.

But that is not the strangest thing.

Its interior seems hollowed out, but not by the claws or teeth of another inconceivable beast.

But by a sharp tool.

Chesterfield Tacuarembo.—

CHAPTER 1

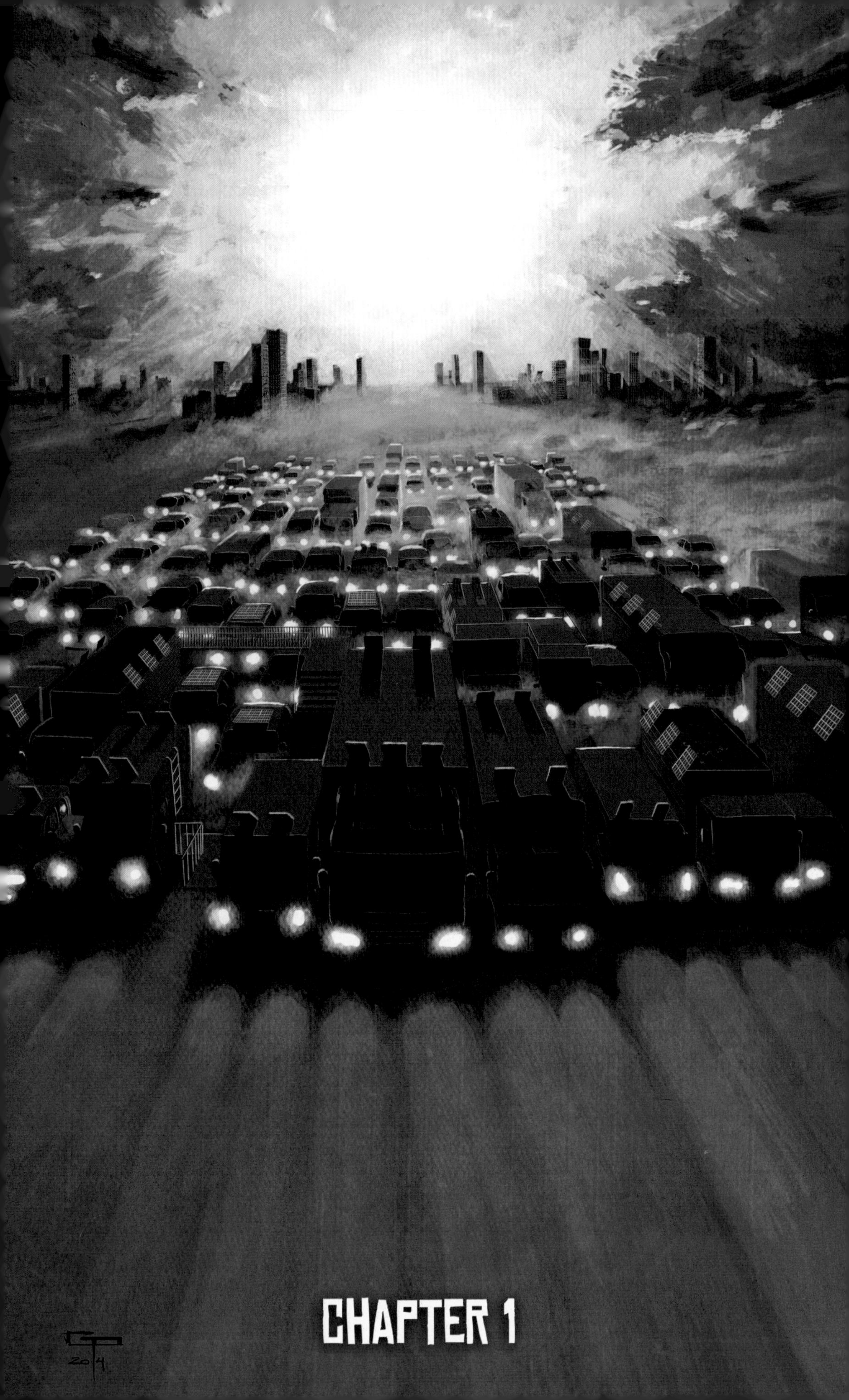

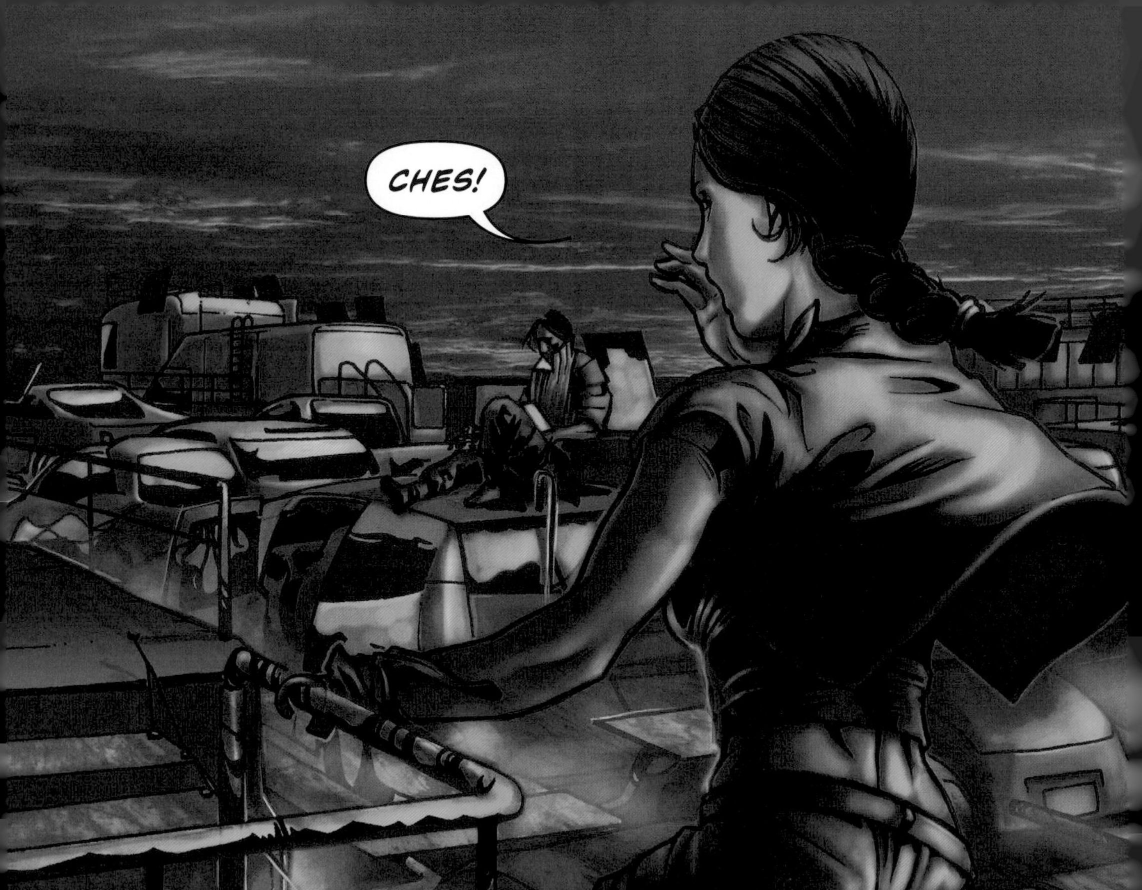
CHES!

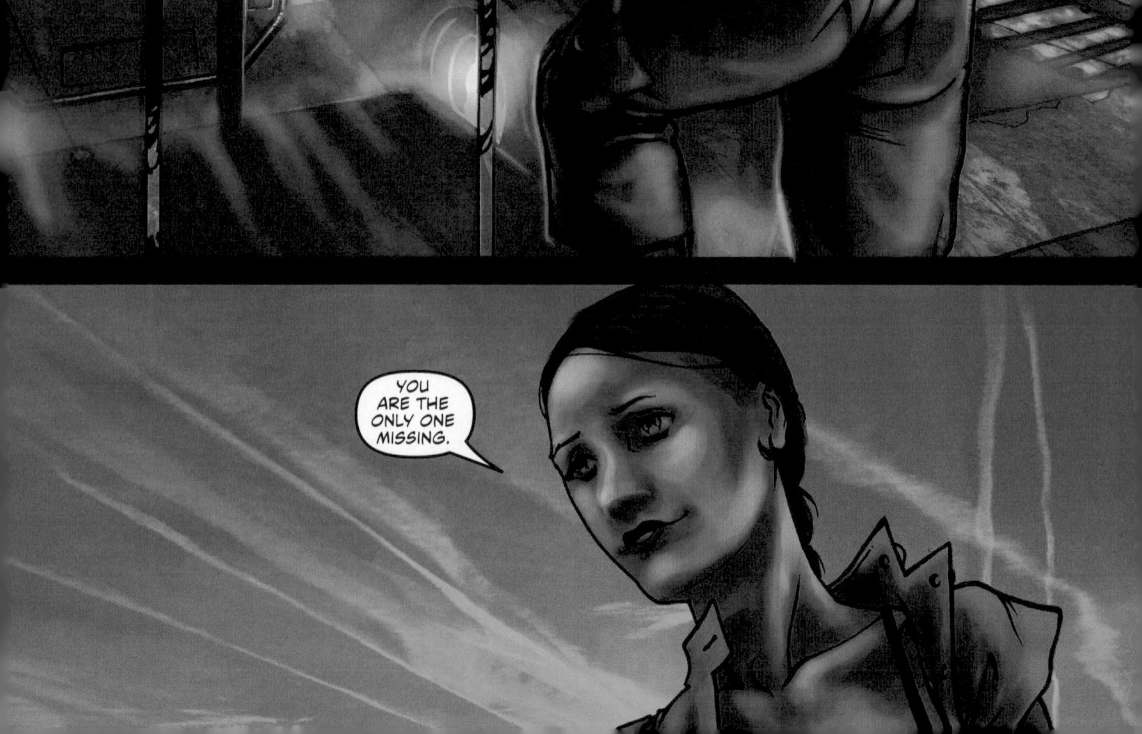
YOU ARE THE ONLY ONE MISSING.

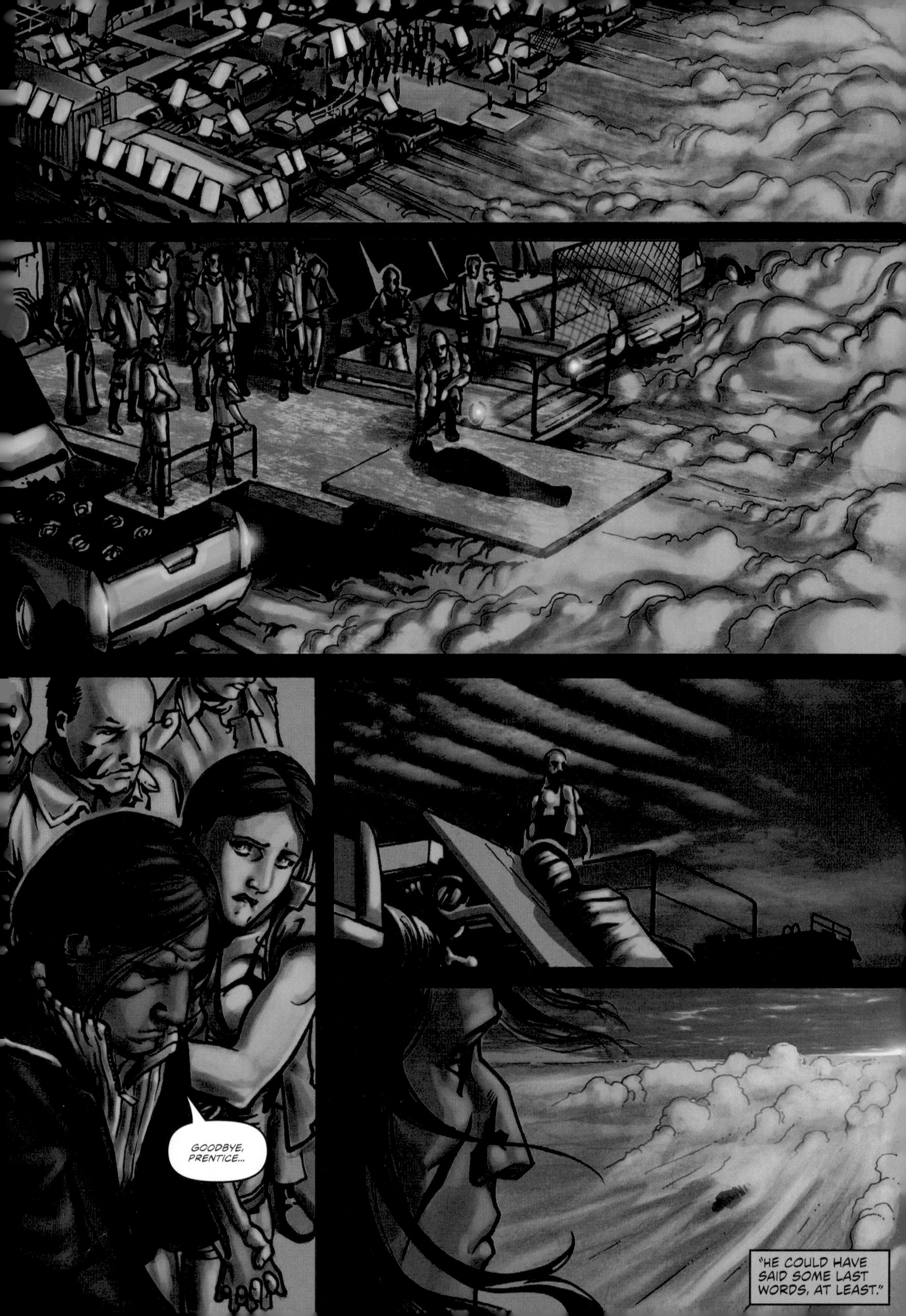
GOODBYE, PRENTICE...
"HE COULD HAVE SAID SOME LAST WORDS, AT LEAST."

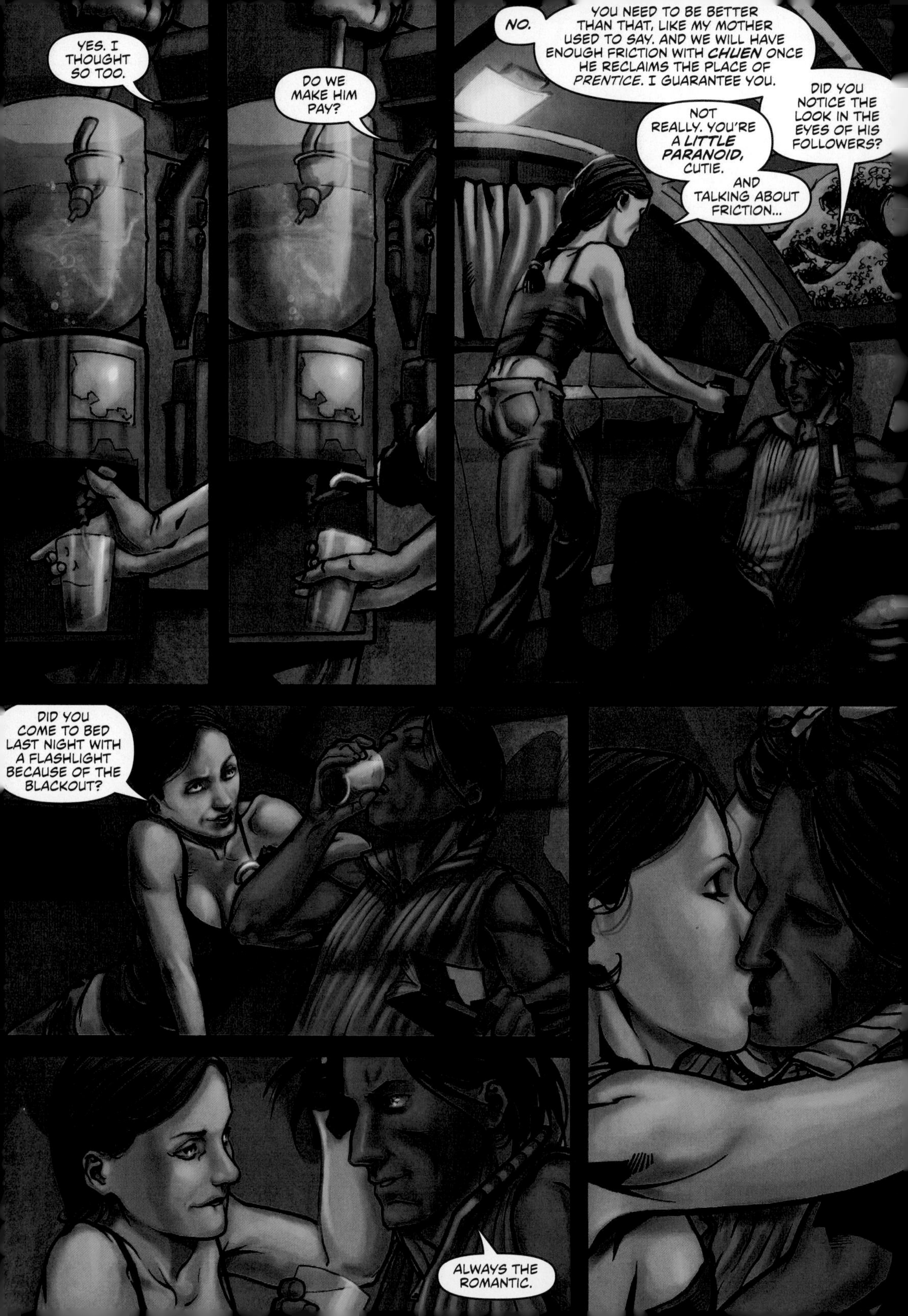
YES. I THOUGHT SO TOO.
DO WE MAKE HIM PAY?
NO.
YOU NEED TO BE BETTER THAN THAT, LIKE MY MOTHER USED TO SAY. AND WE WILL HAVE ENOUGH FRICTION WITH CHUEN ONCE HE RECLAIMS THE PLACE OF PRENTICE. I GUARANTEE YOU.
DID YOU NOTICE THE LOOK IN THE EYES OF HIS FOLLOWERS?
NOT REALLY. YOU'RE A LITTLE PARANOID, CUTIE.
AND TALKING ABOUT FRICTION...
DID YOU COME TO BED LAST NIGHT WITH A FLASHLIGHT BECAUSE OF THE BLACKOUT?
ALWAYS THE ROMANTIC.

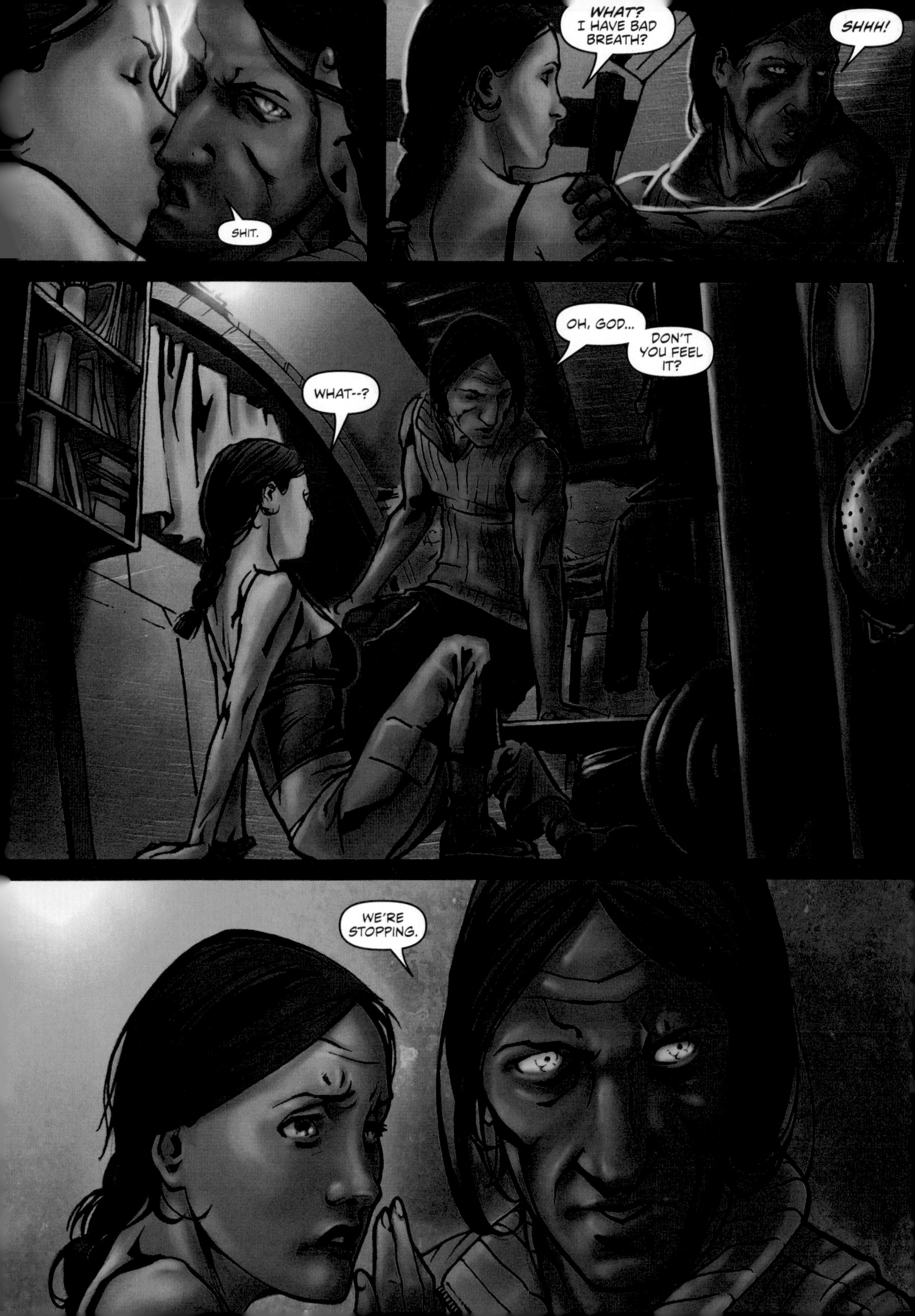
SHIT.
WHAT? I HAVE BAD BREATH?
SHHH!
OH, GOD...
DON'T YOU FEEL IT?
WHAT--?
WE'RE STOPPING.

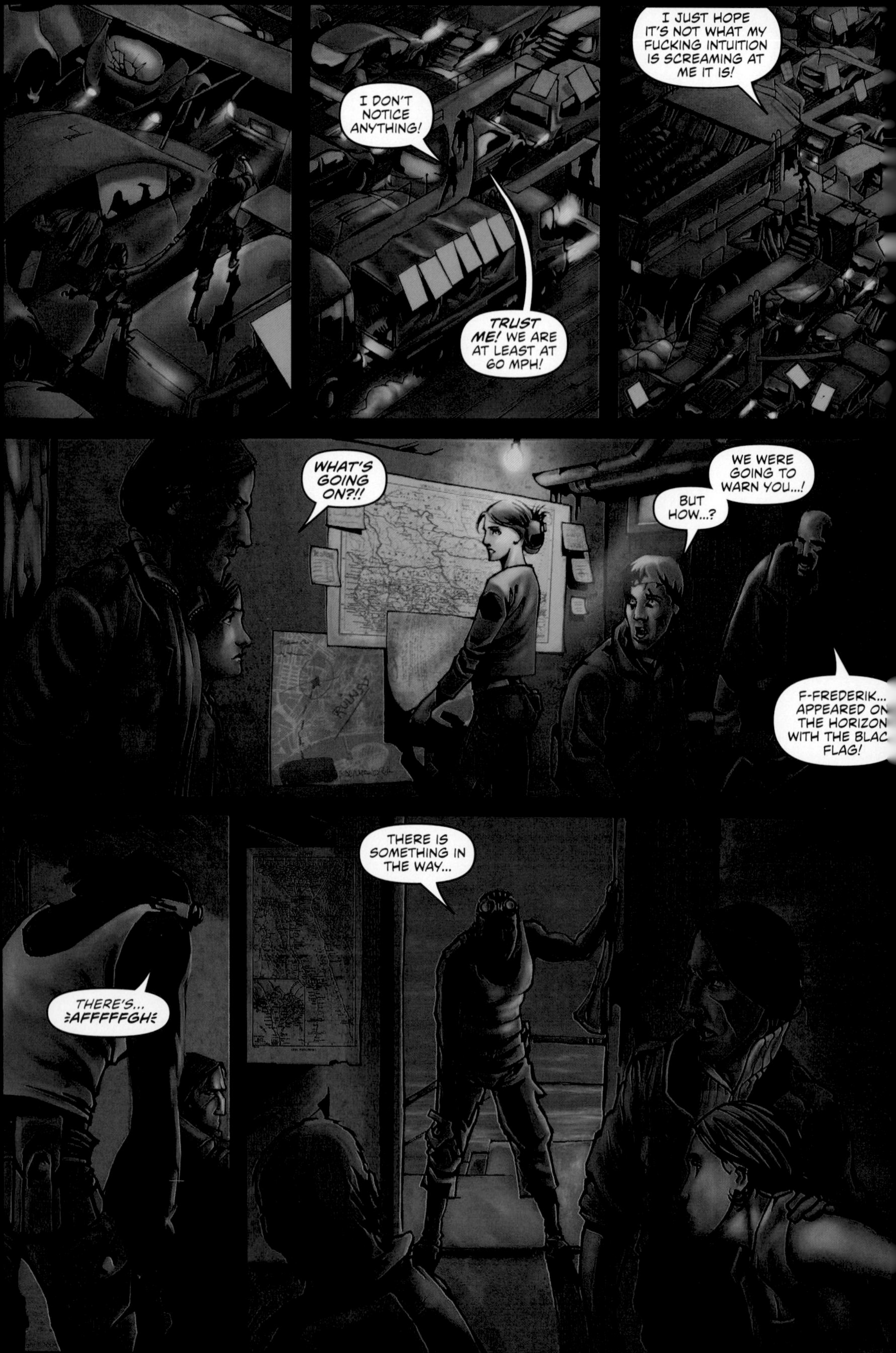
I DON'T NOTICE ANYTHING!
TRUST ME! WE ARE AT LEAST AT 60 MPH!
I JUST HOPE IT'S NOT WHAT MY FUCKING INTUITION IS SCREAMING AT ME IT IS!
WHAT'S GOING ON?!!
WE WERE GOING TO WARN YOU...!
BUT HOW...?
F-FREDERIK... APPEARED ON THE HORIZON WITH THE BLAC FLAG!
THERE IS SOMETHING IN THE WAY...
THERE'S... AFFFFFGH

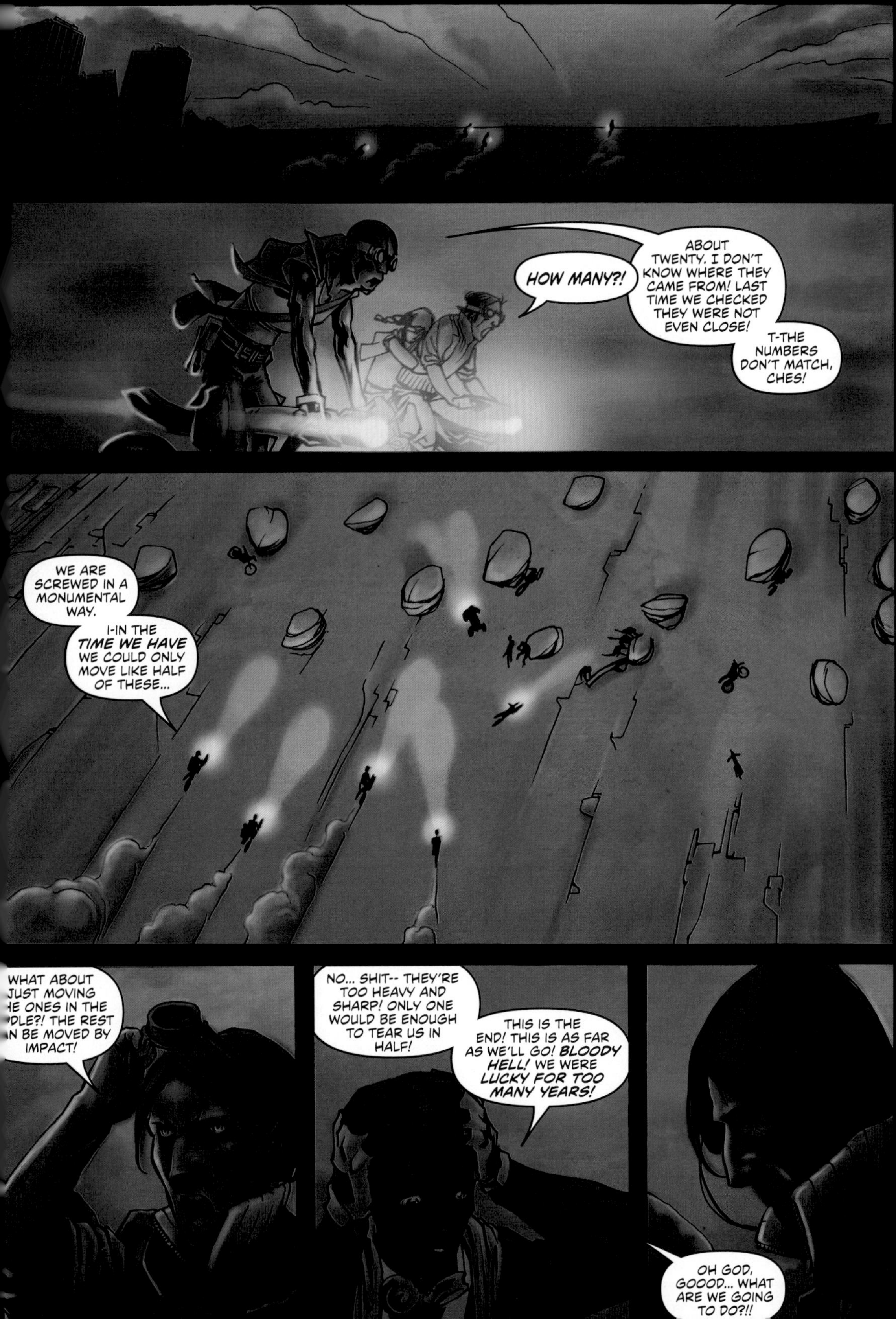
HOW MANY?!
ABOUT TWENTY. I DON'T KNOW WHERE THEY CAME FROM! LAST TIME WE CHECKED THEY WERE NOT EVEN CLOSE!
T-THE NUMBERS DON'T MATCH, CHES!
WE ARE SCREWED IN A MONUMENTAL WAY.
I-IN THE TIME WE HAVE WE COULD ONLY MOVE LIKE HALF OF THESE...
WHAT ABOUT JUST MOVING THE ONES IN THE MIDDLE?! THE REST CAN BE MOVED BY IMPACT!
NO... SHIT-- THEY'RE TOO HEAVY AND SHARP! ONLY ONE WOULD BE ENOUGH TO TEAR US IN HALF!
THIS IS THE END! THIS IS AS FAR AS WE'LL GO! BLOODY HELL! WE WERE LUCKY FOR TOO MANY YEARS!
OH GOD, GOOOD... WHAT ARE WE GOING TO DO?!!

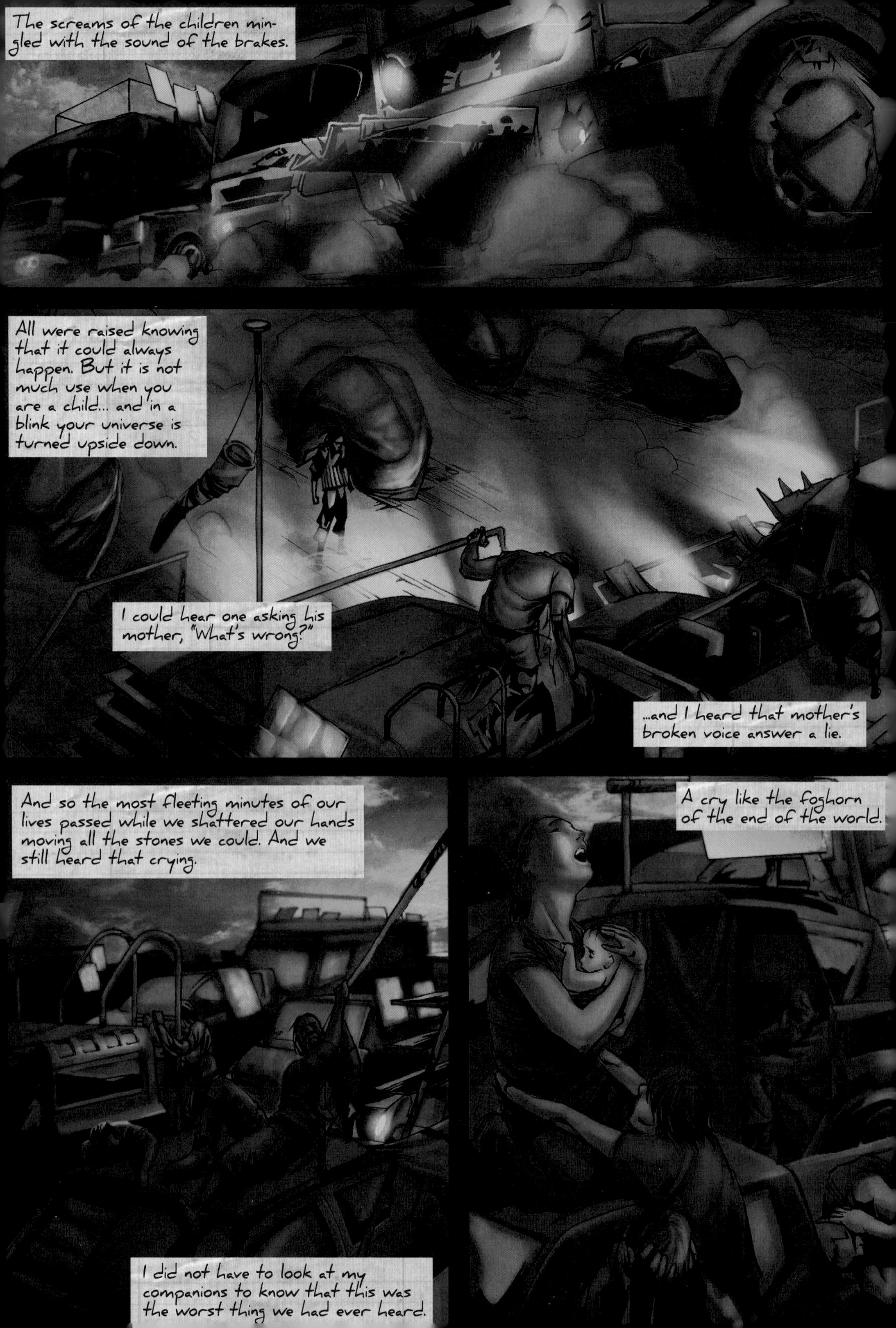
The screams of the children mingled with the sound of the brakes.
All were raised knowing that it could always happen. But it is not much use when you are a child... and in a blink your universe is turned upside down.
I could hear one asking his mother, "What's wrong?"
...and I heard that mother's broken voice answer a lie.
And so the most fleeting minutes of our lives passed while we shattered our hands moving all the stones we could. And we still heard that crying.
I did not have to look at my companions to know that this was the worst thing we had ever heard.
A cry like the foghorn of the end of the world.

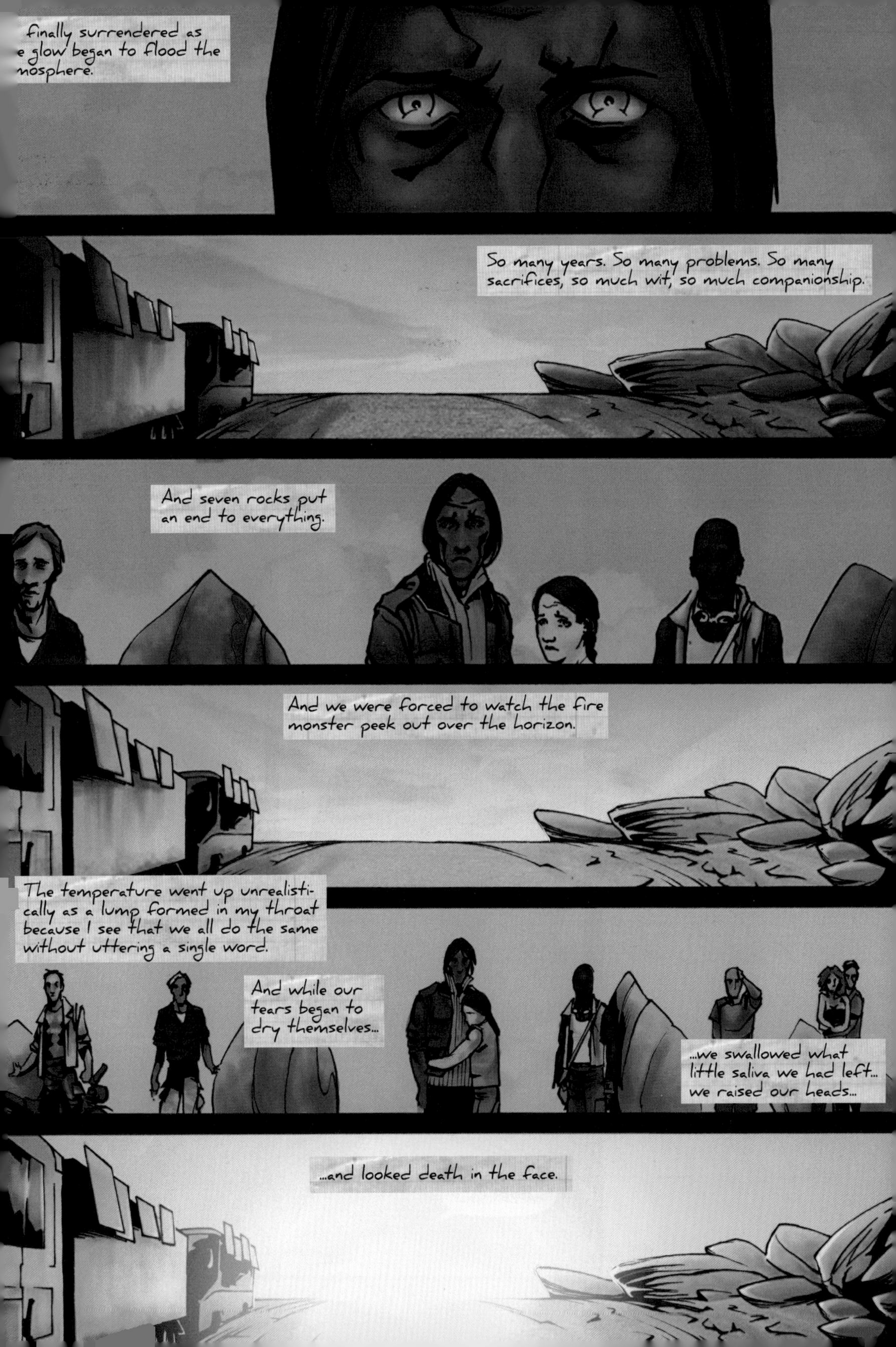
finally surrendered as
e glow began to flood the
nosphere.
So many years. So many problems. So many sacrifices, so much wit, so much companionship.
And seven rocks put an end to everything.
And we were forced to watch the fire monster peek out over the horizon.
The temperature went up unrealistically as a lump formed in my throat because I see that we all do the same without uttering a single word.
And while our tears began to dry themselves...
...we swallowed what little saliva we had left... we raised our heads...
...and looked death in the face.

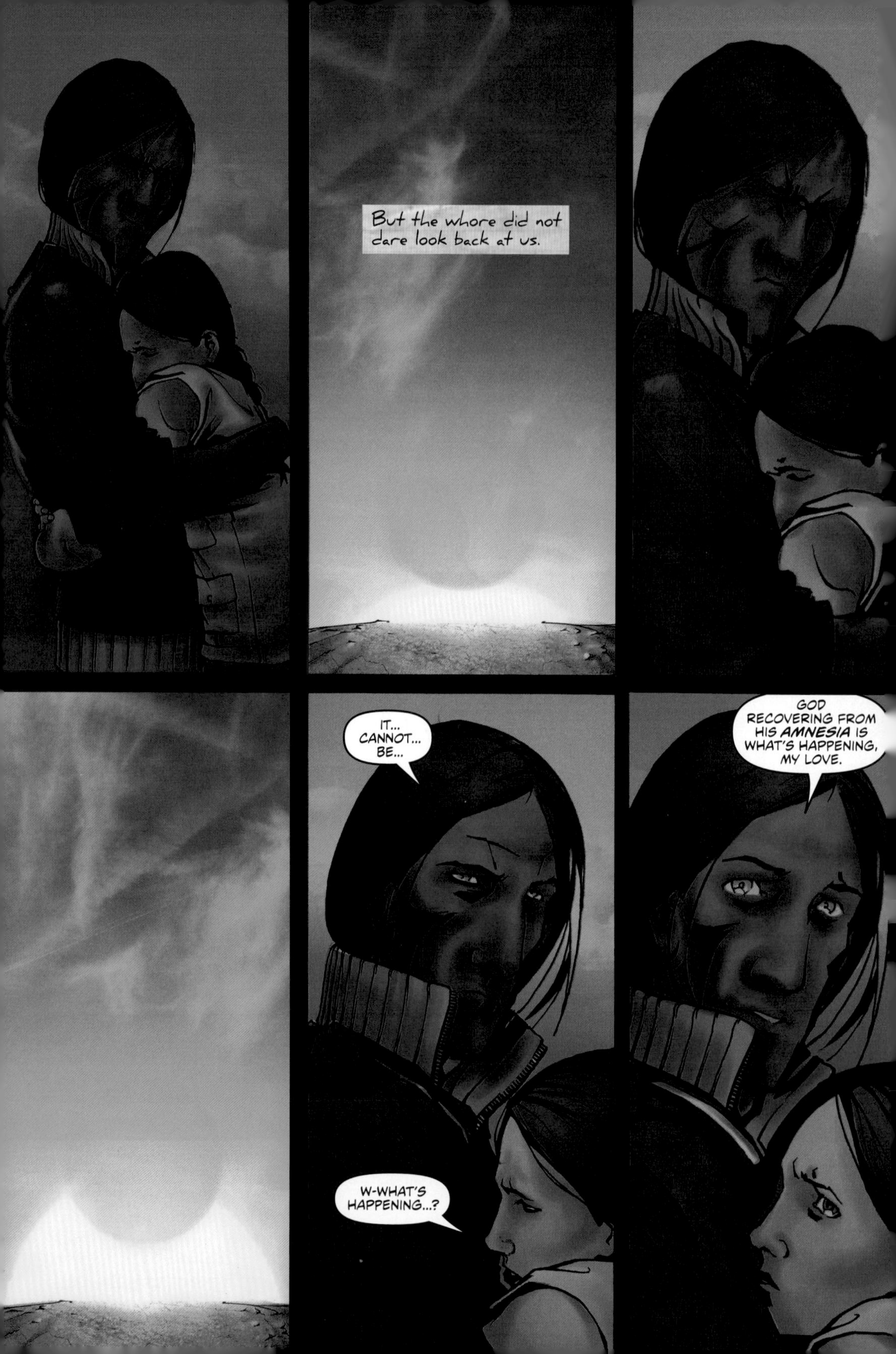
But the whore did not dare look back at us.
IT... CANNOT... BE...
W-WHAT'S HAPPENING...?
GOD RECOVERING FROM HIS AMNESIA IS WHAT'S HAPPENING, MY LOVE.

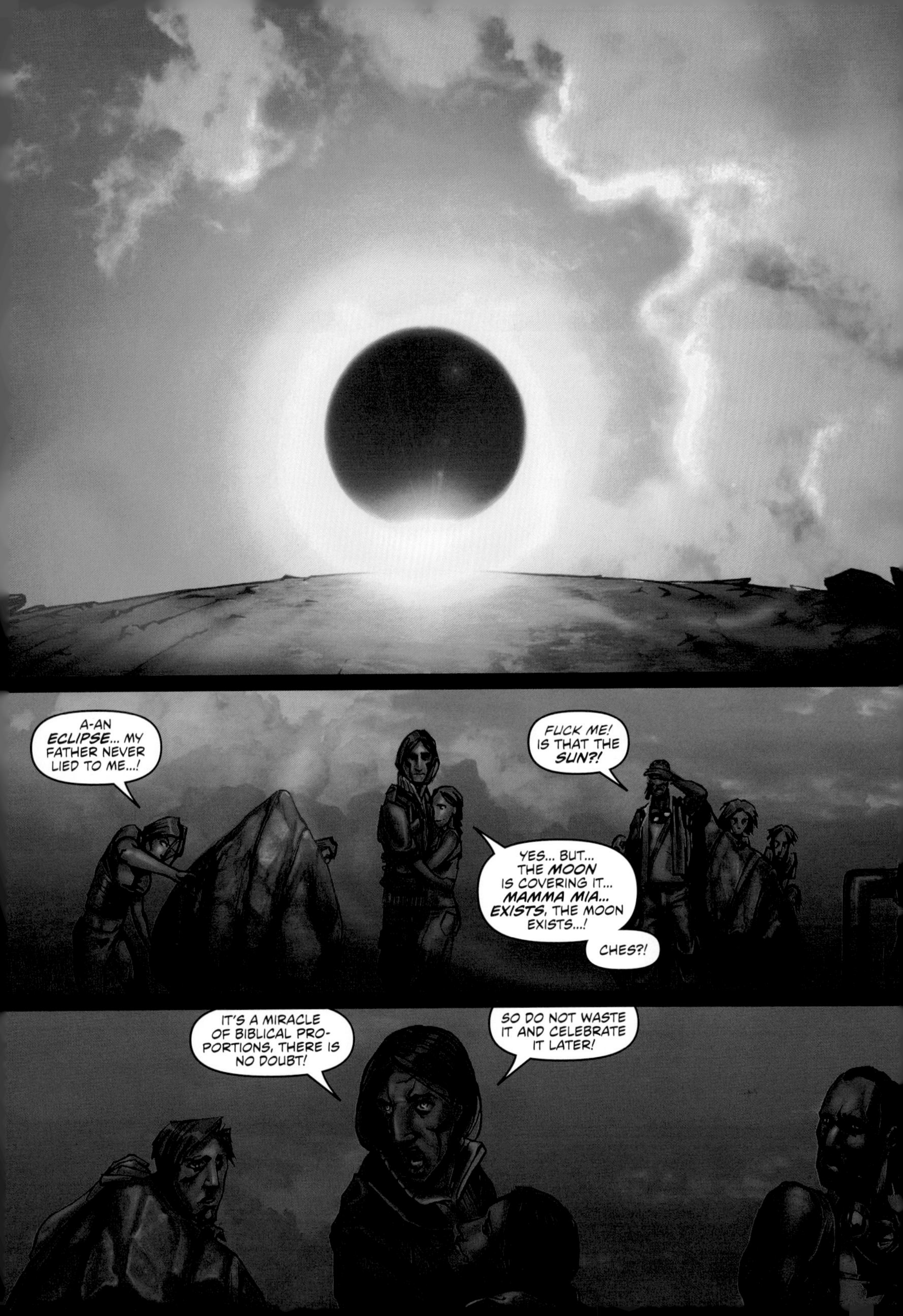
A-AN ECLIPSE... MY FATHER NEVER LIED TO ME...!
FUCK ME! IS THAT THE SUN?!
YES... BUT... THE MOON IS COVERING IT... MAMMA MIA... EXISTS, THE MOON EXISTS...!
CHES?!
IT'S A MIRACLE OF BIBLICAL PRO-PORTIONS, THERE IS NO DOUBT!
SO DO NOT WASTE IT AND CELEBRATE IT LATER!

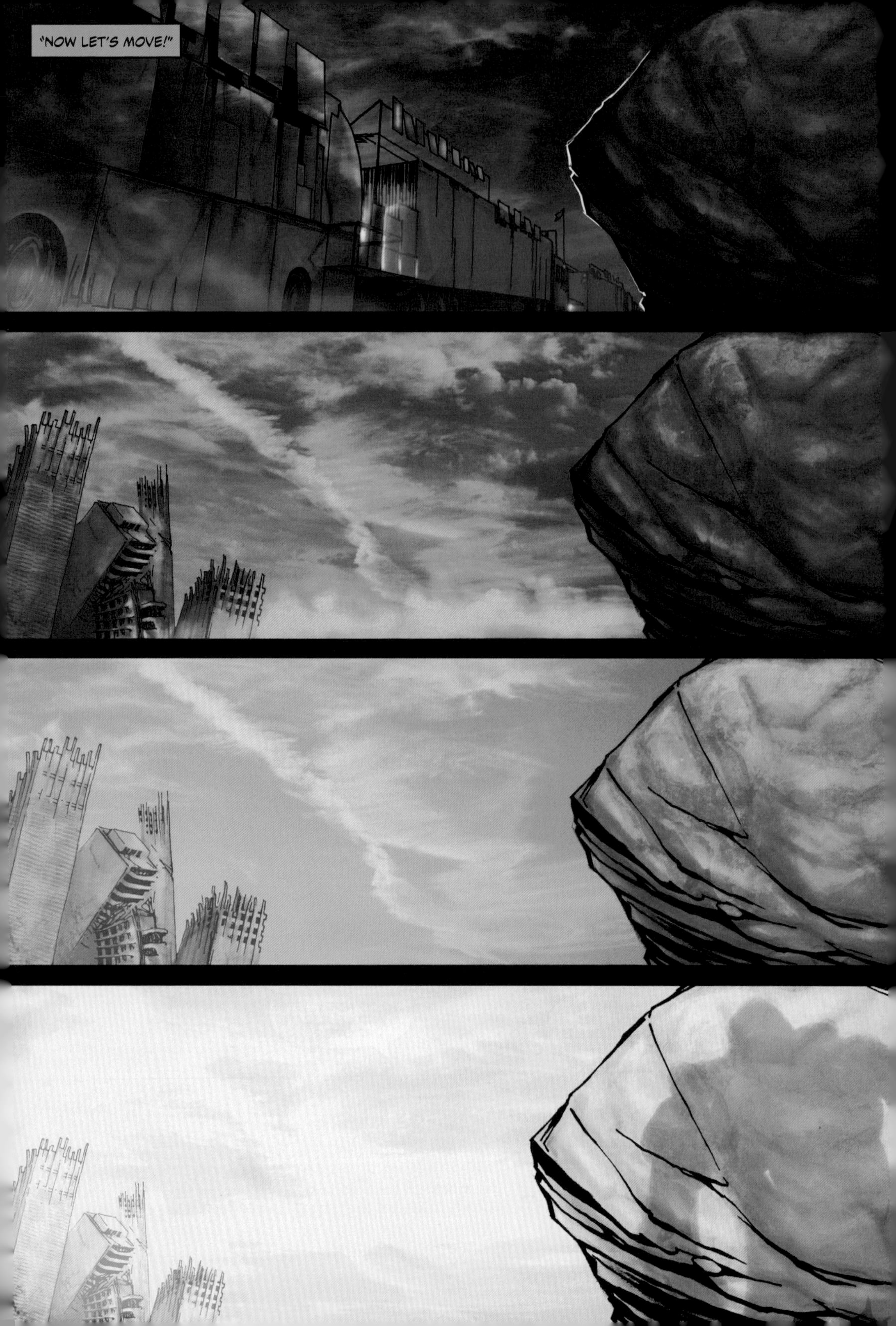
"NOW LET'S MOVE!"

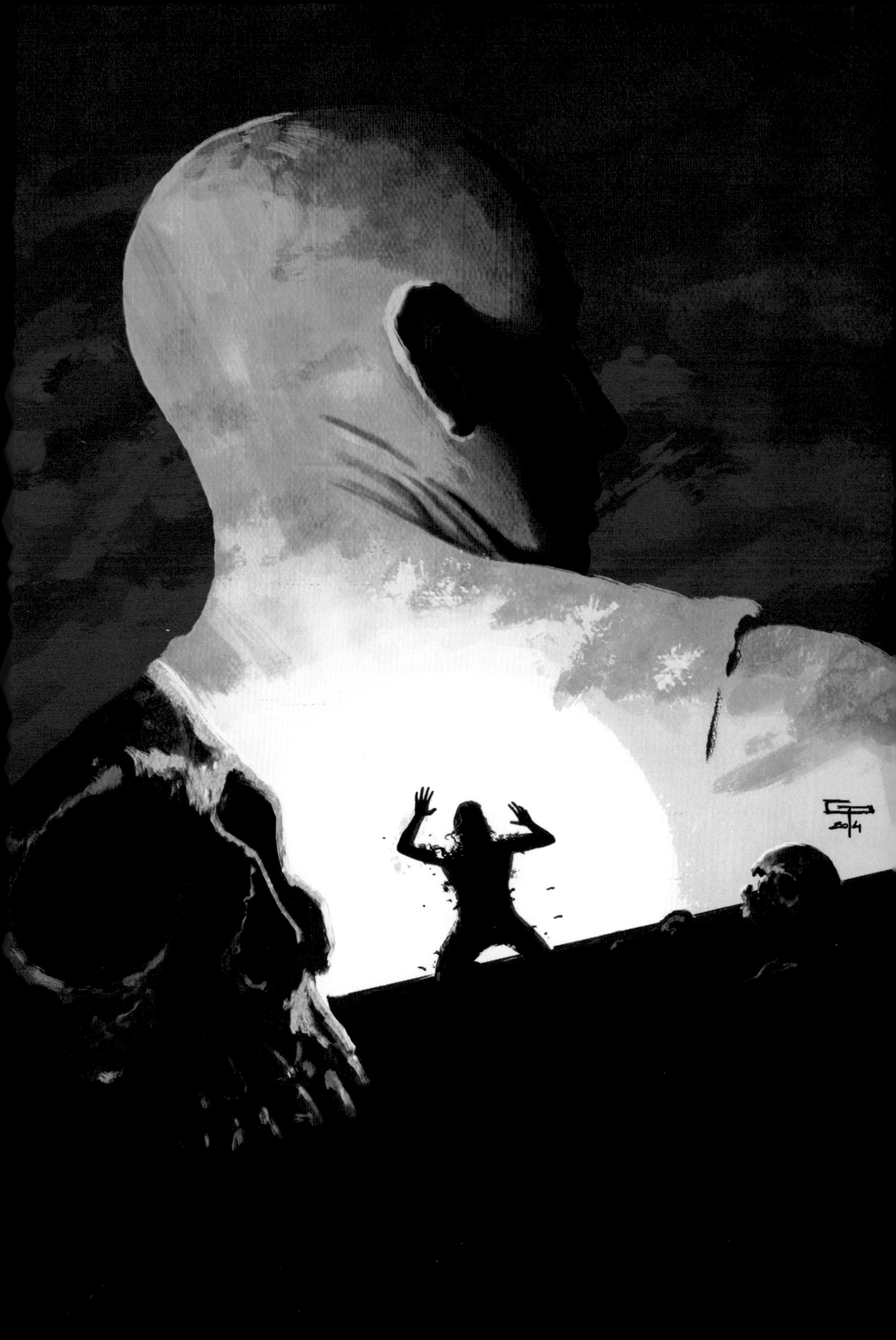

CHAPTER 2

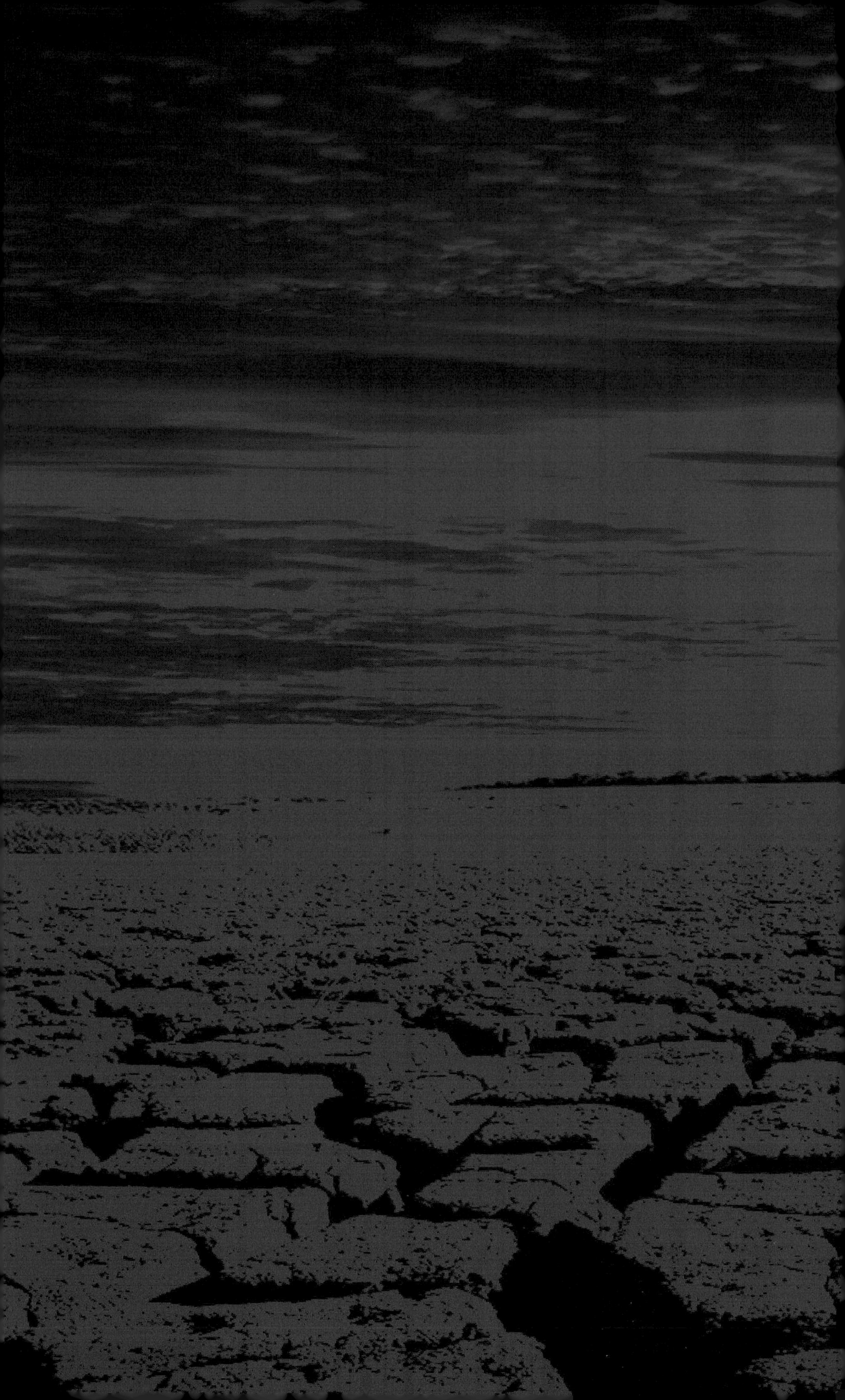

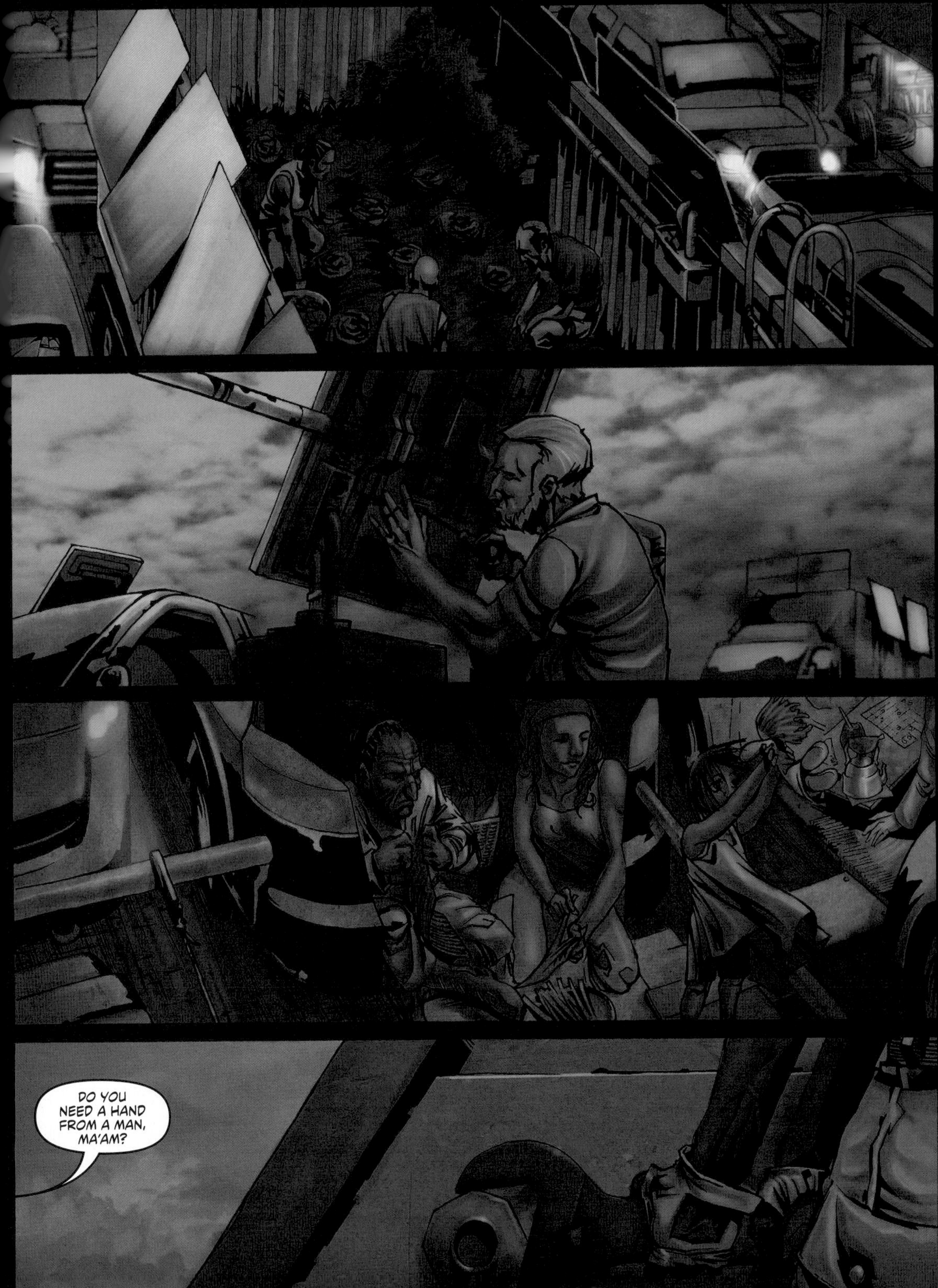
DO YOU NEED A HAND FROM A MAN, MA'AM?

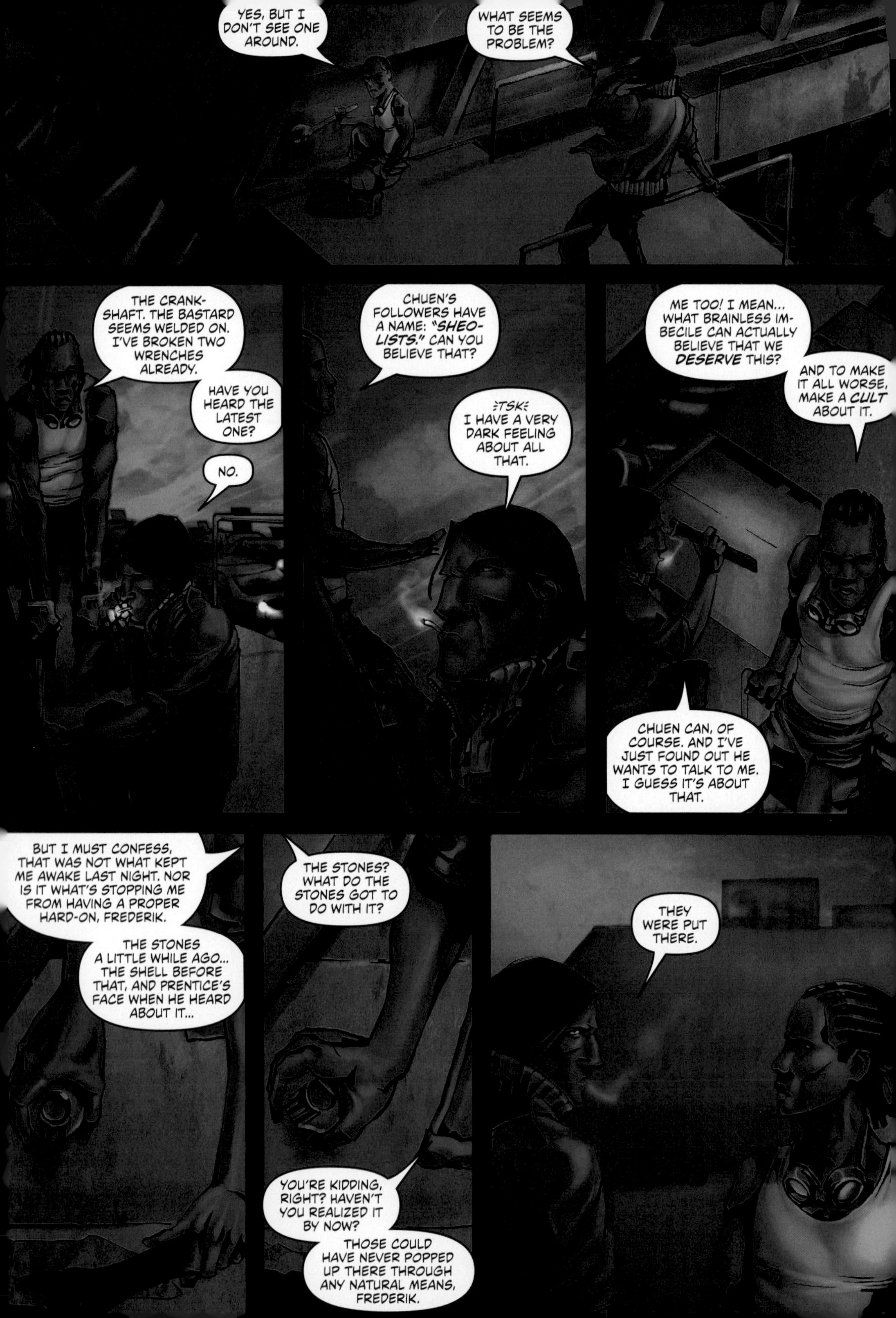
YES, BUT I DON'T SEE ONE AROUND.
WHAT SEEMS TO BE THE PROBLEM?
THE CRANK-SHAFT. THE BASTARD SEEMS WELDED ON. I'VE BROKEN TWO WRENCHES ALREADY.
HAVE YOU HEARD THE LATEST ONE?
NO.
CHUEN'S FOLLOWERS HAVE A NAME: "SHEO-LISTS." CAN YOU BELIEVE THAT?
TSK
I HAVE A VERY DARK FEELING ABOUT ALL THAT.
ME TOO! I MEAN... WHAT BRAINLESS IM-BECILE CAN ACTUALLY BELIEVE THAT WE DESERVE THIS?
AND TO MAKE IT ALL WORSE, MAKE A CULT ABOUT IT.
CHUEN CAN, OF COURSE. AND I'VE JUST FOUND OUT HE WANTS TO TALK TO ME. I GUESS IT'S ABOUT THAT.
BUT I MUST CONFESS, THAT WAS NOT WHAT KEPT ME AWAKE LAST NIGHT. NOR IS IT WHAT'S STOPPING ME FROM HAVING A PROPER HARD-ON, FREDERIK.
THE STONES A LITTLE WHILE AGO... THE SHELL BEFORE THAT, AND PRENTICE'S FACE WHEN HE HEARD ABOUT IT...
THE STONES? WHAT DO THE STONES GOT TO DO WITH IT?
YOU'RE KIDDING, RIGHT? HAVEN'T YOU REALIZED IT BY NOW?
THOSE COULD HAVE NEVER POPPED UP THERE THROUGH ANY NATURAL MEANS, FREDERIK.
THEY WERE PUT THERE.

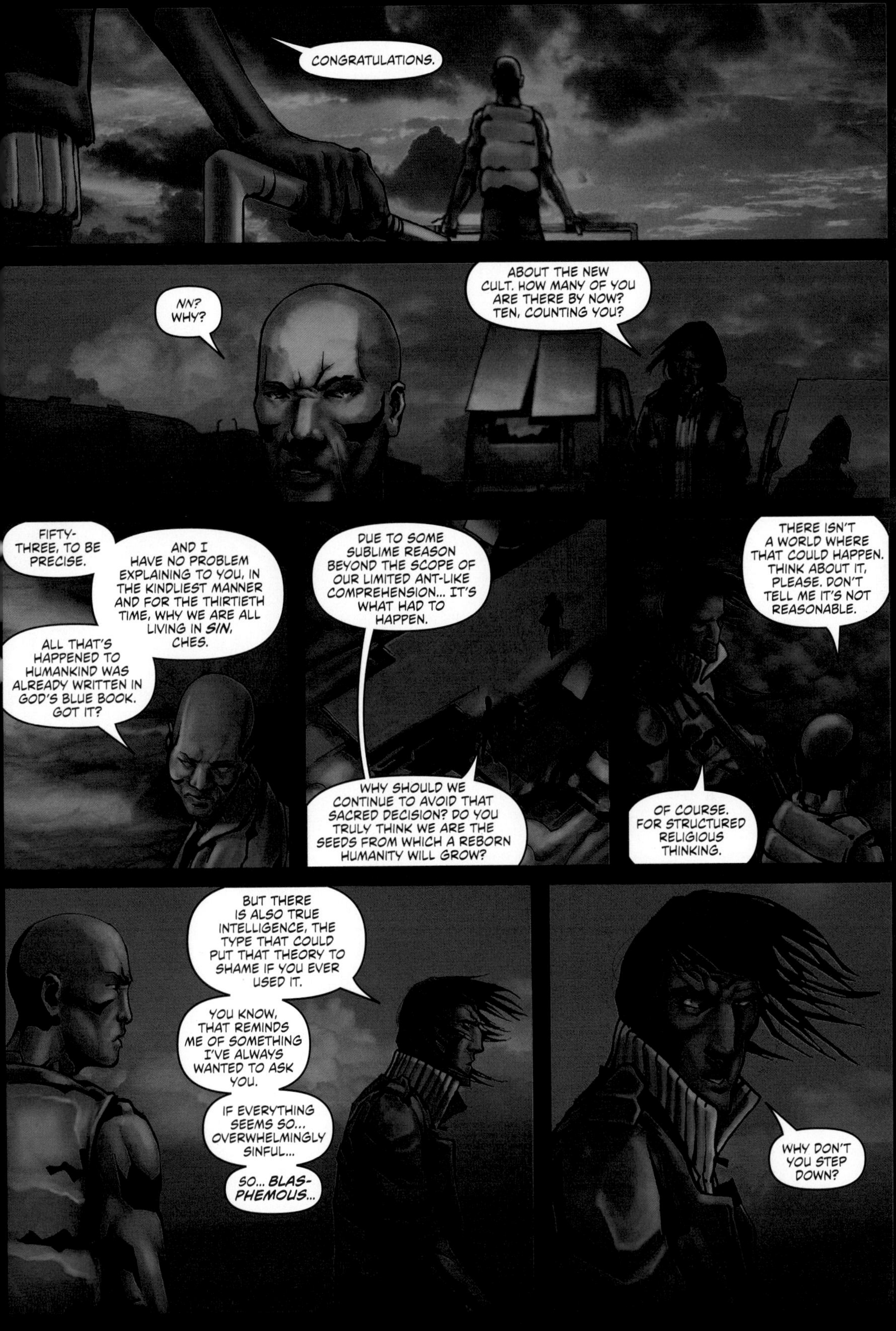
CONGRATULATIONS.
NN? WHY?
ABOUT THE NEW CULT. HOW MANY OF YOU ARE THERE BY NOW? TEN, COUNTING YOU?
FIFTY-THREE, TO BE PRECISE.
AND I HAVE NO PROBLEM EXPLAINING TO YOU, IN THE KINDLIEST MANNER AND FOR THE THIRTIETH TIME, WHY WE ARE ALL LIVING IN *SIN*, CHES.
ALL THAT'S HAPPENED TO HUMANKIND WAS ALREADY WRITTEN IN GOD'S BLUE BOOK. GOT IT?
DUE TO SOME SUBLIME REASON BEYOND THE SCOPE OF OUR LIMITED ANT-LIKE COMPREHENSION... IT'S WHAT HAD TO HAPPEN.
WHY SHOULD WE CONTINUE TO AVOID THAT SACRED DECISION? DO YOU TRULY THINK WE ARE THE SEEDS FROM WHICH A REBORN HUMANITY WILL GROW?
THERE ISN'T A WORLD WHERE THAT COULD HAPPEN. THINK ABOUT IT, PLEASE. DON'T TELL ME IT'S NOT REASONABLE.
OF COURSE. FOR STRUCTURED RELIGIOUS THINKING.
BUT THERE IS ALSO TRUE INTELLIGENCE, THE TYPE THAT COULD PUT THAT THEORY TO SHAME IF YOU EVER USED IT.
YOU KNOW, THAT REMINDS ME OF SOMETHING I'VE ALWAYS WANTED TO ASK YOU.
IF EVERYTHING SEEMS SO... OVERWHELMINGLY SINFUL...
SO... *BLASPHEMOUS*...
WHY DON'T YOU STEP DOWN?

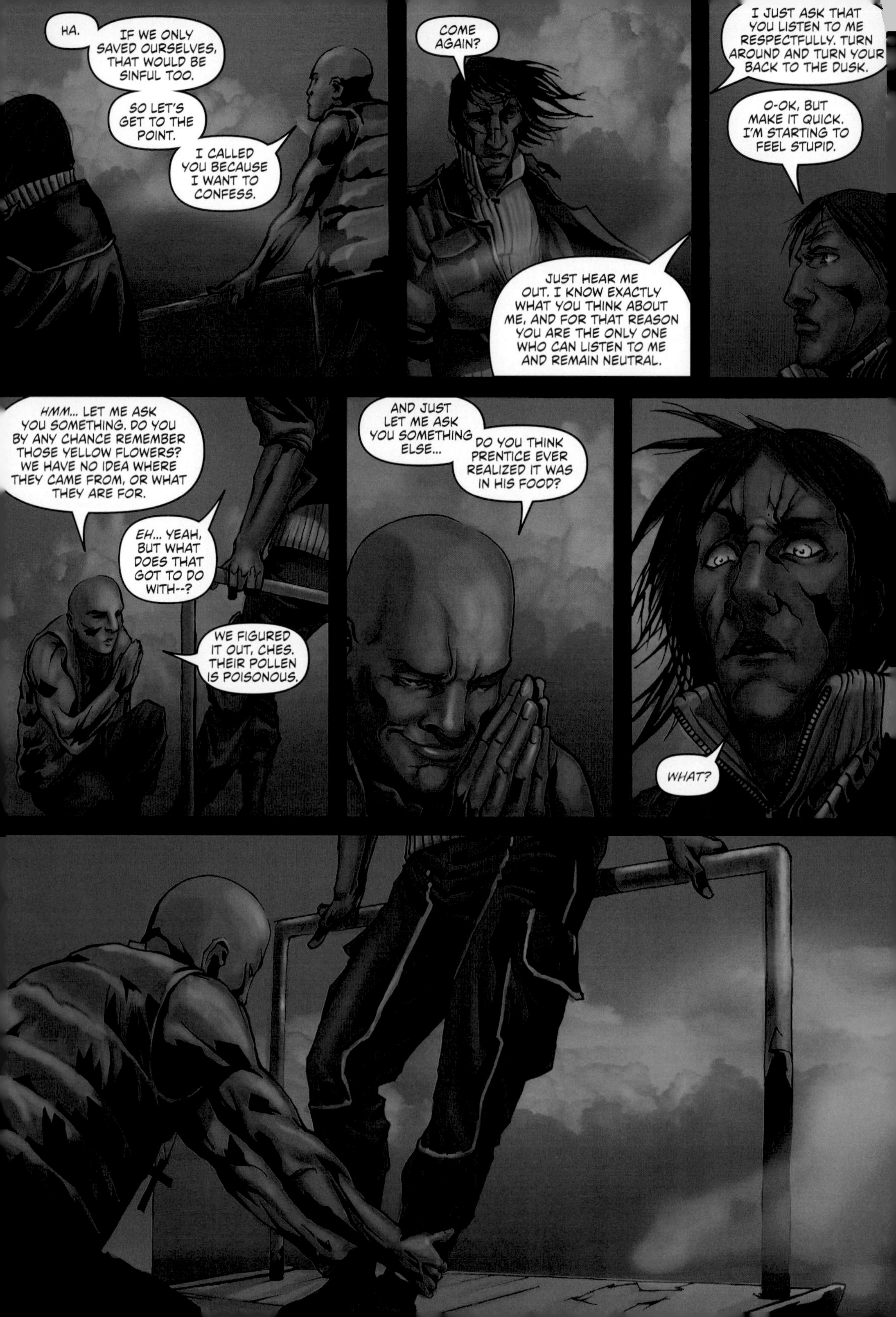
HA.
IF WE ONLY SAVED OURSELVES, THAT WOULD BE SINFUL TOO.
SO LET'S GET TO THE POINT.
I CALLED YOU BECAUSE I WANT TO CONFESS.
COME AGAIN?
JUST HEAR ME OUT. I KNOW EXACTLY WHAT YOU THINK ABOUT ME, AND FOR THAT REASON YOU ARE THE ONLY ONE WHO CAN LISTEN TO ME AND REMAIN NEUTRAL.
I JUST ASK THAT YOU LISTEN TO ME RESPECTFULLY. TURN AROUND AND TURN YOUR BACK TO THE DUSK.
O-OK, BUT MAKE IT QUICK. I'M STARTING TO FEEL STUPID.
HMM... LET ME ASK YOU SOMETHING. DO YOU BY ANY CHANCE REMEMBER THOSE YELLOW FLOWERS? WE HAVE NO IDEA WHERE THEY CAME FROM, OR WHAT THEY ARE FOR.
EH... YEAH, BUT WHAT DOES THAT GOT TO DO WITH--?
WE FIGURED IT OUT, CHES. THEIR POLLEN IS POISONOUS.
AND JUST LET ME ASK YOU SOMETHING ELSE...
DO YOU THINK PRENTICE EVER REALIZED IT WAS IN HIS FOOD?
WHAT?

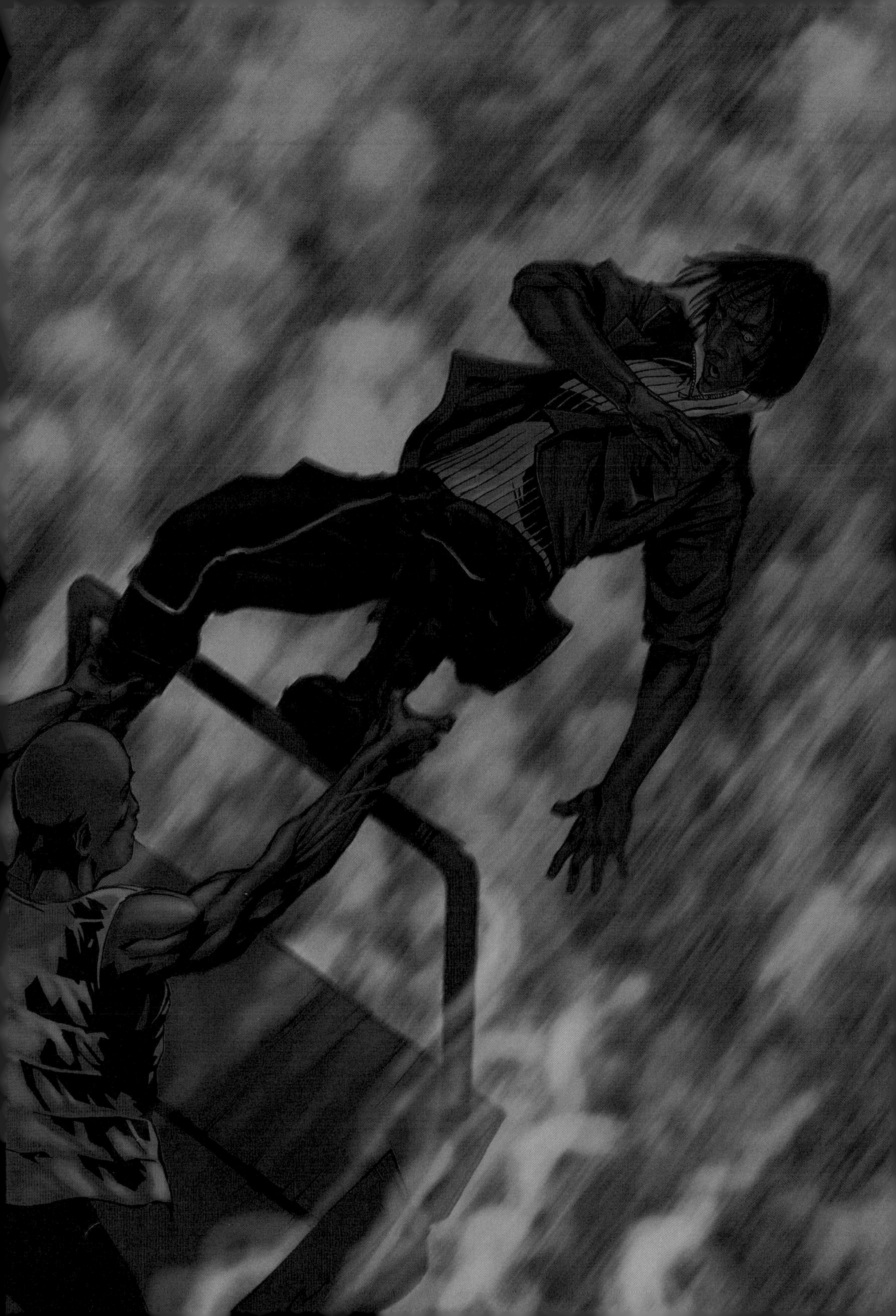

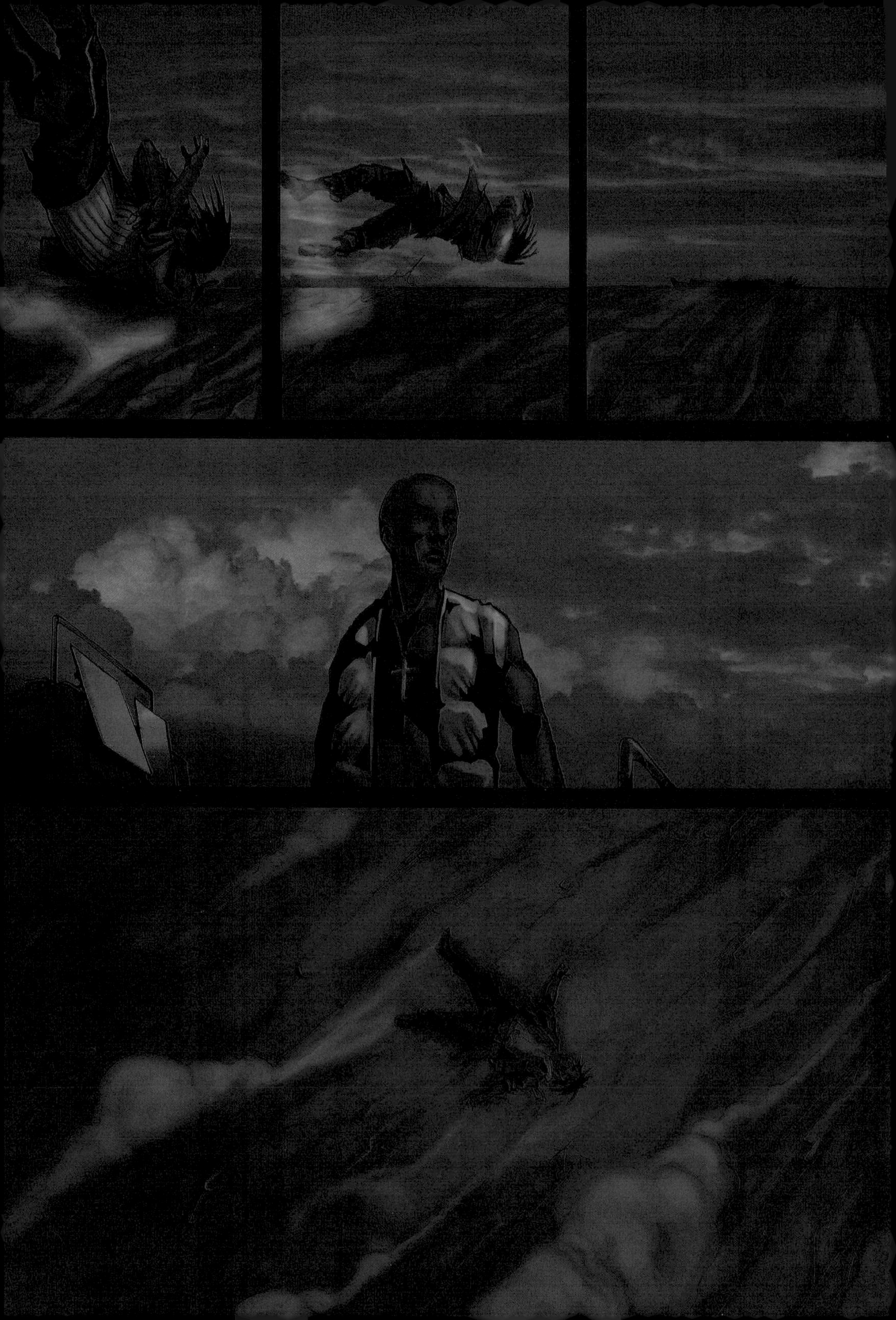

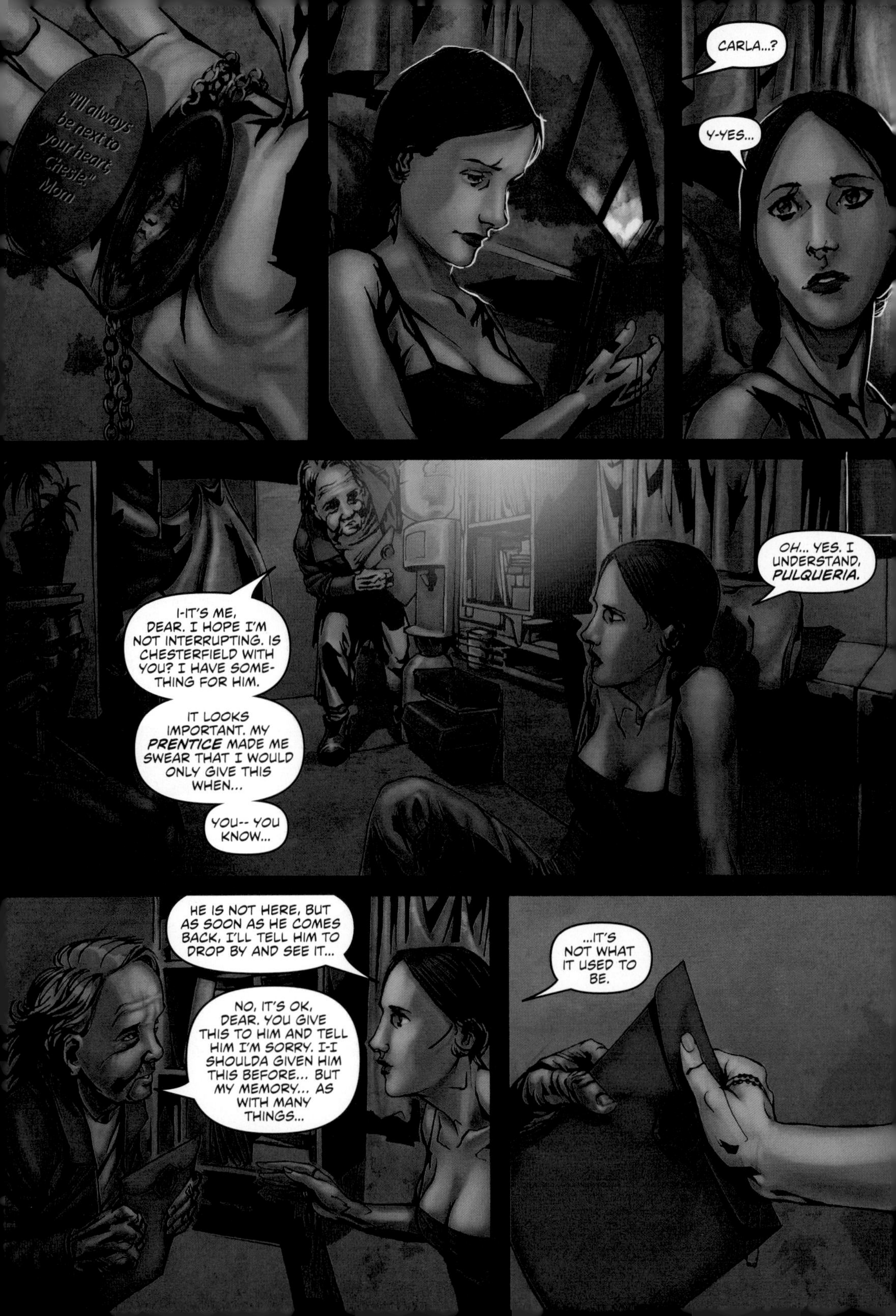

"I'll always be next to your heart, Chesle." Mom
CARLA...?
Y-YES...
I-IT'S ME, DEAR. I HOPE I'M NOT INTERRUPTING. IS CHESTERFIELD WITH YOU? I HAVE SOME-THING FOR HIM.
IT LOOKS IMPORTANT. MY PRENTICE MADE ME SWEAR THAT I WOULD ONLY GIVE THIS WHEN...
YOU-- YOU KNOW...
OH... YES. I UNDERSTAND, PULQUERIA.
HE IS NOT HERE, BUT AS SOON AS HE COMES BACK, I'LL TELL HIM TO DROP BY AND SEE IT...
NO, IT'S OK, DEAR. YOU GIVE THIS TO HIM AND TELL HIM I'M SORRY. I-I SHOULDA GIVEN HIM THIS BEFORE... BUT MY MEMORY... AS WITH MANY THINGS...
...IT'S NOT WHAT IT USED TO BE.

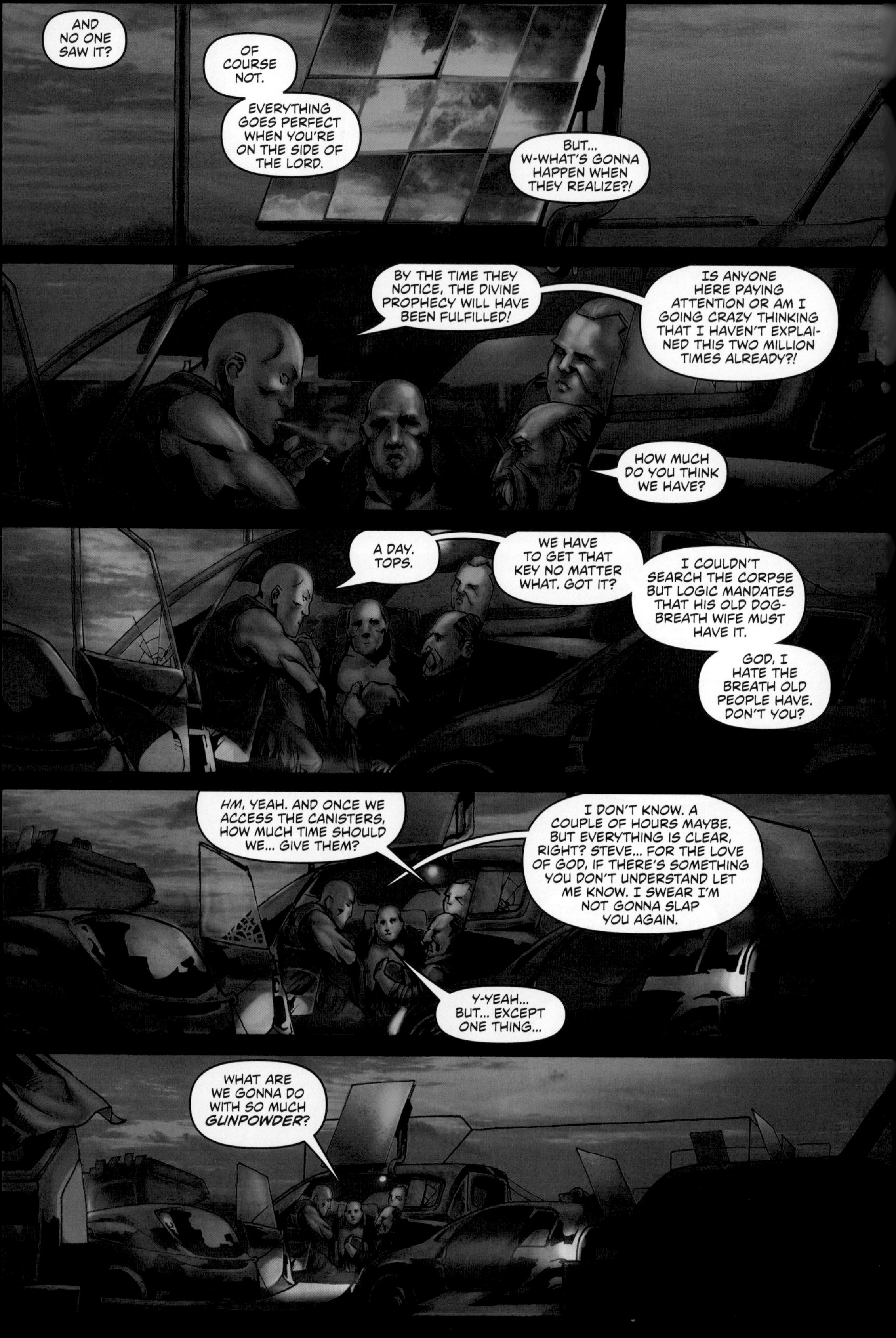
AND NO ONE SAW IT?
OF COURSE NOT.
EVERYTHING GOES PERFECT WHEN YOU'RE ON THE SIDE OF THE LORD.
BUT... W-WHAT'S GONNA HAPPEN WHEN THEY REALIZE?!
BY THE TIME THEY NOTICE, THE DIVINE PROPHECY WILL HAVE BEEN FULFILLED!
IS ANYONE HERE PAYING ATTENTION OR AM I GOING CRAZY THINKING THAT I HAVEN'T EXPLAINED THIS TWO MILLION TIMES ALREADY?!
HOW MUCH DO YOU THINK WE HAVE?
A DAY. TOPS.
WE HAVE TO GET THAT KEY NO MATTER WHAT. GOT IT?
I COULDN'T SEARCH THE CORPSE BUT LOGIC MANDATES THAT HIS OLD DOG-BREATH WIFE MUST HAVE IT.
GOD, I HATE THE BREATH OLD PEOPLE HAVE. DON'T YOU?
HM, YEAH. AND ONCE WE ACCESS THE CANISTERS, HOW MUCH TIME SHOULD WE... GIVE THEM?
I DON'T KNOW. A COUPLE OF HOURS MAYBE. BUT EVERYTHING IS CLEAR, RIGHT? STEVE... FOR THE LOVE OF GOD, IF THERE'S SOMETHING YOU DON'T UNDERSTAND LET ME KNOW. I SWEAR I'M NOT GONNA SLAP YOU AGAIN.
Y-YEAH... BUT... EXCEPT ONE THING...
WHAT ARE WE GONNA DO WITH SO MUCH GUNPOWDER?

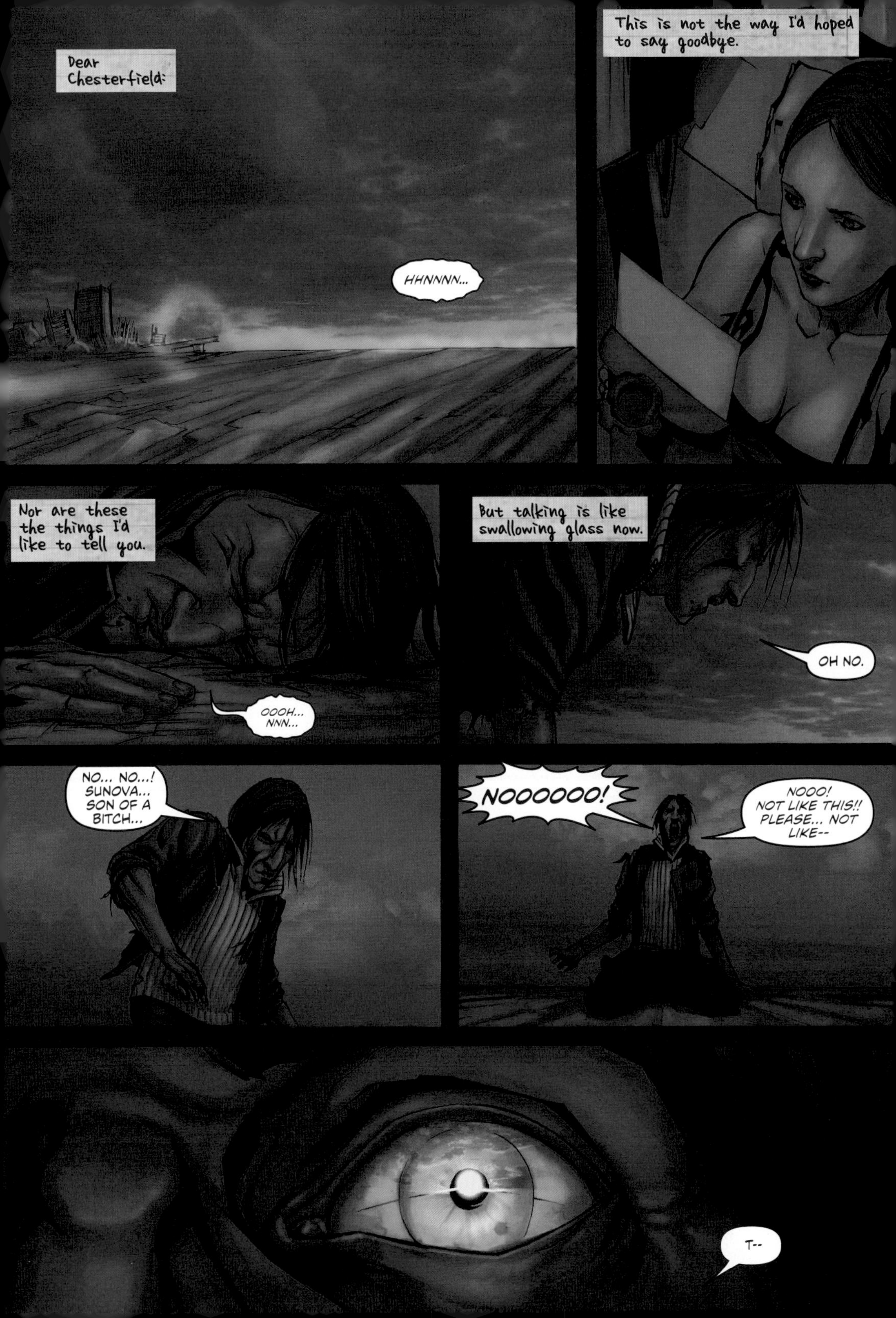
Dear Chesterfield:
HHNNNN...
This is not the way I'd hoped to say goodbye.
Nor are these the things I'd like to tell you.
OOOH... NNN...
But talking is like swallowing glass now.
OH NO.
NO... NO...! SUNOVA... SON OF A BITCH...
NOOOOOO!
NOOO! NOT LIKE THIS!! PLEASE... NOT LIKE--
T--

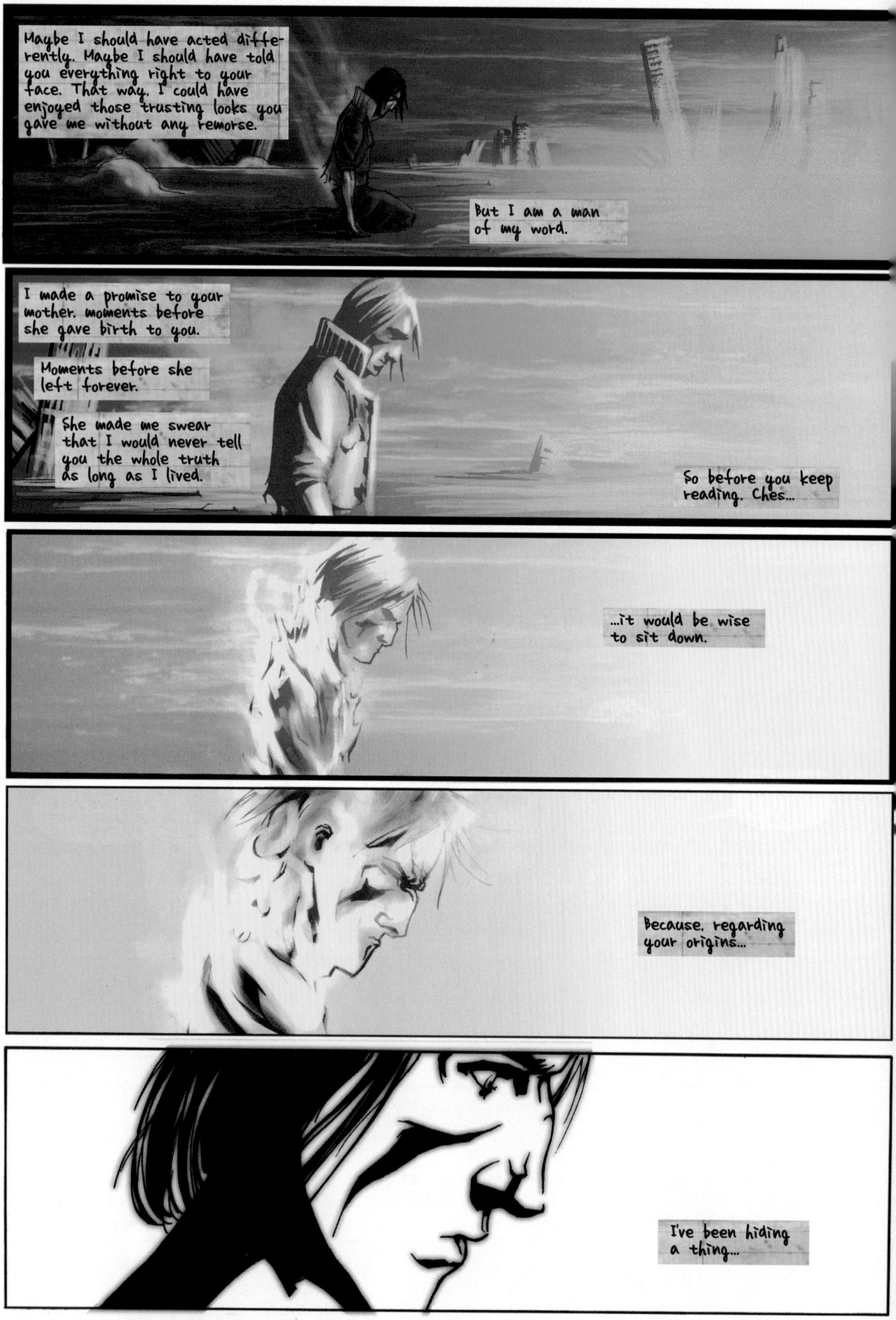

Maybe I should have acted differently. Maybe I should have told you everything right to your face. That way, I could have enjoyed those trusting looks you gave me without any remorse.
But I am a man of my word.
I made a promise to your mother, moments before she gave birth to you.
Moments before she left forever.
She made me swear that I would never tell you the whole truth as long as I lived.
So before you keep reading, Ches...
...it would be wise to sit down.
Because, regarding your origins...
I've been hiding a thing...

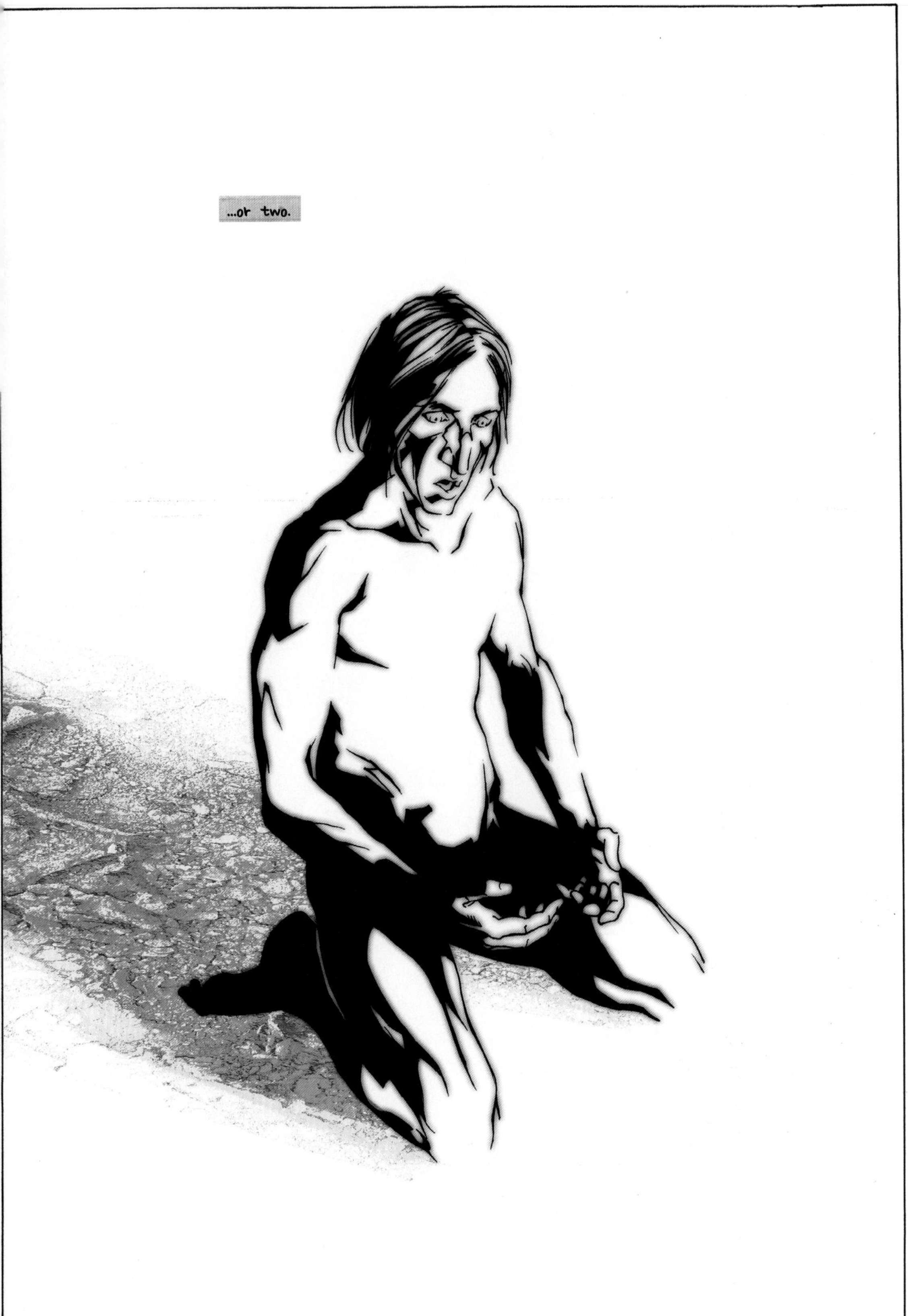
...or two.

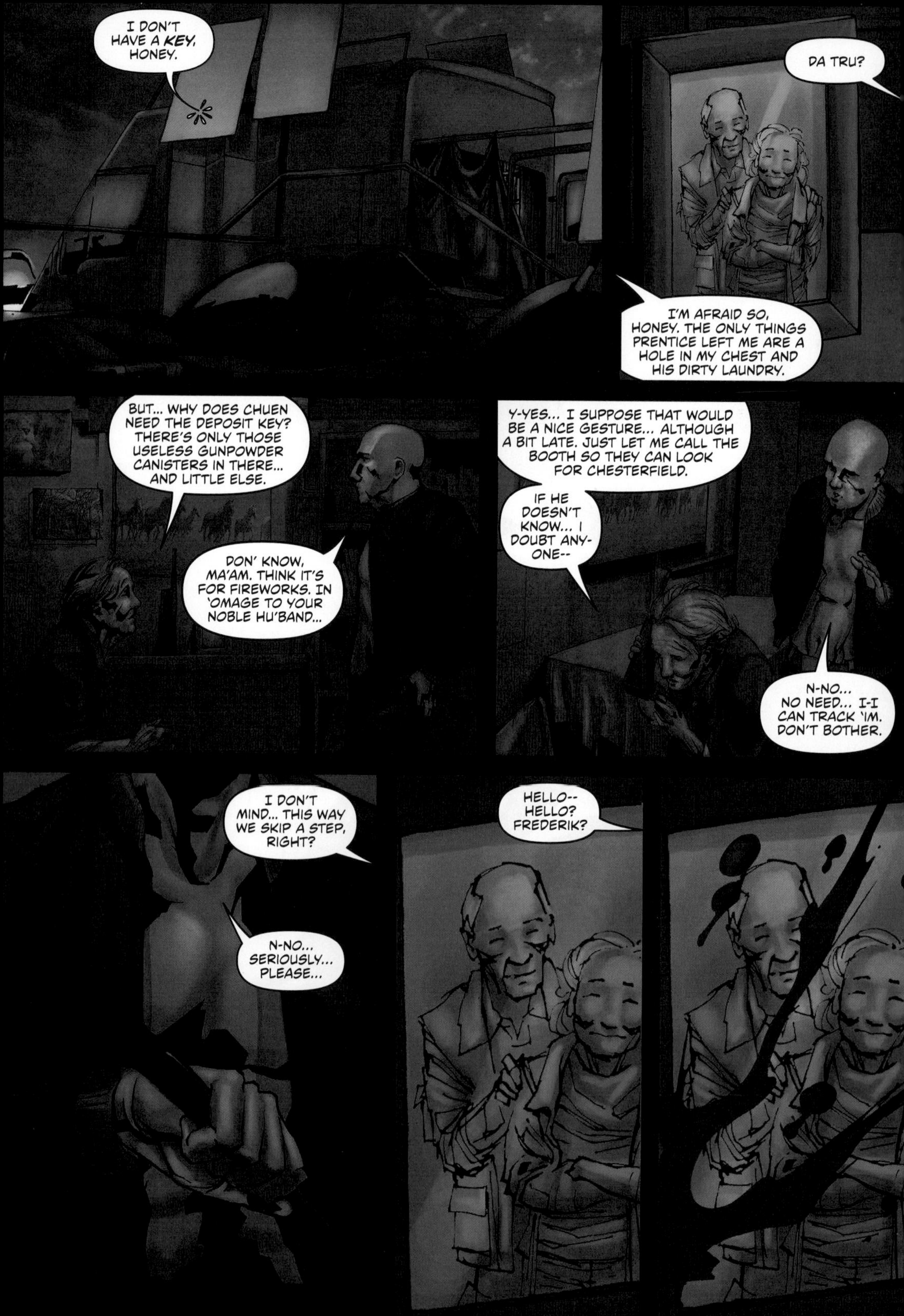
I DON'T HAVE A KEY, HONEY.
DA TRU?
I'M AFRAID SO, HONEY. THE ONLY THINGS PRENTICE LEFT ME ARE A HOLE IN MY CHEST AND HIS DIRTY LAUNDRY.
BUT... WHY DOES CHUEN NEED THE DEPOSIT KEY? THERE'S ONLY THOSE USELESS GUNPOWDER CANISTERS IN THERE... AND LITTLE ELSE.
DON' KNOW, MA'AM. THINK IT'S FOR FIREWORKS. IN 'OMAGE TO YOUR NOBLE HU'BAND...
Y-YES... I SUPPOSE THAT WOULD BE A NICE GESTURE... ALTHOUGH A BIT LATE. JUST LET ME CALL THE BOOTH SO THEY CAN LOOK FOR CHESTERFIELD.
IF HE DOESN'T KNOW... I DOUBT ANY-ONE--
N-NO... NO NEED... I-I CAN TRACK 'IM. DON'T BOTHER.
I DON'T MIND... THIS WAY WE SKIP A STEP, RIGHT?
N-NO... SERIOUSLY... PLEASE...
HELLO-- HELLO? FREDERIK?

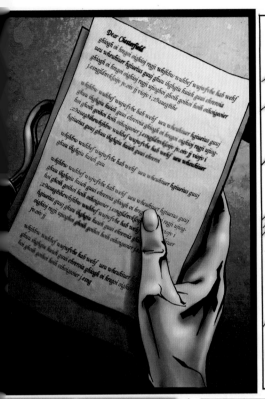

Dear Chesterfield

Of course, it all began with your poor mother. Ches.

Everything I ever told you about her is true.

Except one thing.

She was not born on the Salamander.

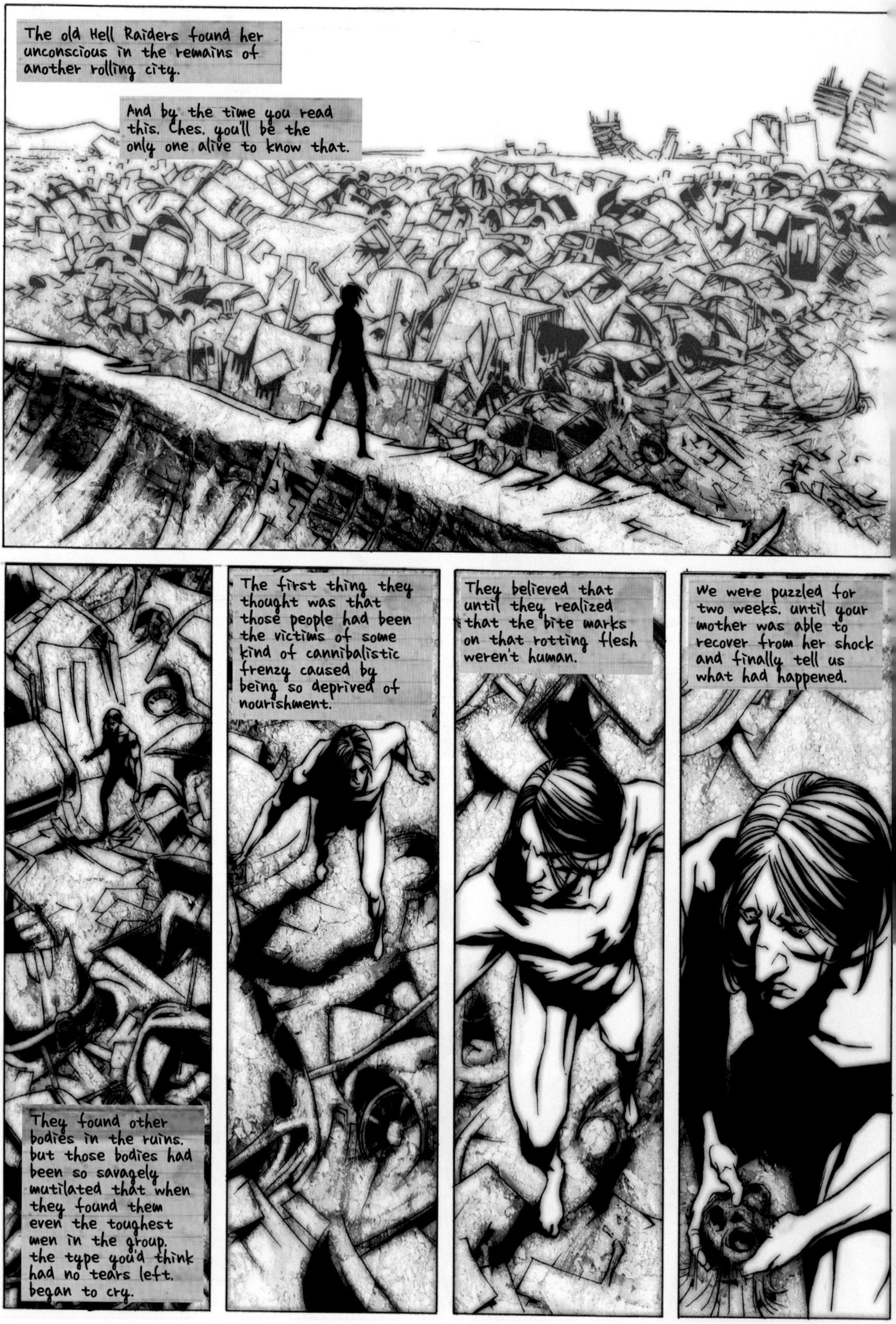
The old Hell Raiders found her unconscious in the remains of another rolling city.
And by the time you read this, Ches, you'll be the only one alive to know that.
They found other bodies in the ruins, but those bodies had been so savagely mutilated that when they found them even the toughest men in the group, the type you'd think had no tears left, began to cry.
The first thing they thought was that those people had been the victims of some kind of cannibalistic frenzy caused by being so deprived of nourishment.
They believed that until they realized that the bite marks on that rotting flesh weren't human.
We were puzzled for two weeks, until your mother was able to recover from her shock and finally tell us what had happened.

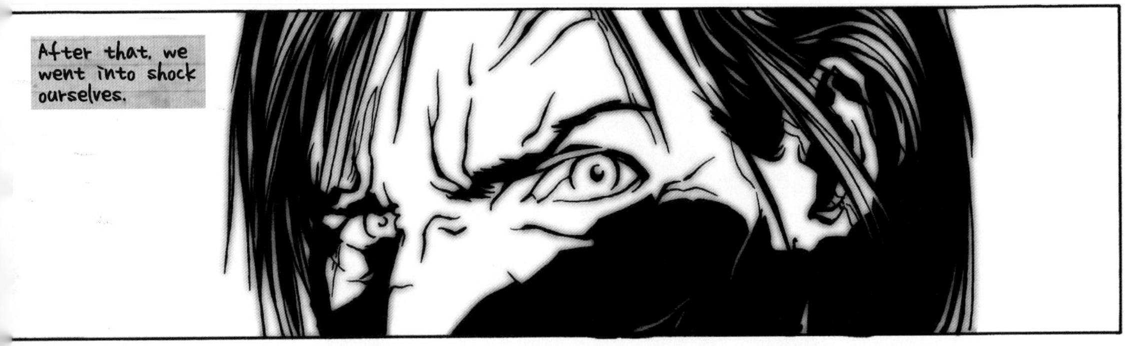
After that, we went into shock ourselves.

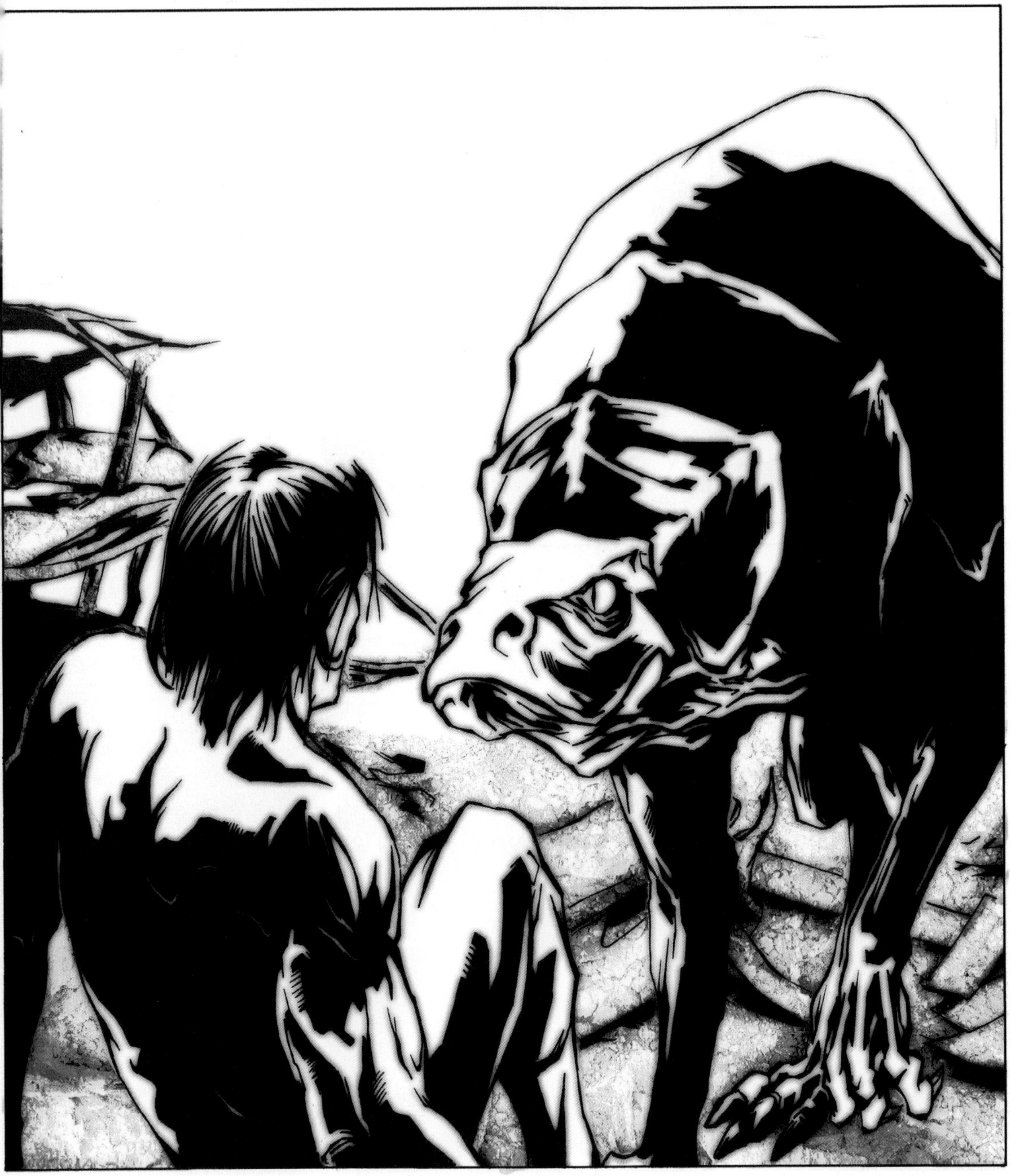

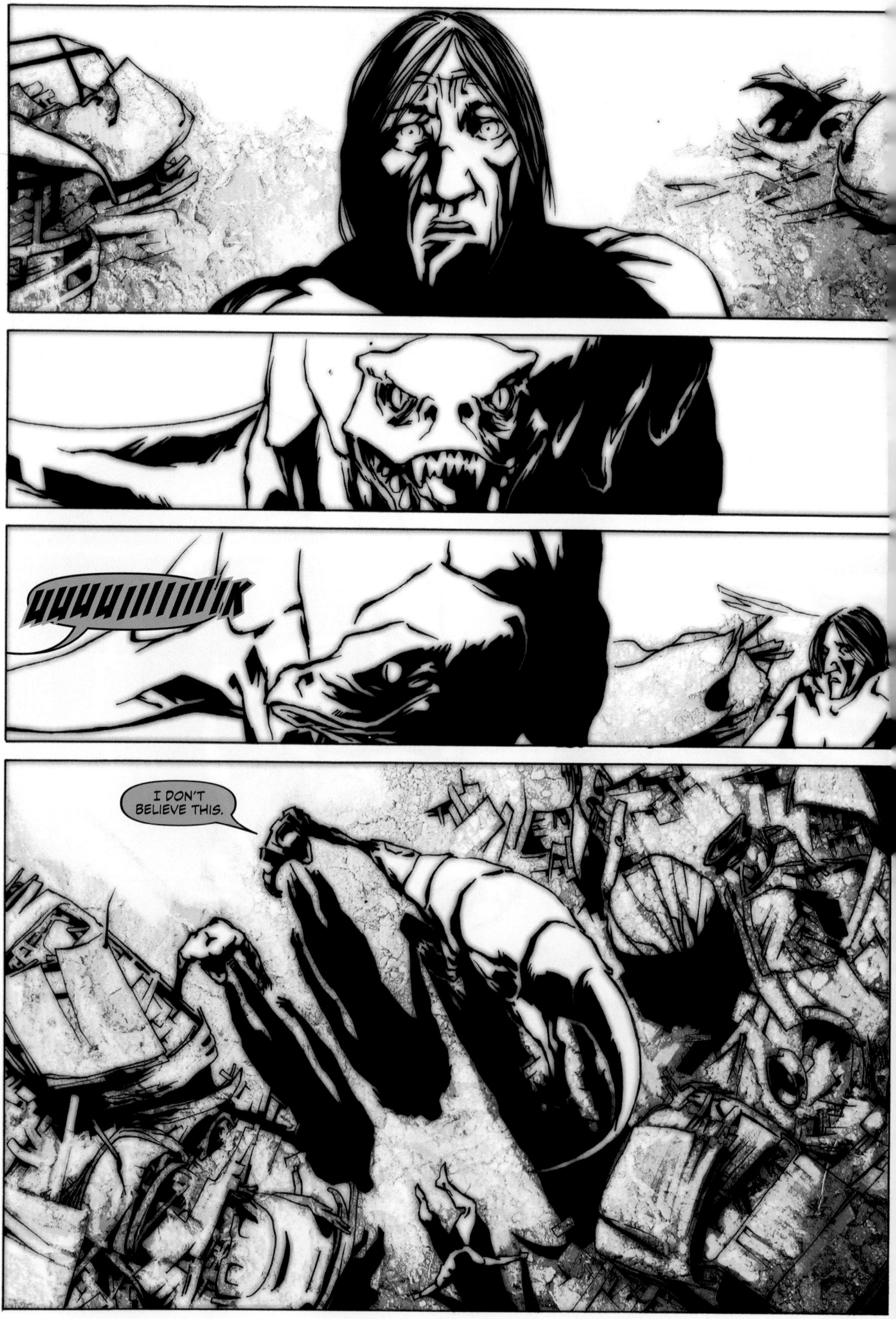
UUUUNNNNK
I DON'T BELIEVE THIS.

At least two species seem to have survived and adapted.

HOLY...

One is like an animal. Your mother described them as "monstrous armadillos". I assume that the shell they found recently belonged to one of their young.

...SHIT.

The other is humanoid.

In a sense.

HOW CAN HE BE BREATHING?

I HAVE NO IDEA, PLUTARCH.

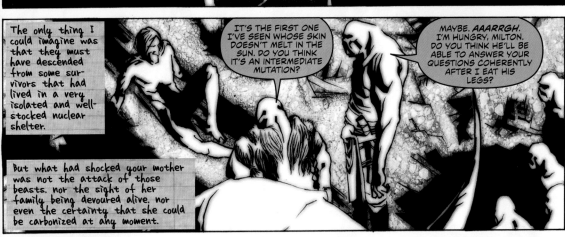

The only thing I could imagine was that they must have descended from some survivors that had lived in a very isolated and well-stocked nuclear shelter.

IT'S THE FIRST ONE I'VE SEEN WHOSE SKIN DOESN'T MELT IN THE SUN. DO YOU THINK IT'S AN INTERMEDIATE MUTATION?

MAYBE. AAARRGH. I'M HUNGRY, MILTON. DO YOU THINK HE'LL BE ABLE TO ANSWER YOUR QUESTIONS COHERENTLY AFTER I EAT HIS LEGS?

But what had shocked your mother was not the attack of those beasts, nor the sight of her family being devoured alive, nor even the certainty that she could be carbonized at any moment.

BUT... LOOKING AT HIM UP CLOSE... HIS FACE...

MMMM...

It was something else entirely, which we couldn't even fathom until we saw the blood dripping down her legs.

Then we understood that what terrified her the most wasn't what had happened, but what was going to happen...

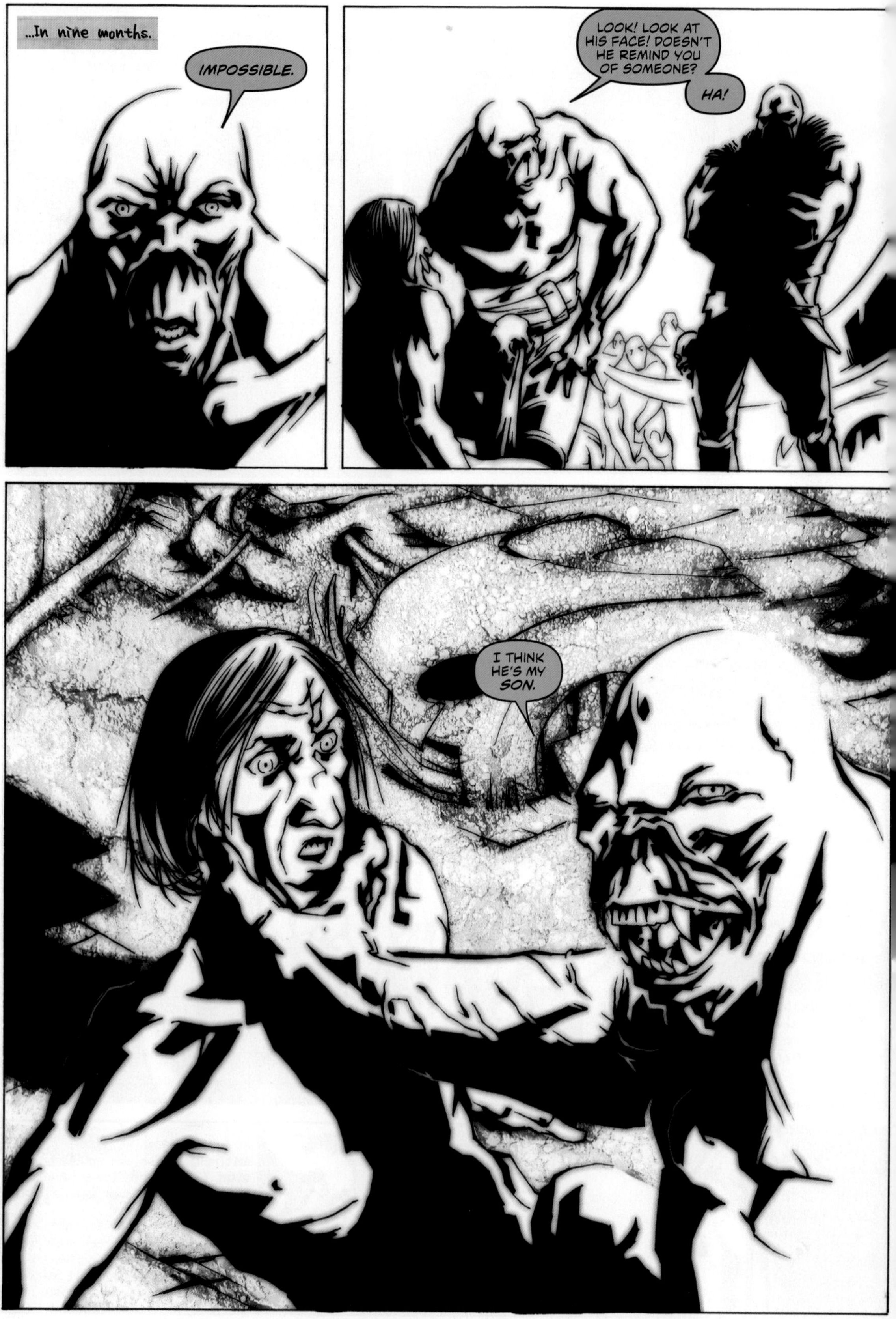
...In nine months.
IMPOSSIBLE.
LOOK! LOOK AT HIS FACE! DOESN'T HE REMIND YOU OF SOMEONE?
HA!
I THINK HE'S MY SON.

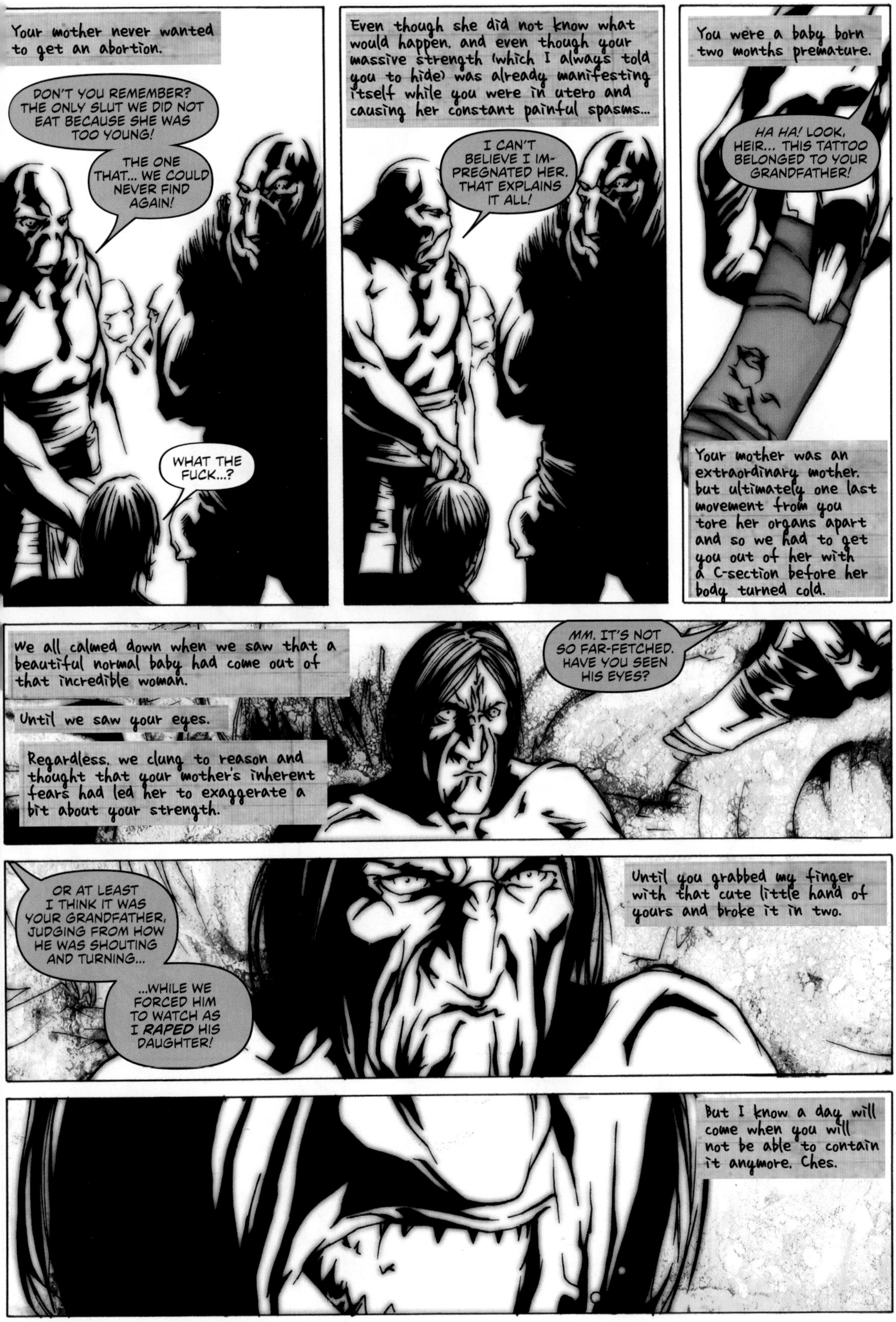
Your mother never wanted to get an abortion.
DON'T YOU REMEMBER? THE ONLY SLUT WE DID NOT EAT BECAUSE SHE WAS TOO YOUNG!
THE ONE THAT... WE COULD NEVER FIND AGAIN!
WHAT THE FUCK...?
Even though she did not know what would happen, and even though your massive strength (which I always told you to hide) was already manifesting itself while you were in utero and causing her constant painful spasms...
I CAN'T BELIEVE I IMPREGNATED HER. THAT EXPLAINS IT ALL!
You were a baby born two months premature.
HA HA! LOOK, HEIR... THIS TATTOO BELONGED TO YOUR GRANDFATHER!
Your mother was an extraordinary mother, but ultimately one last movement from you tore her organs apart and so we had to get you out of her with a C-section before her body turned cold.
We all calmed down when we saw that a beautiful normal baby had come out of that incredible woman.
Until we saw your eyes.
Regardless, we clung to reason and thought that your mother's inherent fears had led her to exaggerate a bit about your strength.
MM. IT'S NOT SO FAR-FETCHED. HAVE YOU SEEN HIS EYES?
OR AT LEAST I THINK IT WAS YOUR GRANDFATHER, JUDGING FROM HOW HE WAS SHOUTING AND TURNING...
...WHILE WE FORCED HIM TO WATCH AS I RAPED HIS DAUGHTER!
Until you grabbed my finger with that cute little hand of yours and broke it in two.
But I know a day will come when you will not be able to contain it anymore, Ches.

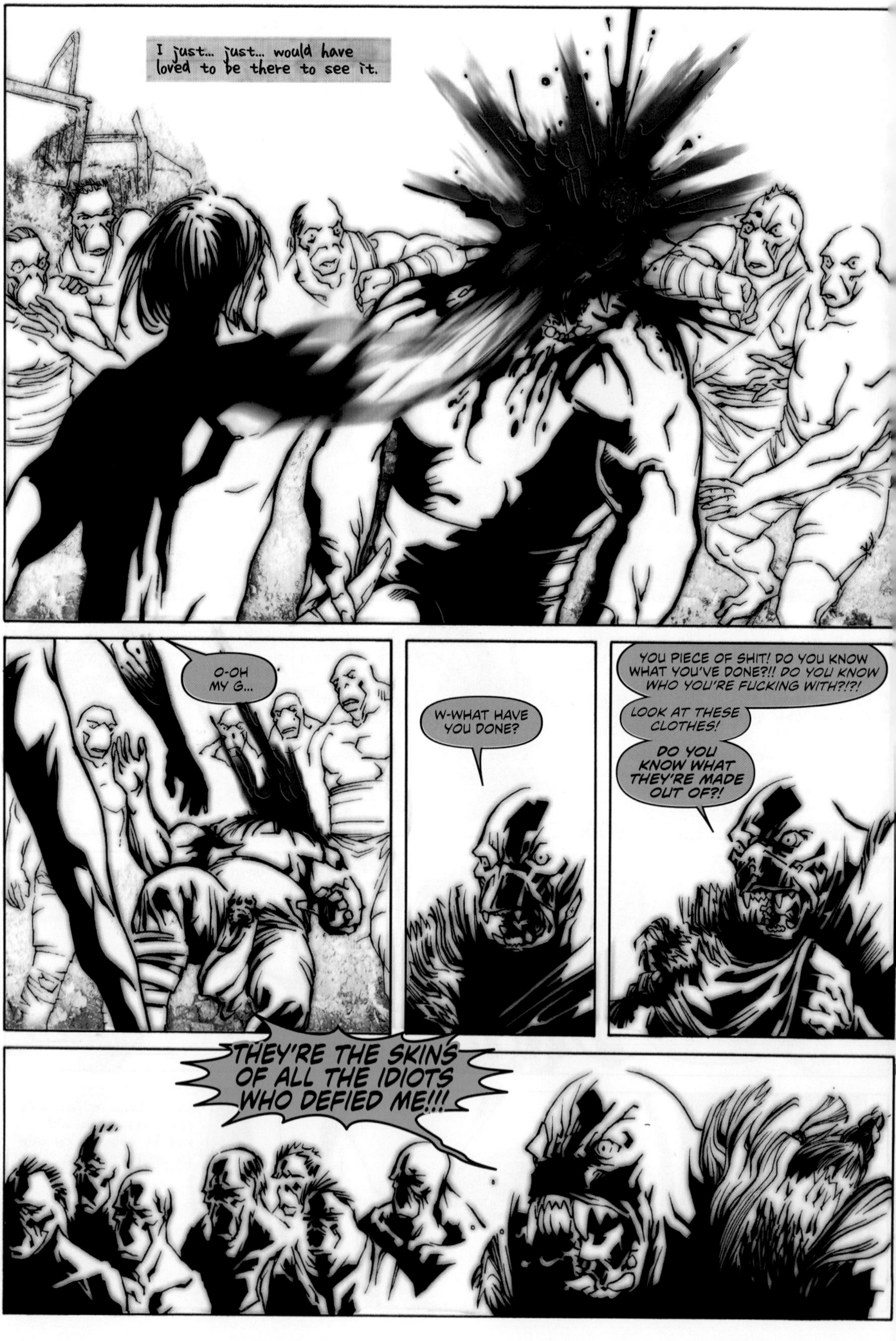
I just... just... would have loved to be there to see it.
O-OH MY G...
W-WHAT HAVE YOU DONE?
YOU PIECE OF SHIT! DO YOU KNOW WHAT YOU'VE DONE?!! DO YOU KNOW WHO YOU'RE FUCKING WITH?!?!
LOOK AT THESE CLOTHES!
DO YOU KNOW WHAT THEY'RE MADE OUT OF?!
THEY'RE THE SKINS OF ALL THE IDIOTS WHO DEFIED ME!!!

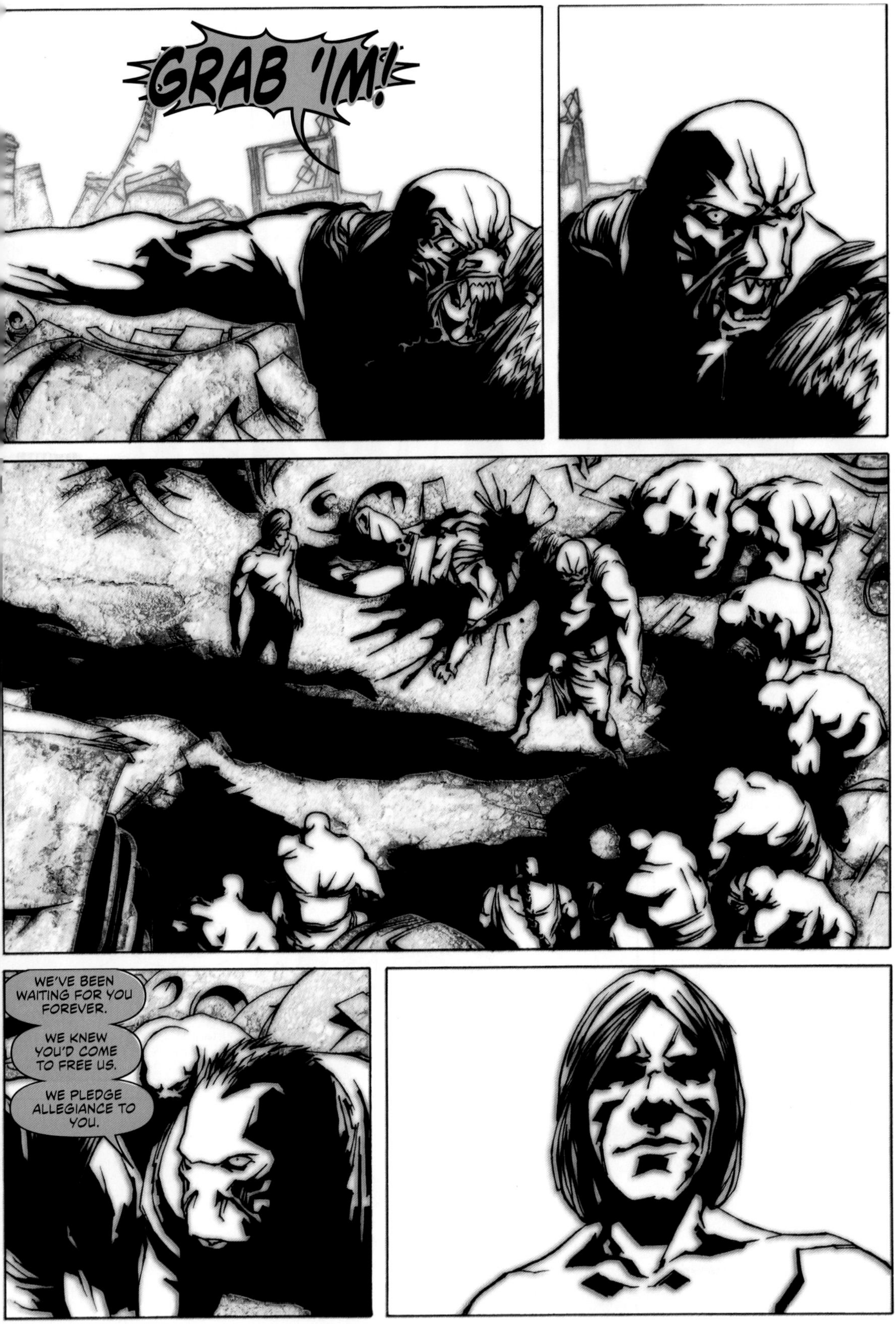
GRAB 'IM!
WE'VE BEEN WAITING FOR YOU FOREVER.
WE KNEW YOU'D COME TO FREE US.
WE PLEDGE ALLEGIANCE TO YOU.

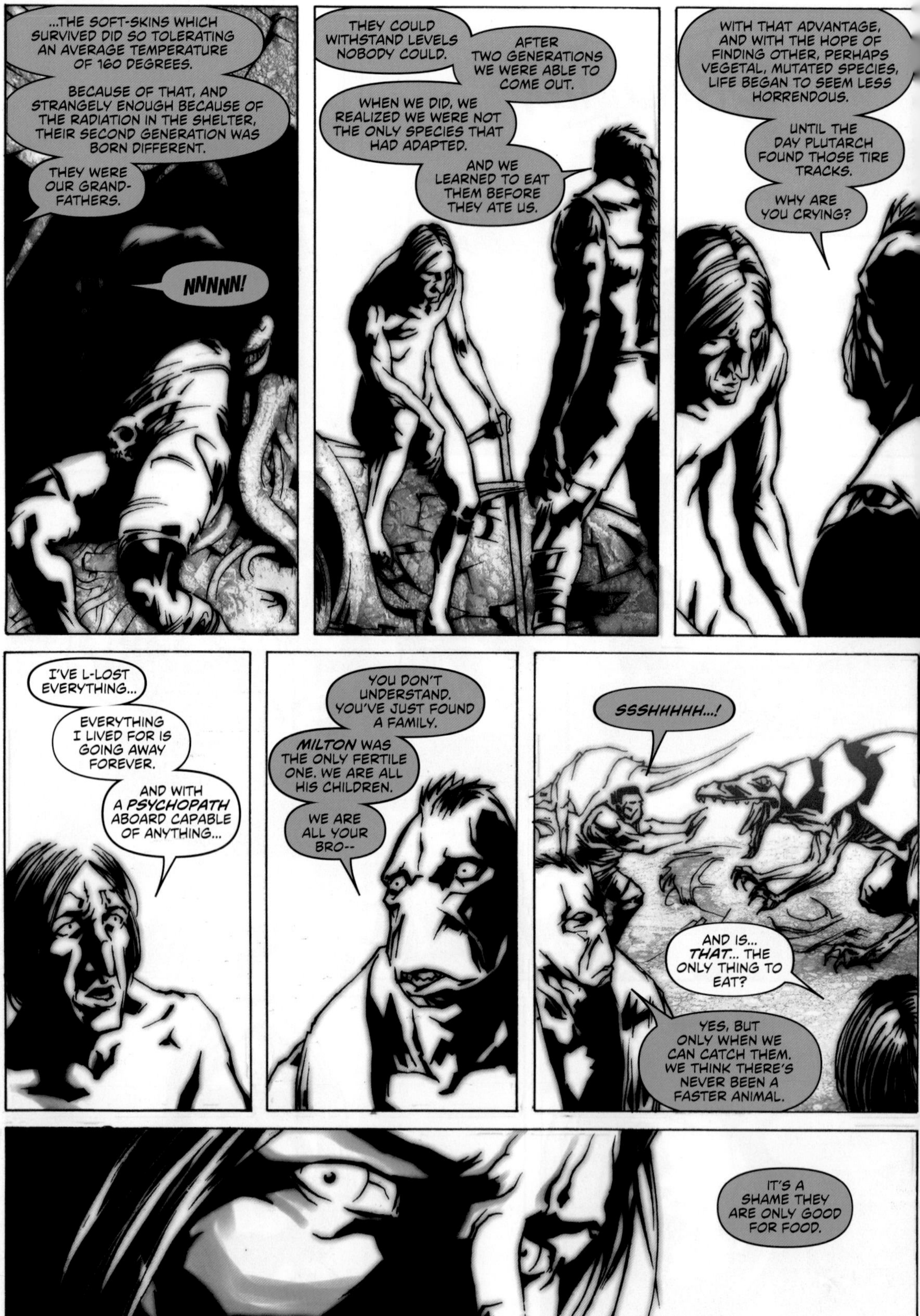
...THE SOFT-SKINS WHICH SURVIVED DID SO TOLERATING AN AVERAGE TEMPERATURE OF 160 DEGREES.
BECAUSE OF THAT, AND STRANGELY ENOUGH BECAUSE OF THE RADIATION IN THE SHELTER, THEIR SECOND GENERATION WAS BORN DIFFERENT.
THEY WERE OUR GRAND-FATHERS.
NNNNN!
THEY COULD WITHSTAND LEVELS NOBODY COULD.
AFTER TWO GENERATIONS WE WERE ABLE TO COME OUT.
WHEN WE DID, WE REALIZED WE WERE NOT THE ONLY SPECIES THAT HAD ADAPTED.
AND WE LEARNED TO EAT THEM BEFORE THEY ATE US.
WITH THAT ADVANTAGE, AND WITH THE HOPE OF FINDING OTHER, PERHAPS VEGETAL, MUTATED SPECIES, LIFE BEGAN TO SEEM LESS HORRENDOUS.
UNTIL THE DAY PLUTARCH FOUND THOSE TIRE TRACKS.
WHY ARE YOU CRYING?
I'VE L-LOST EVERYTHING...
EVERYTHING I LIVED FOR IS GOING AWAY FOREVER.
AND WITH A PSYCHOPATH ABOARD CAPABLE OF ANYTHING...
YOU DON'T UNDERSTAND. YOU'VE JUST FOUND A FAMILY.
MILTON WAS THE ONLY FERTILE ONE. WE ARE ALL HIS CHILDREN.
WE ARE ALL YOUR BRO--
SSSHHHHH...!
AND IS... THAT... THE ONLY THING TO EAT?
YES, BUT ONLY WHEN WE CAN CATCH THEM. WE THINK THERE'S NEVER BEEN A FASTER ANIMAL.
IT'S A SHAME THEY ARE ONLY GOOD FOR FOOD.

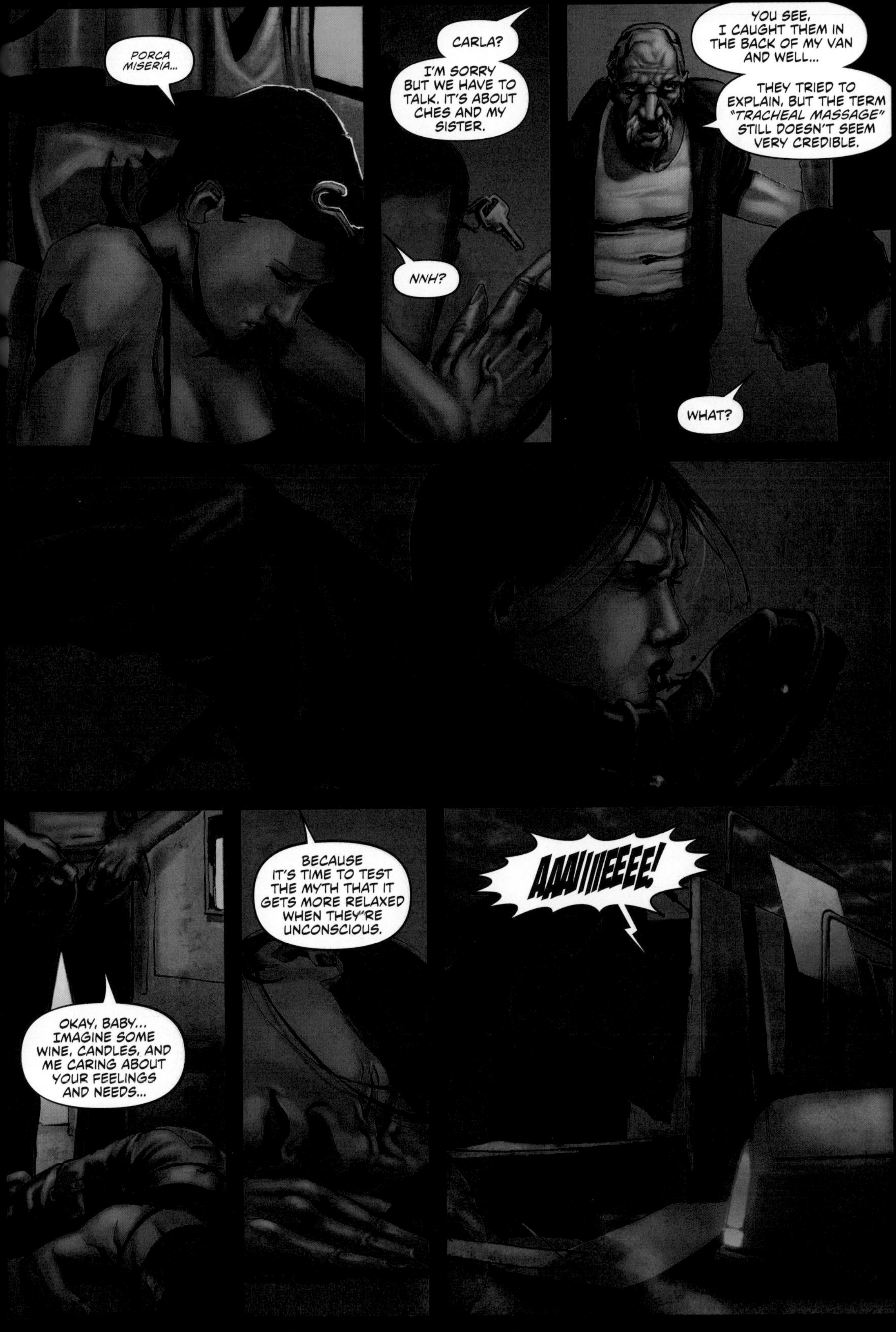
PORCA MISERIA...
CARLA?
I'M SORRY BUT WE HAVE TO TALK. IT'S ABOUT CHES AND MY SISTER.
NNH?
YOU SEE, I CAUGHT THEM IN THE BACK OF MY VAN AND WELL...
THEY TRIED TO EXPLAIN, BUT THE TERM "TRACHEAL MASSAGE" STILL DOESN'T SEEM VERY CREDIBLE.
WHAT?
OKAY, BABY... IMAGINE SOME WINE, CANDLES, AND ME CARING ABOUT YOUR FEELINGS AND NEEDS...
BECAUSE IT'S TIME TO TEST THE MYTH THAT IT GETS MORE RELAXED WHEN THEY'RE UNCONSCIOUS.
AAAIIIEEEE!

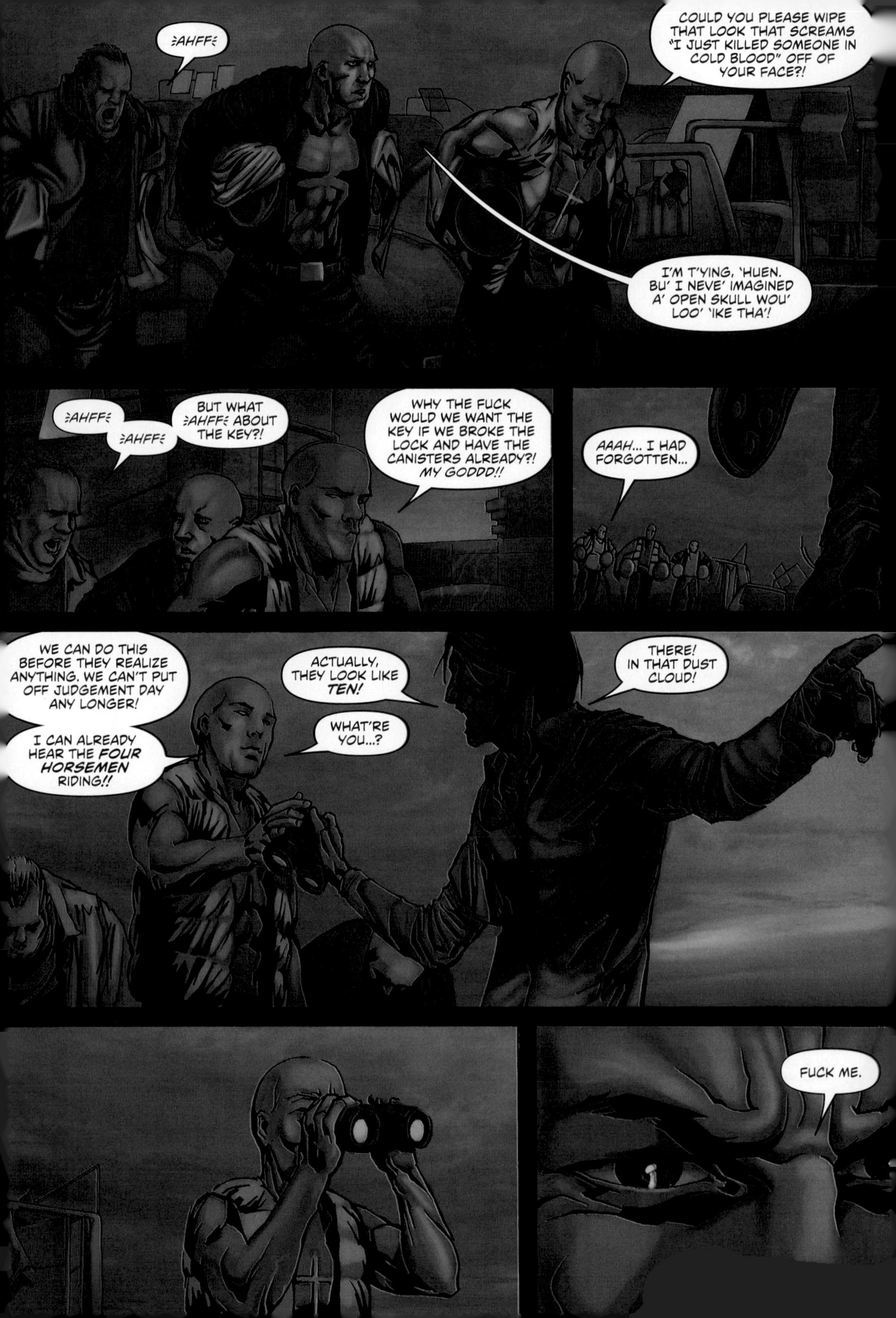

ƎAHFFƎ
COULD YOU PLEASE WIPE THAT LOOK THAT SCREAMS "I JUST KILLED SOMEONE IN COLD BLOOD" OFF OF YOUR FACE?!
I'M T'YING, 'HUEN. BU' I NEVE' IMAGINED A' OPEN SKULL WOU' LOO' 'IKE THA'!
ƎAHFFƎ
ƎAHFFƎ
BUT WHAT ƎAHFFƎ ABOUT THE KEY?!
WHY THE FUCK WOULD WE WANT THE KEY IF WE BROKE THE LOCK AND HAVE THE CANISTERS ALREADY?! MY GODDD!!
AAAH... I HAD FORGOTTEN...
WE CAN DO THIS BEFORE THEY REALIZE ANYTHING. WE CAN'T PUT OFF JUDGEMENT DAY ANY LONGER!
I CAN ALREADY HEAR THE FOUR HORSEMEN RIDING!!
ACTUALLY, THEY LOOK LIKE TEN!
WHAT'RE YOU...?
THERE! IN THAT DUST CLOUD!
FUCK ME.

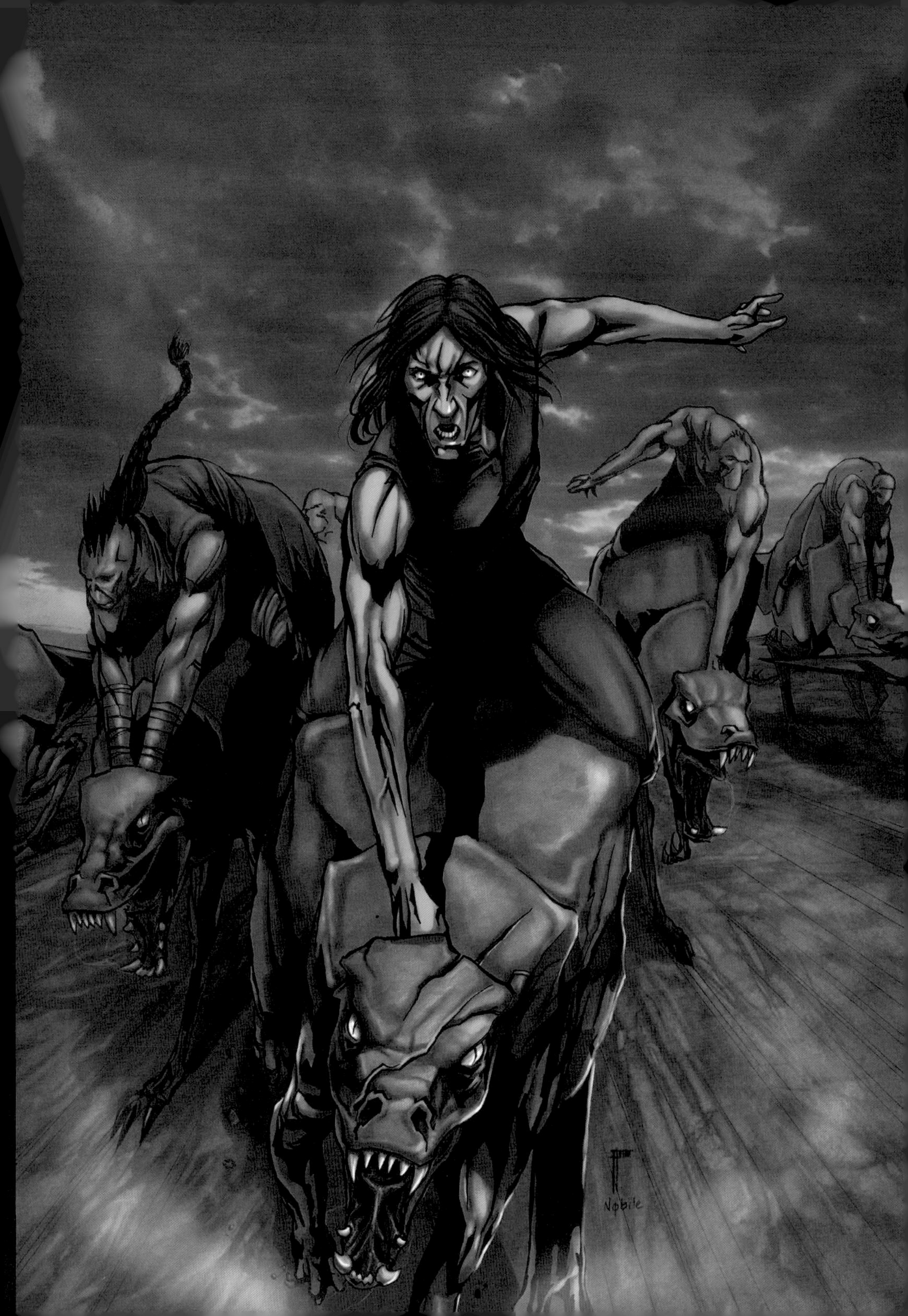

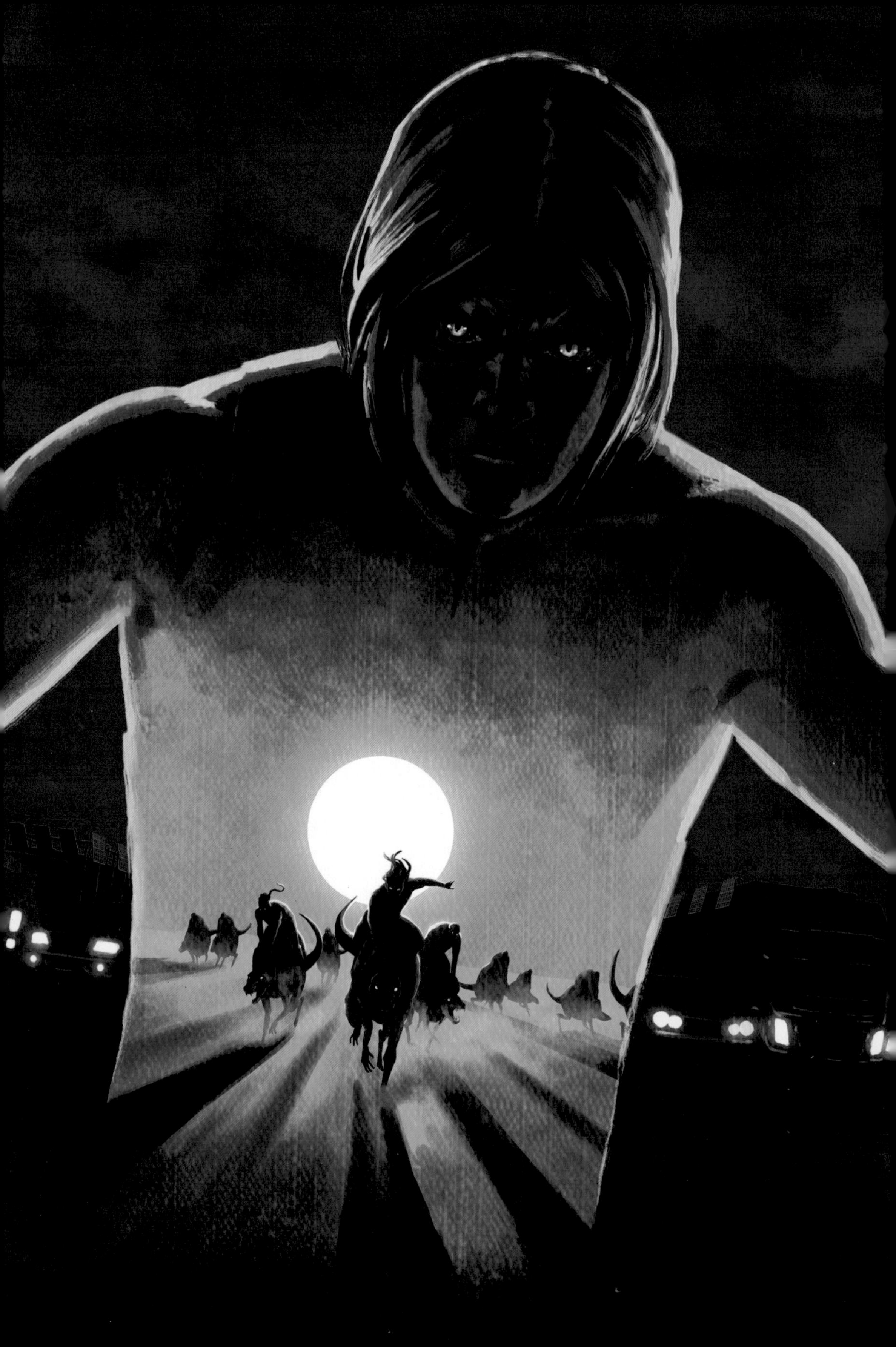

CHAPTER 3

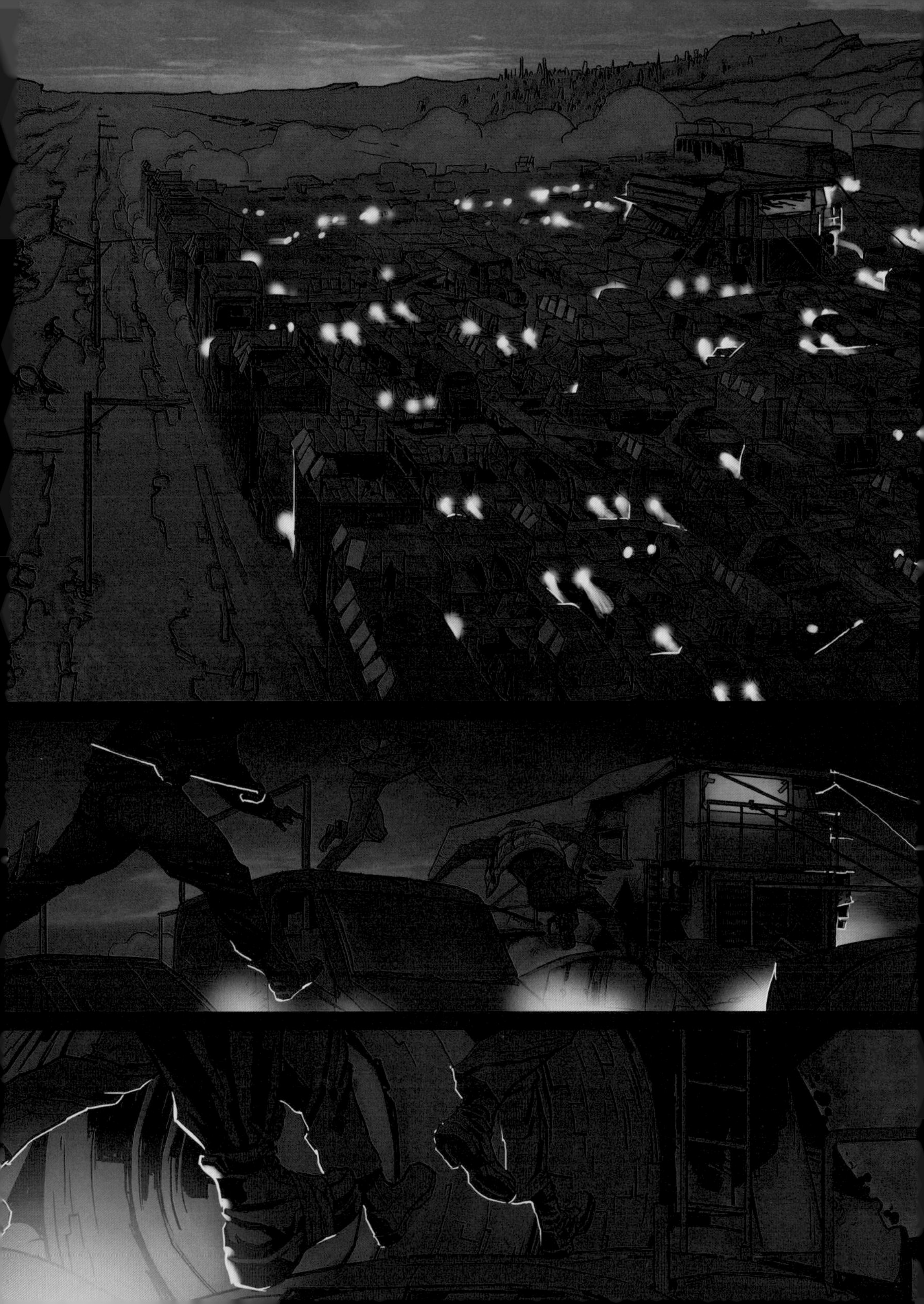

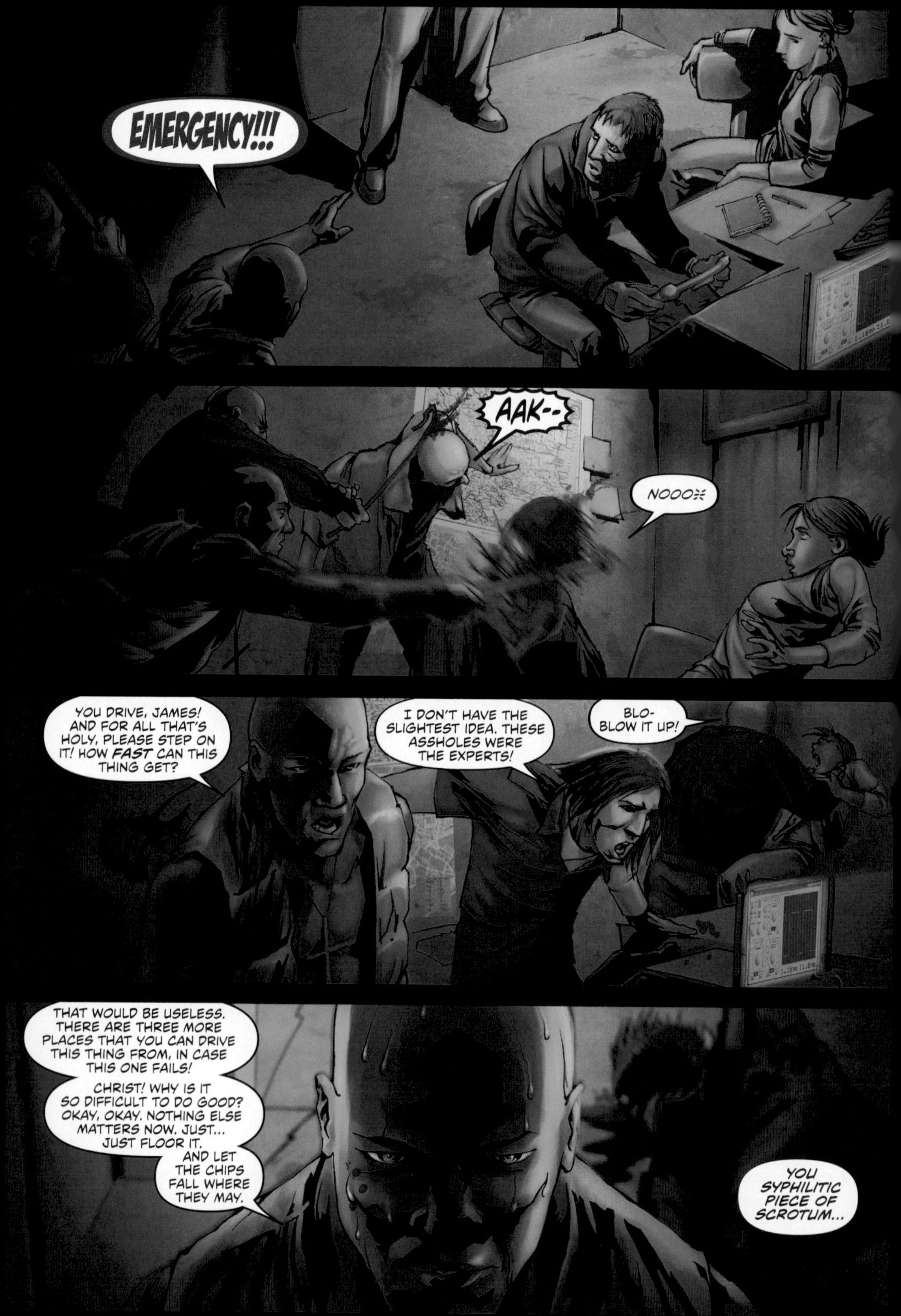
EMERGENCY!!!
AAK--
NOOO※
YOU DRIVE, JAMES! AND FOR ALL THAT'S HOLY, PLEASE STEP ON IT! HOW FAST CAN THIS THING GET?
I DON'T HAVE THE SLIGHTEST IDEA. THESE ASSHOLES WERE THE EXPERTS!
BLO- BLOW IT UP!
THAT WOULD BE USELESS. THERE ARE THREE MORE PLACES THAT YOU CAN DRIVE THIS THING FROM, IN CASE THIS ONE FAILS!
CHRIST! WHY IS IT SO DIFFICULT TO DO GOOD? OKAY, OKAY. NOTHING ELSE MATTERS NOW. JUST... JUST FLOOR IT.
AND LET THE CHIPS FALL WHERE THEY MAY.
YOU SYPHILITIC PIECE OF SCROTUM...

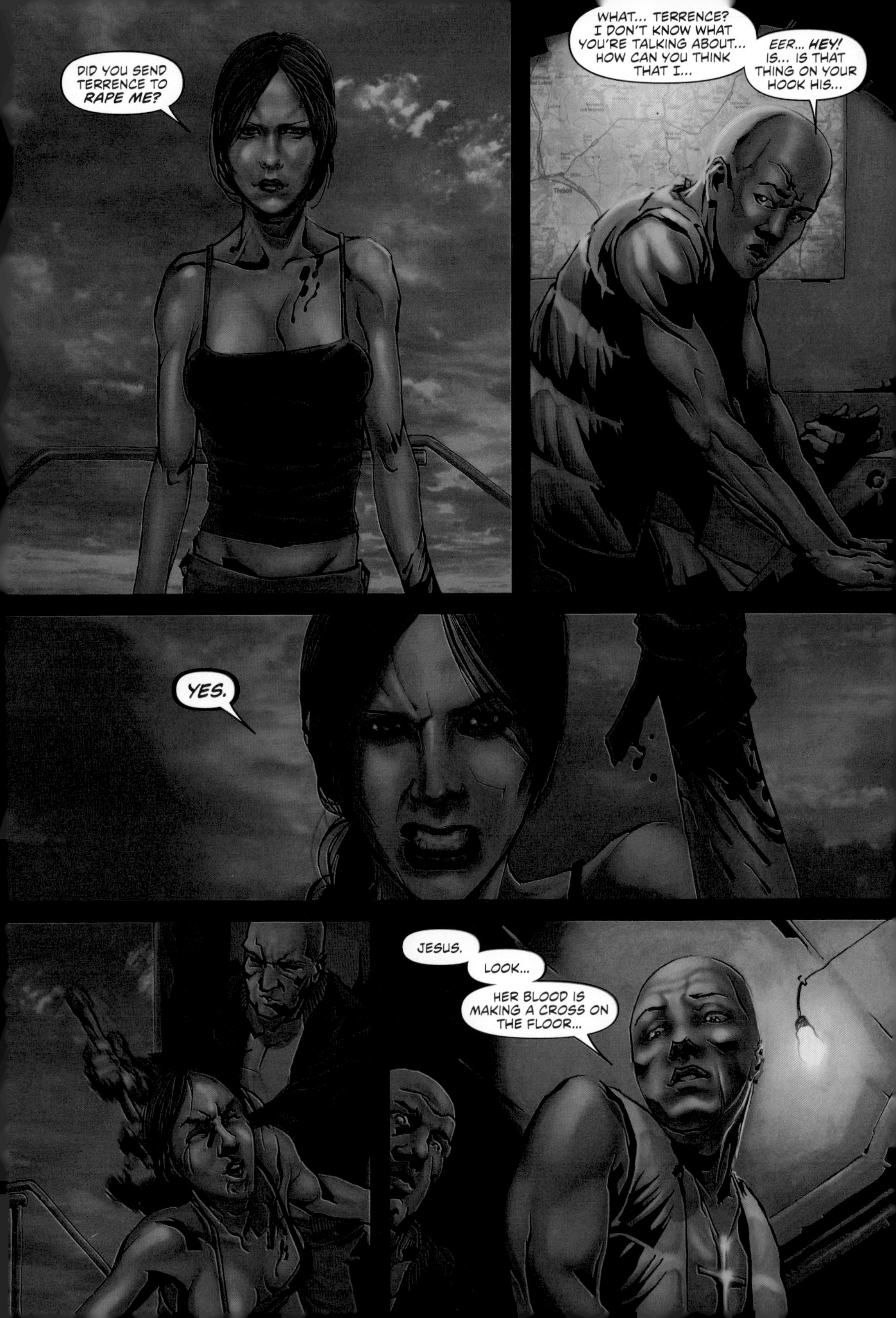
DID YOU SEND TERRENCE TO RAPE ME?
WHAT... TERRENCE? I DON'T KNOW WHAT YOU'RE TALKING ABOUT... HOW CAN YOU THINK THAT I...
EER... HEY! IS... IS THAT THING ON YOUR HOOK HIS...
YES.
JESUS.
LOOK...
HER BLOOD IS MAKING A CROSS ON THE FLOOR...

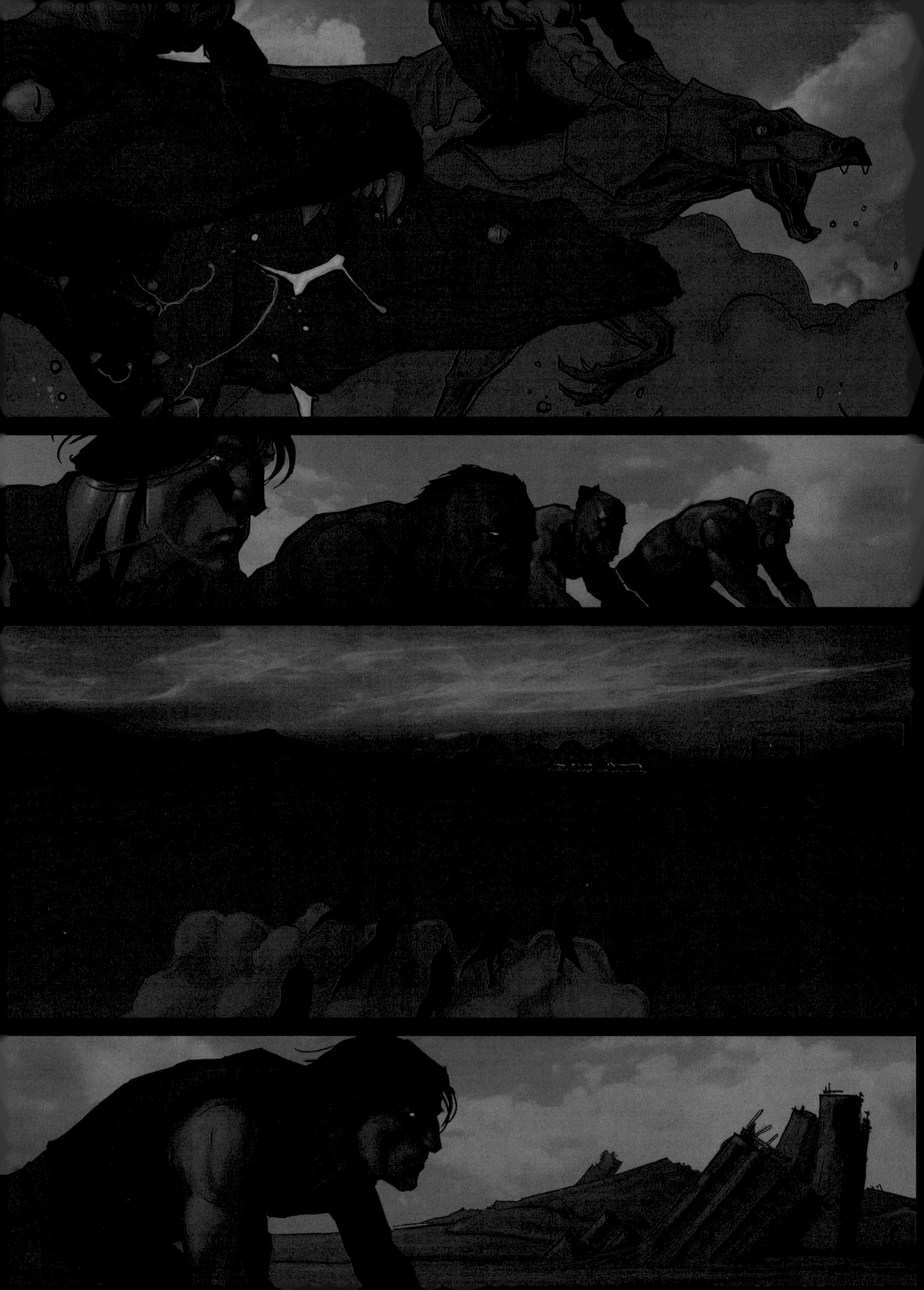

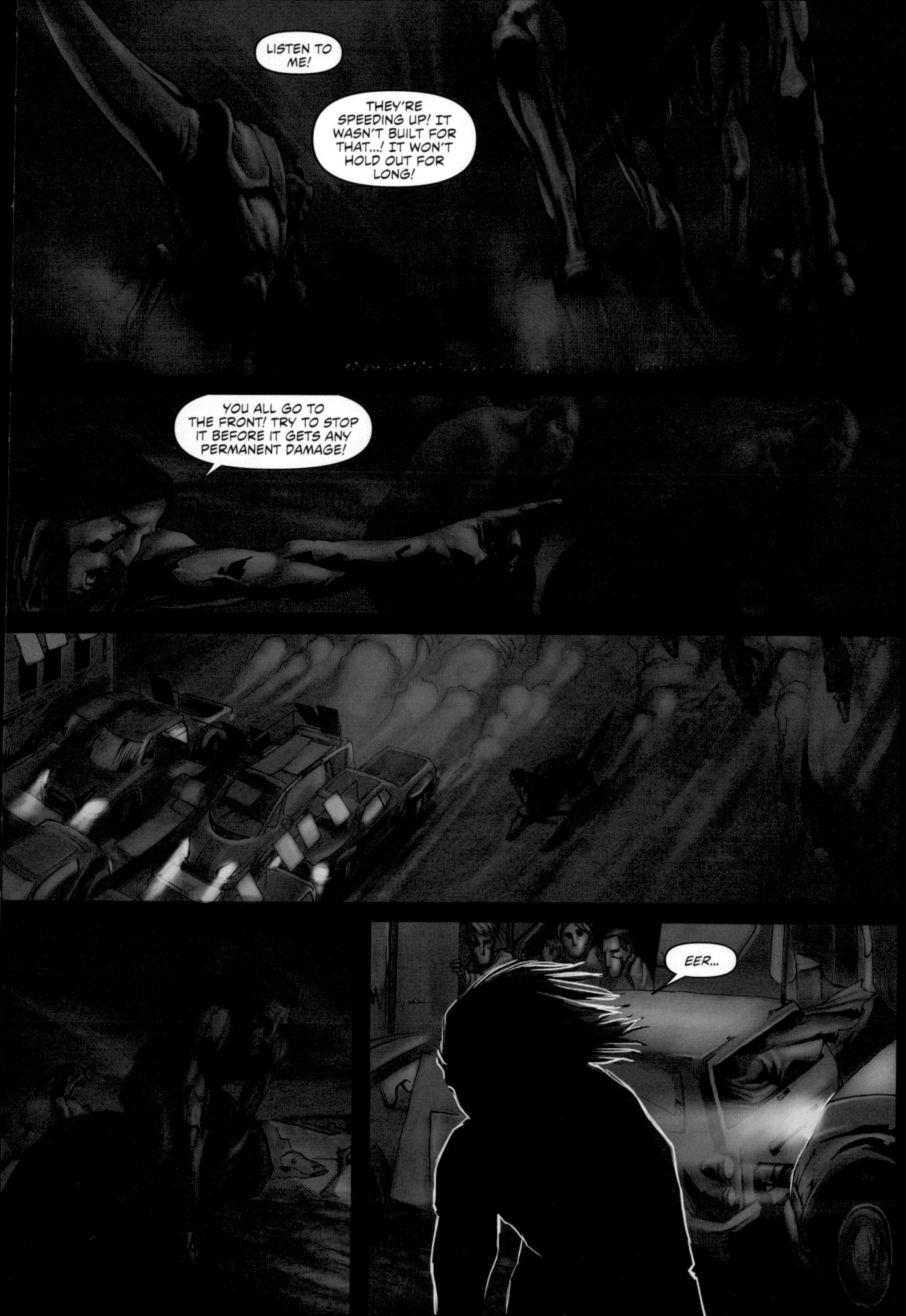
LISTEN TO ME!
THEY'RE SPEEDING UP! IT WASN'T BUILT FOR THAT...! IT WON'T HOLD OUT FOR LONG!
YOU ALL GO TO THE FRONT! TRY TO STOP IT BEFORE IT GETS ANY PERMANENT DAMAGE!
EER...

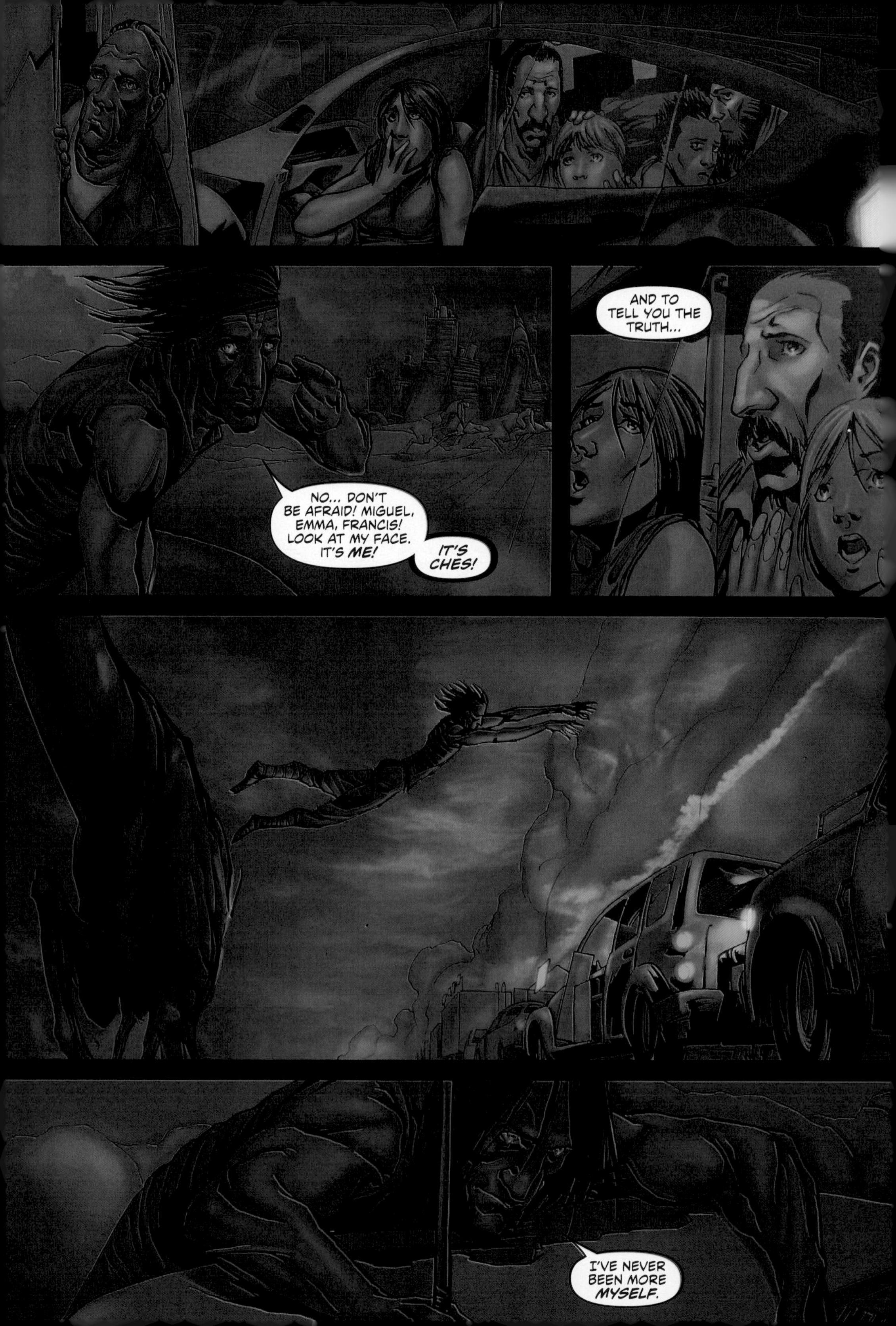
NO... DON'T BE AFRAID! MIGUEL, EMMA, FRANCIS! LOOK AT MY FACE. IT'S *ME!*
IT'S CHES!
AND TO TELL YOU THE TRUTH...
I'VE NEVER BEEN MORE *MYSELF*.

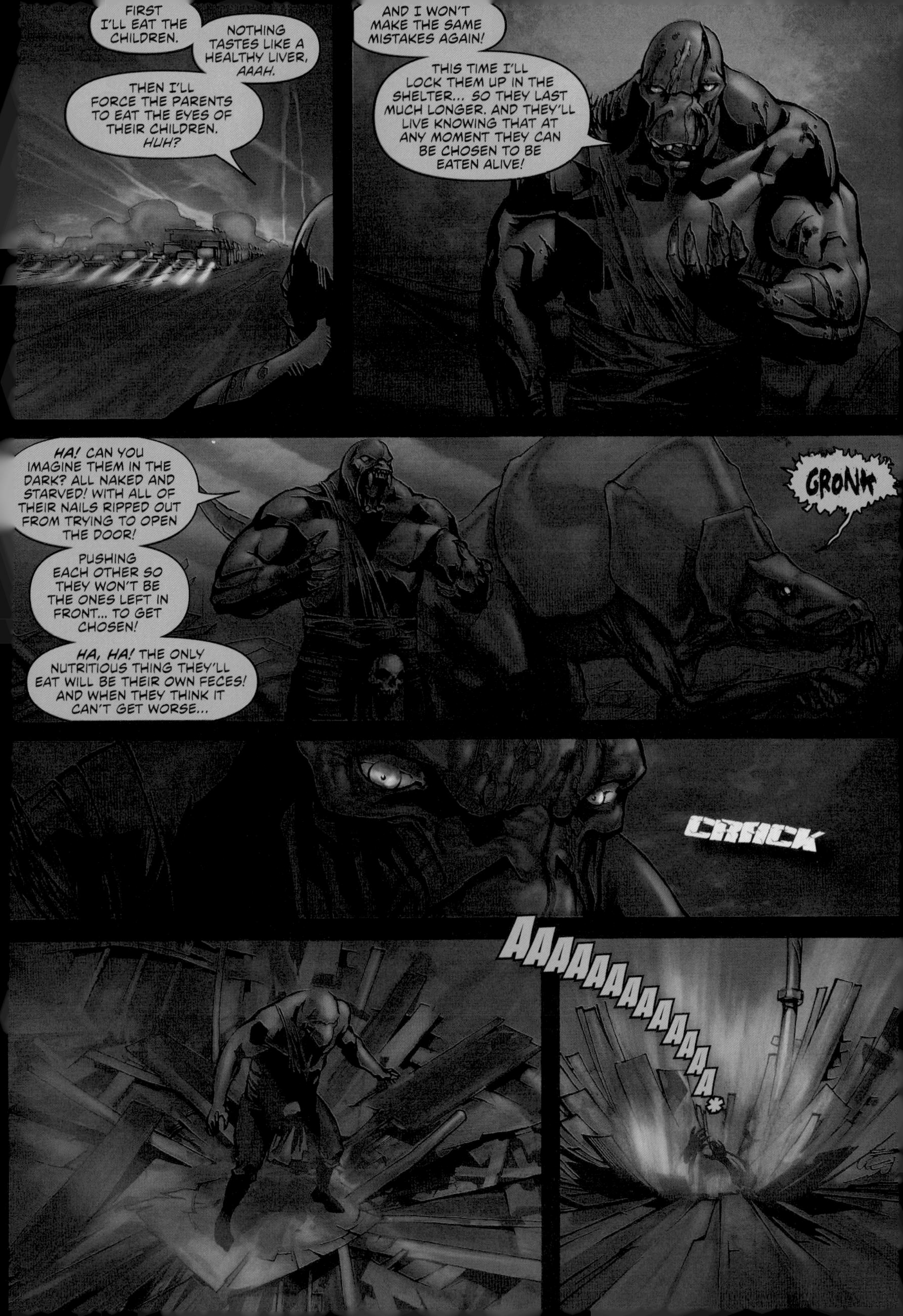
FIRST I'LL EAT THE CHILDREN.
NOTHING TASTES LIKE A HEALTHY LIVER, AAAH.
THEN I'LL FORCE THE PARENTS TO EAT THE EYES OF THEIR CHILDREN. HUH?
AND I WON'T MAKE THE SAME MISTAKES AGAIN!
THIS TIME I'LL LOCK THEM UP IN THE SHELTER... SO THEY LAST MUCH LONGER. AND THEY'LL LIVE KNOWING THAT AT ANY MOMENT THEY CAN BE CHOSEN TO BE EATEN ALIVE!
HA! CAN YOU IMAGINE THEM IN THE DARK? ALL NAKED AND STARVED! WITH ALL OF THEIR NAILS RIPPED OUT FROM TRYING TO OPEN THE DOOR!
PUSHING EACH OTHER SO THEY WON'T BE THE ONES LEFT IN FRONT... TO GET CHOSEN!
HA, HA! THE ONLY NUTRITIOUS THING THEY'LL EAT WILL BE THEIR OWN FECES! AND WHEN THEY THINK IT CAN'T GET WORSE...
GRONK
CRACK
AAAAAAAAAAAAAAA*

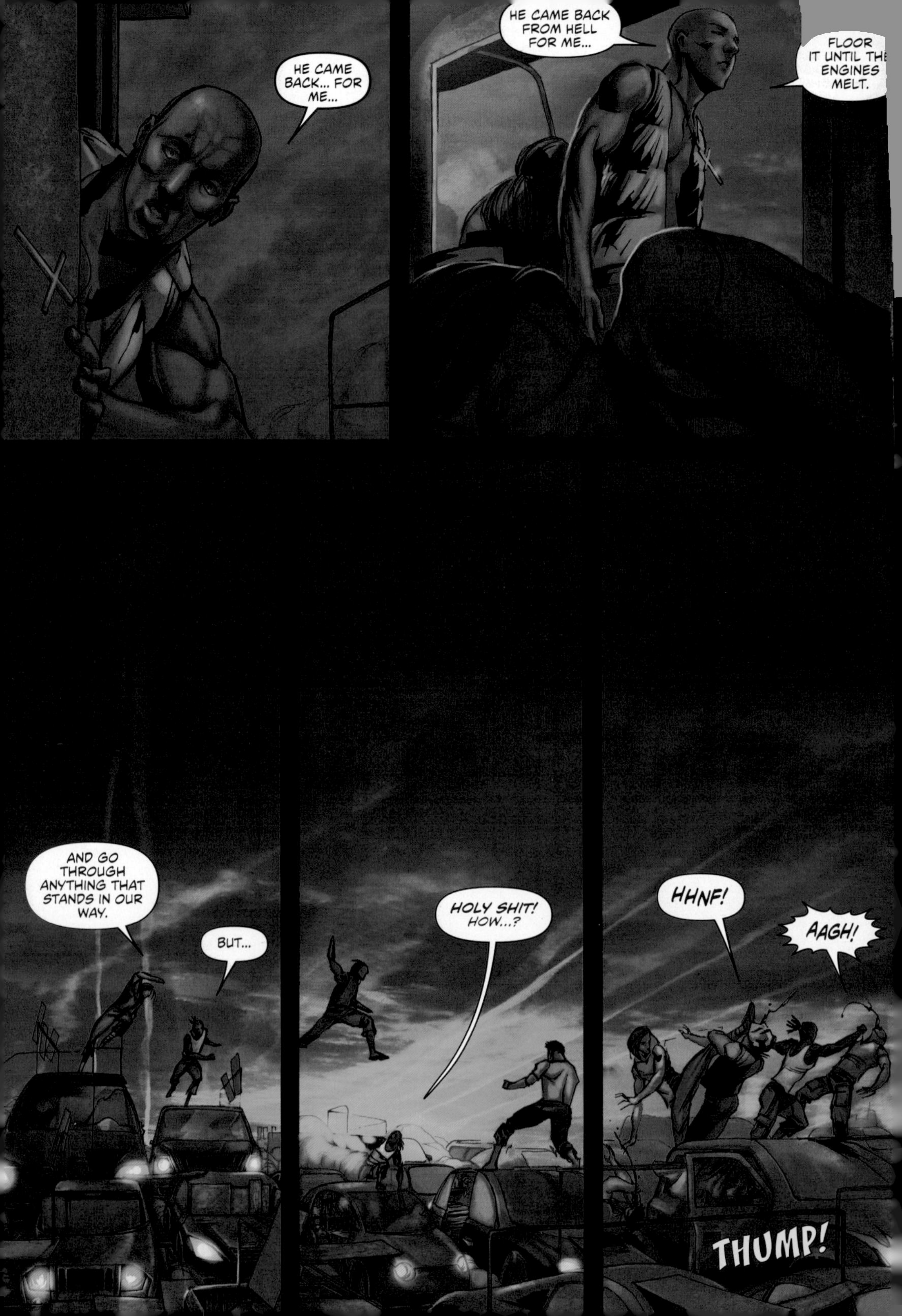
HE CAME BACK... FOR ME...
HE CAME BACK FROM HELL FOR ME...
FLOOR IT UNTIL THE ENGINES MELT.
AND GO THROUGH ANYTHING THAT STANDS IN OUR WAY.
BUT...
HOLY SHIT! HOW...?
HHNF!
AAGH!
THUMP!

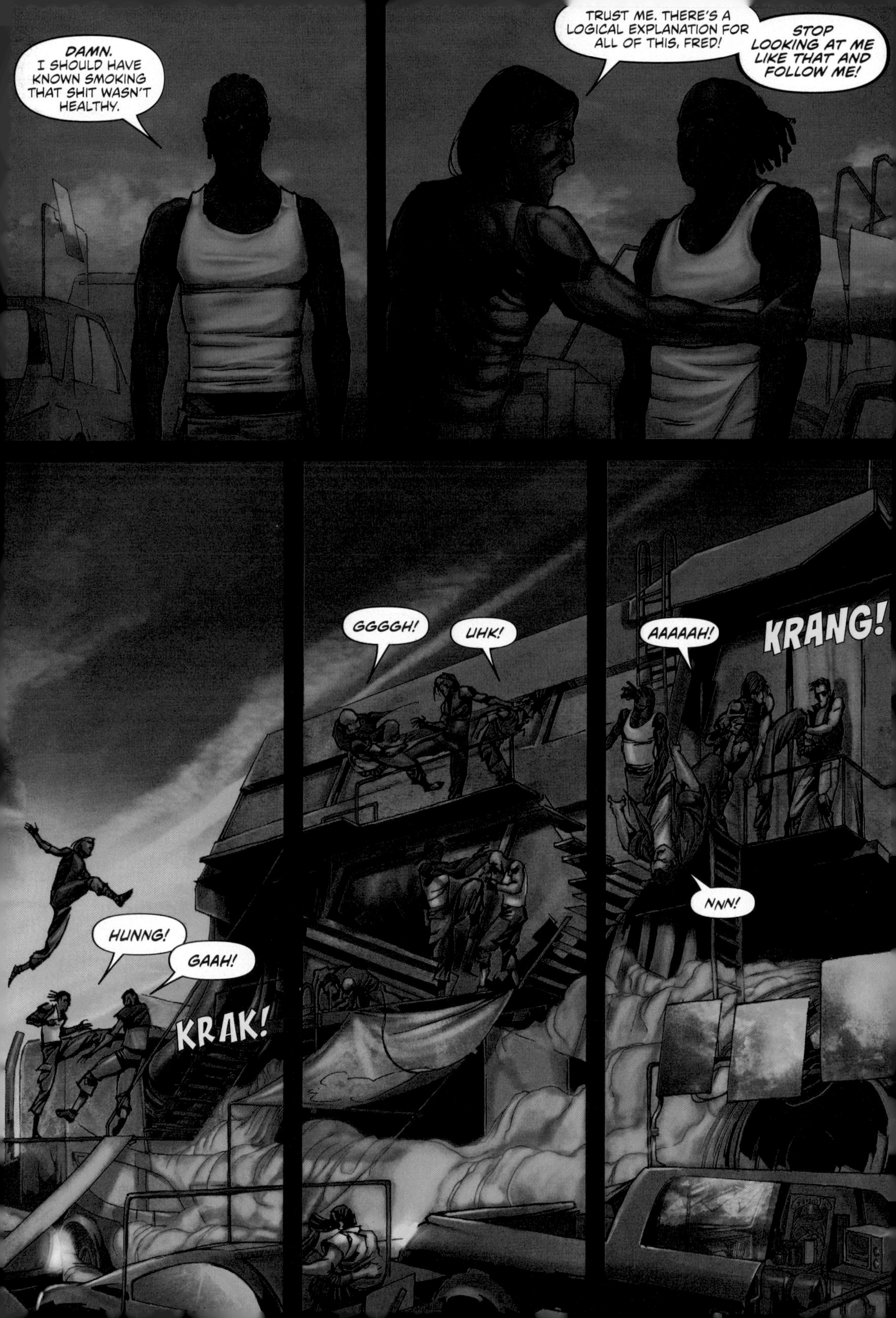
DAMN. I SHOULD HAVE KNOWN SMOKING THAT SHIT WASN'T HEALTHY.
TRUST ME. THERE'S A LOGICAL EXPLANATION FOR ALL OF THIS, FRED!
STOP LOOKING AT ME LIKE THAT AND FOLLOW ME!
HUNNG!
GAAH!
KRAK!
GGGGH!
UHK!
AAAAAH!
KRANG!
NNN!

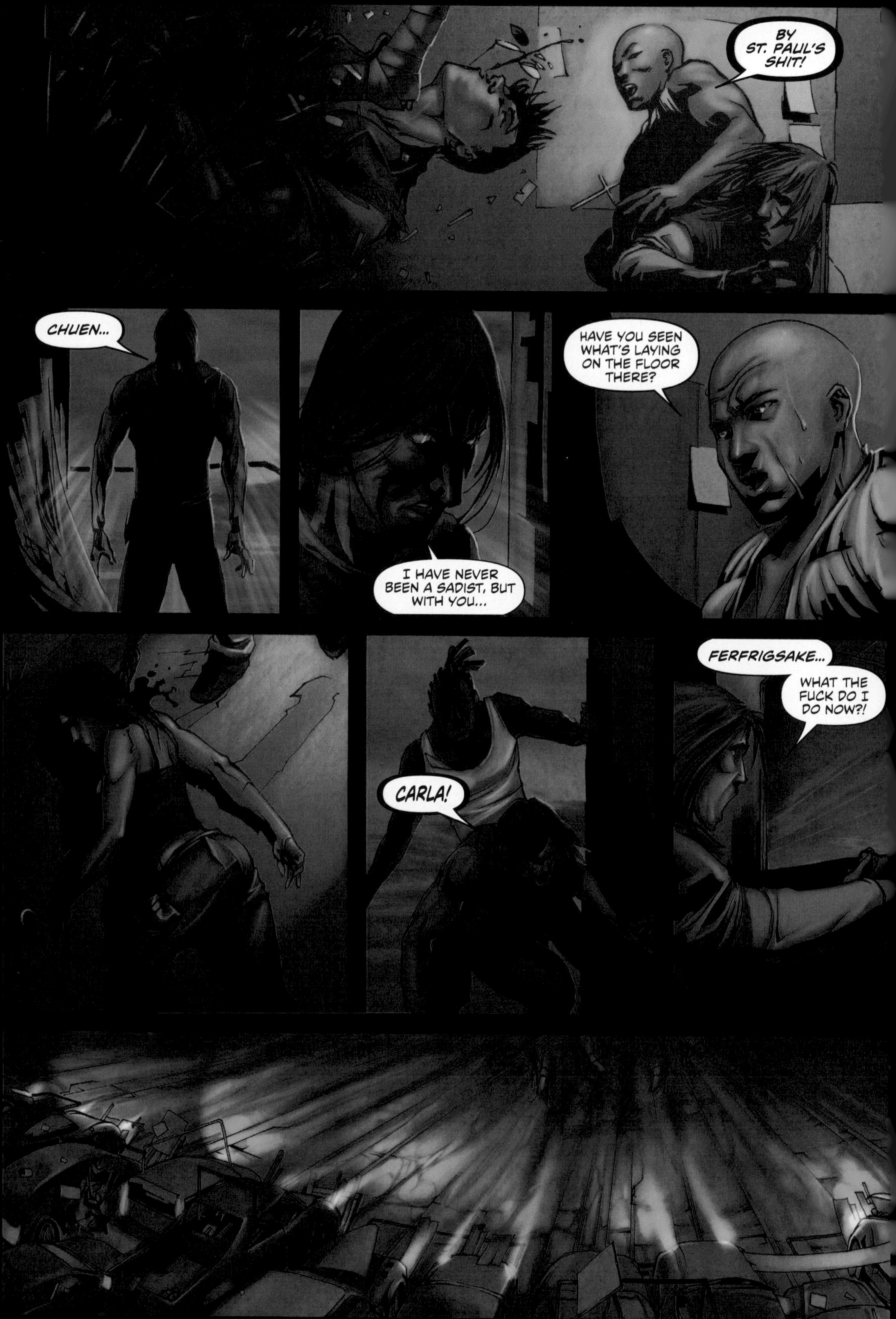
BY ST. PAUL'S SHIT!
CHUEN...
I HAVE NEVER BEEN A SADIST, BUT WITH YOU...
HAVE YOU SEEN WHAT'S LAYING ON THE FLOOR THERE?
CARLA!
FERFRIGSAKE...
WHAT THE FUCK DO I DO NOW?!

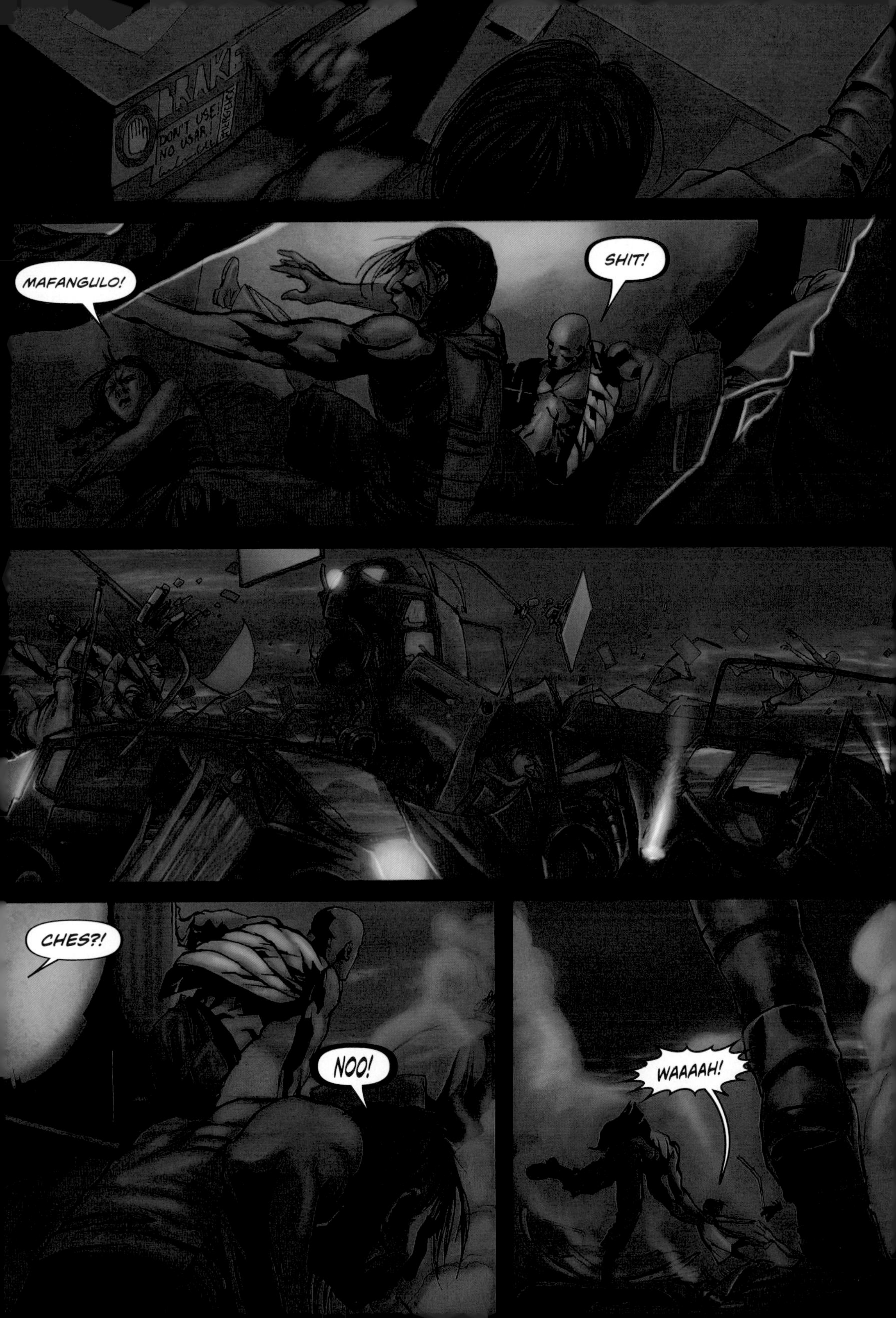
BRAKE
DON'T USE!
NO USAR!
MAFANGULO!
SHIT!
CHES?!
NOO!
WAAAAH!

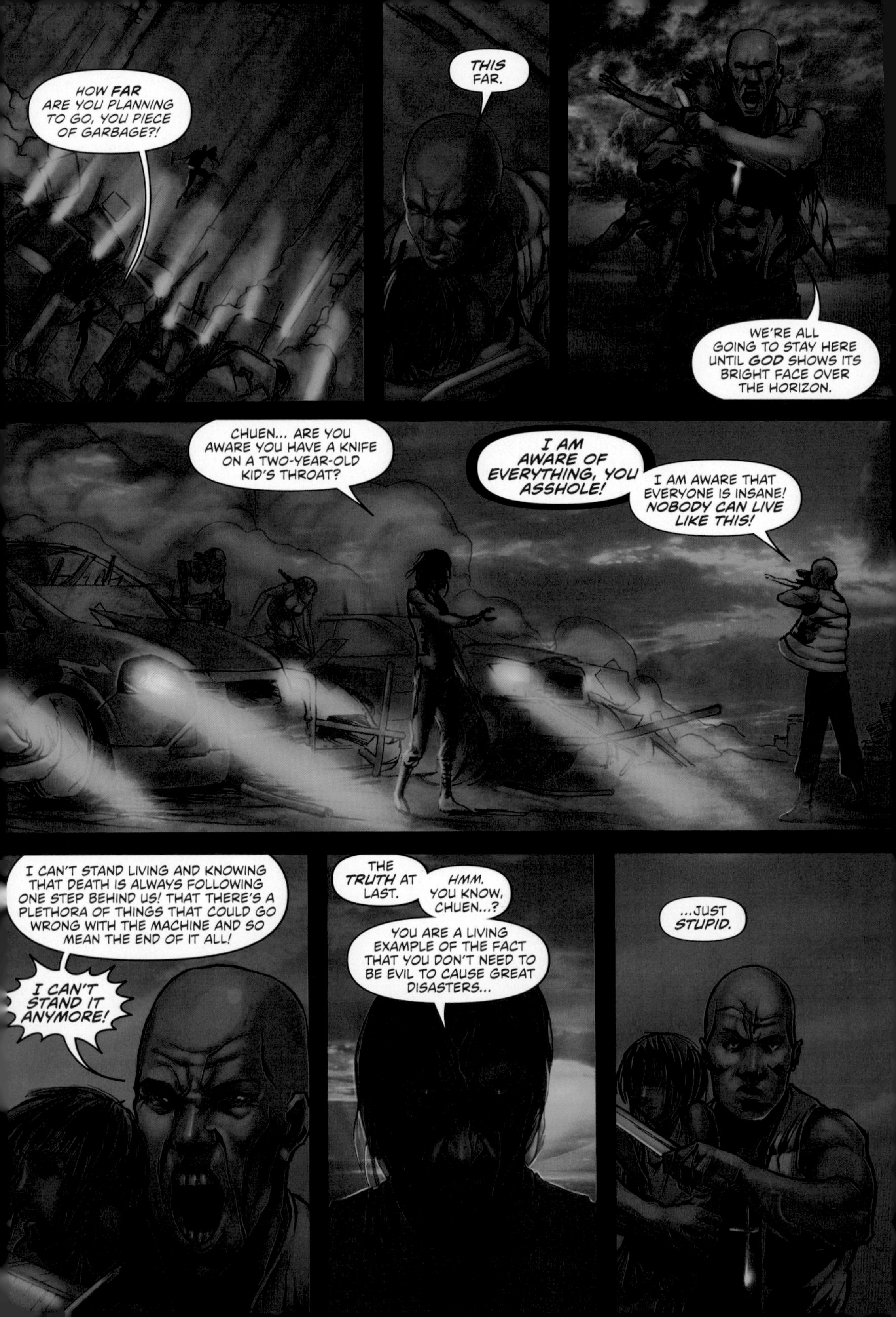
HOW FAR ARE YOU PLANNING TO GO, YOU PIECE OF GARBAGE?!
THIS FAR.
WE'RE ALL GOING TO STAY HERE UNTIL GOD SHOWS ITS BRIGHT FACE OVER THE HORIZON.
CHUEN... ARE YOU AWARE YOU HAVE A KNIFE ON A TWO-YEAR-OLD KID'S THROAT?
I AM AWARE OF EVERYTHING, YOU ASSHOLE!
I AM AWARE THAT EVERYONE IS INSANE! NOBODY CAN LIVE LIKE THIS!
I CAN'T STAND LIVING AND KNOWING THAT DEATH IS ALWAYS FOLLOWING ONE STEP BEHIND US! THAT THERE'S A PLETHORA OF THINGS THAT COULD GO WRONG WITH THE MACHINE AND SO MEAN THE END OF IT ALL!
I CAN'T STAND IT ANYMORE!
THE TRUTH AT LAST.
HMM. YOU KNOW, CHUEN...?
YOU ARE A LIVING EXAMPLE OF THE FACT THAT YOU DON'T NEED TO BE EVIL TO CAUSE GREAT DISASTERS...
...JUST STUPID.

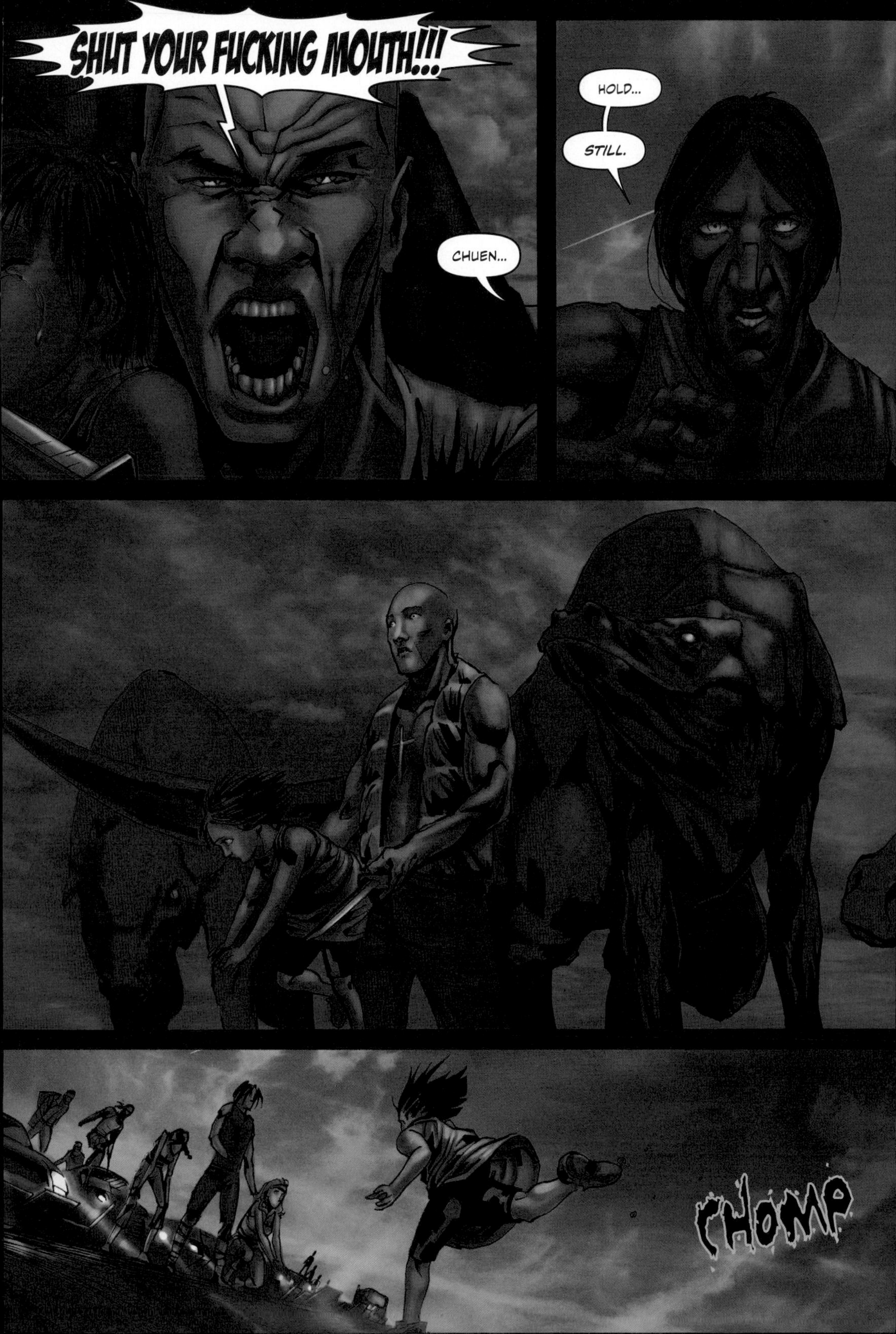
SHUT YOUR FUCKING MOUTH!!!
CHUEN...
HOLD...
STILL.
CHOMP

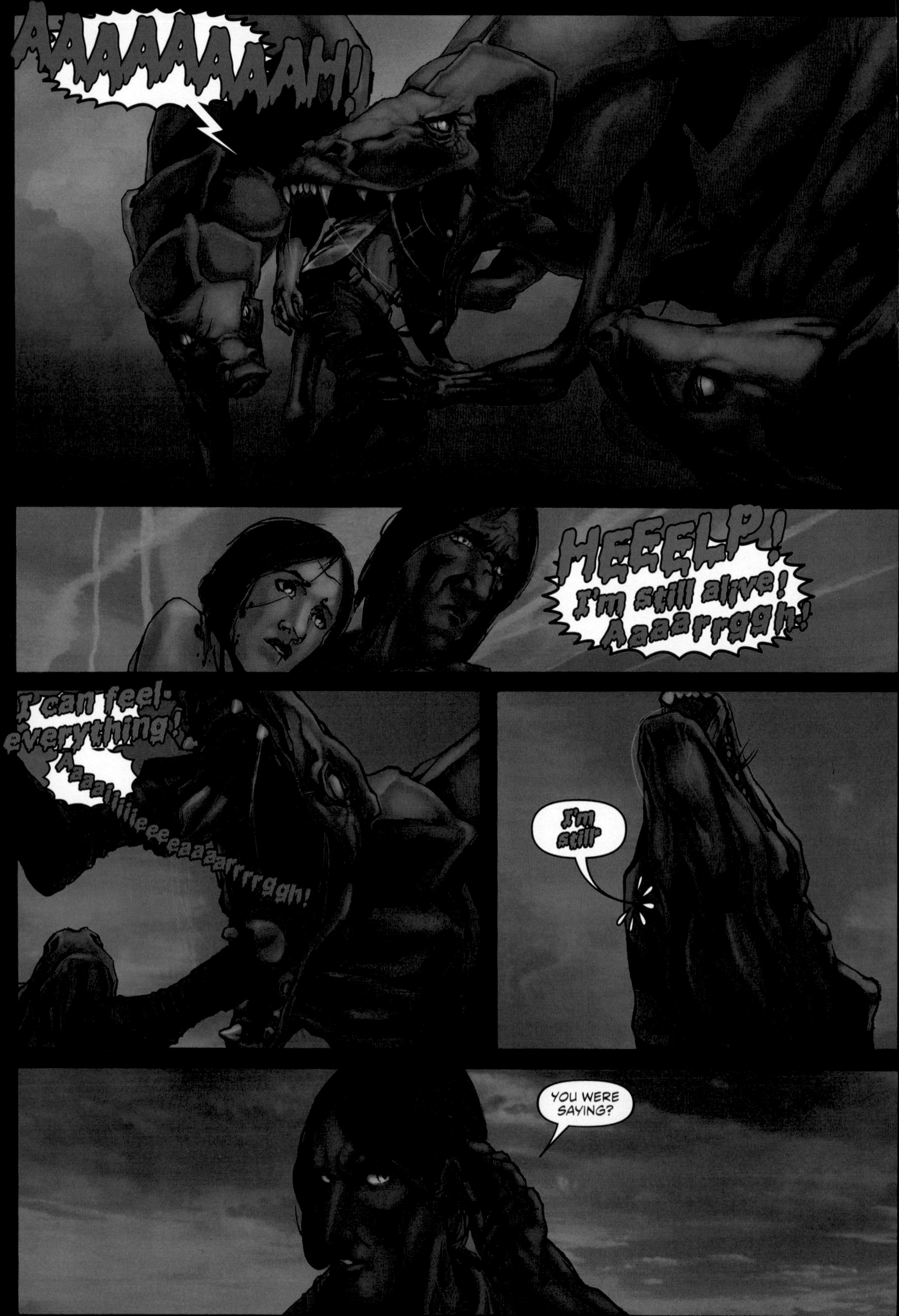
AAAAAAAAAH!
HEEELP! I'm still alive! Aaaarrggh!
I can feel everything! Aaaaiiiiieeeeaaaarrrrgggh!
I'm still
YOU WERE SAYING?

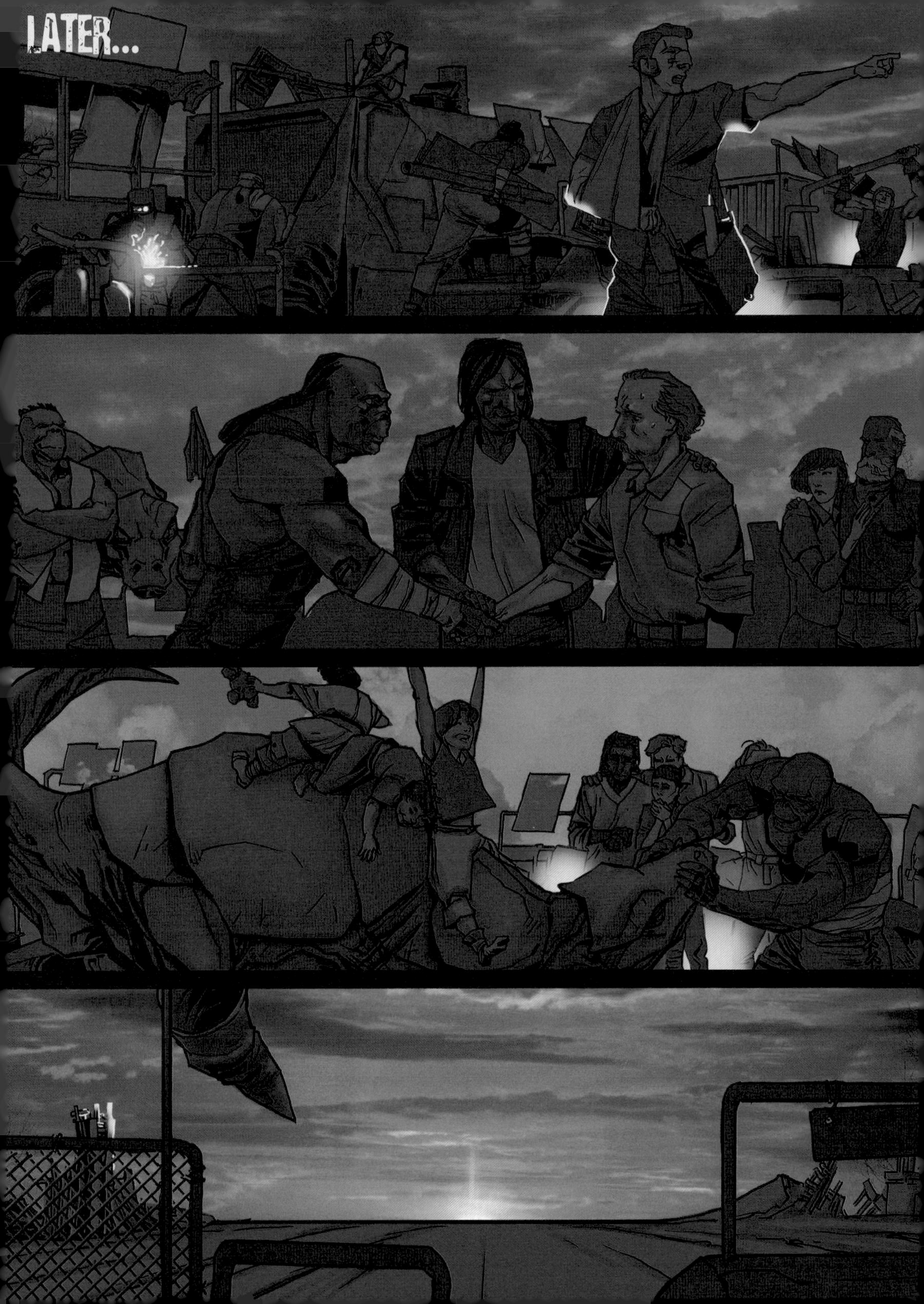
LATER...

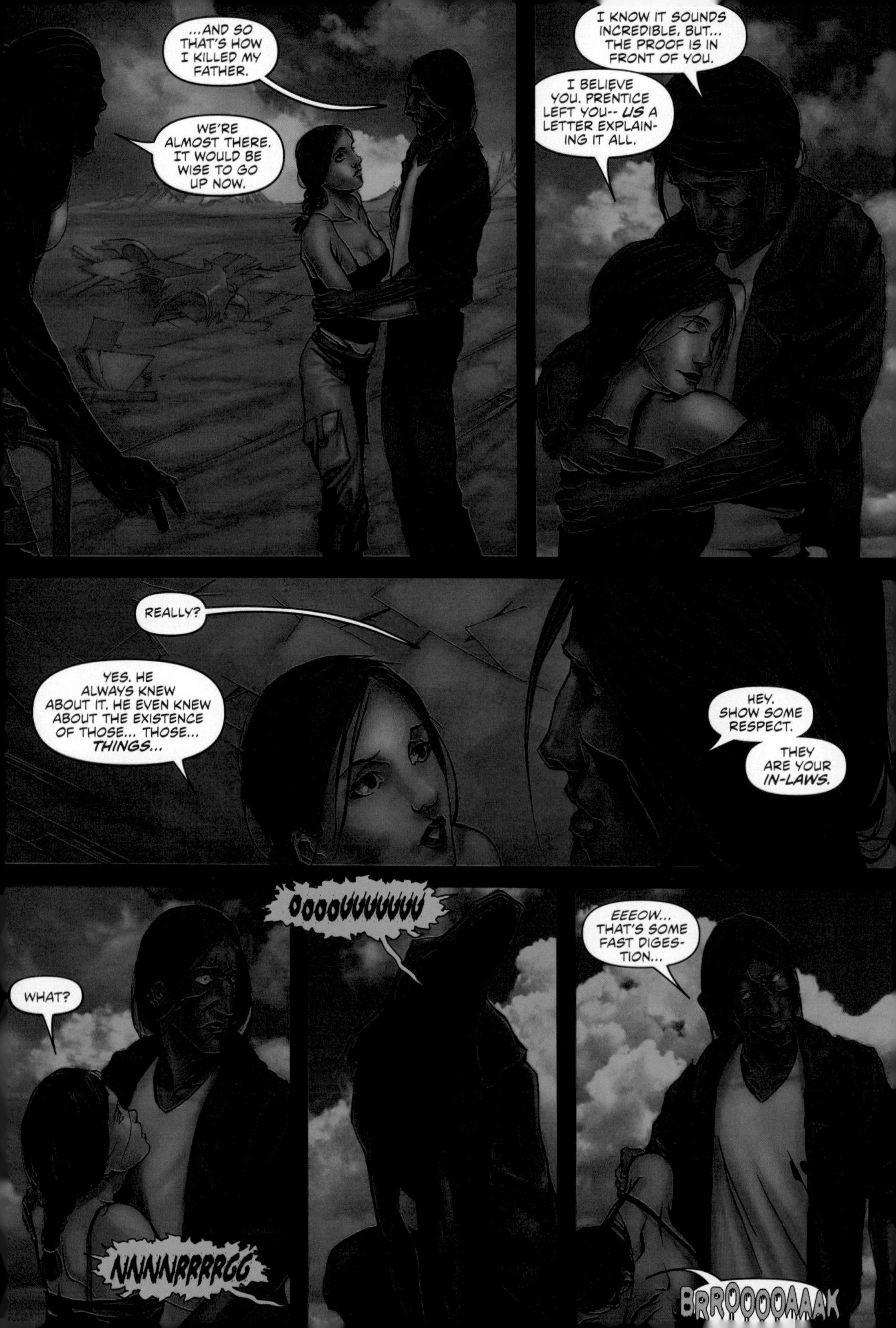
...AND SO THAT'S HOW I KILLED MY FATHER.
WE'RE ALMOST THERE. IT WOULD BE WISE TO GO UP NOW.
I KNOW IT SOUNDS INCREDIBLE, BUT... THE PROOF IS IN FRONT OF YOU.
I BELIEVE YOU. PRENTICE LEFT YOU-- *US* A LETTER EXPLAINING IT ALL.
REALLY?
YES. HE ALWAYS KNEW ABOUT IT. HE EVEN KNEW ABOUT THE EXISTENCE OF THOSE... THOSE... *THINGS*...
HEY. SHOW SOME RESPECT.
THEY ARE YOUR *IN-LAWS*.
WHAT?
NNNNRRRRGG
OOOOUUUUUUU
EEEOW... THAT'S SOME FAST DIGESTION...
BRROOOOAAAK

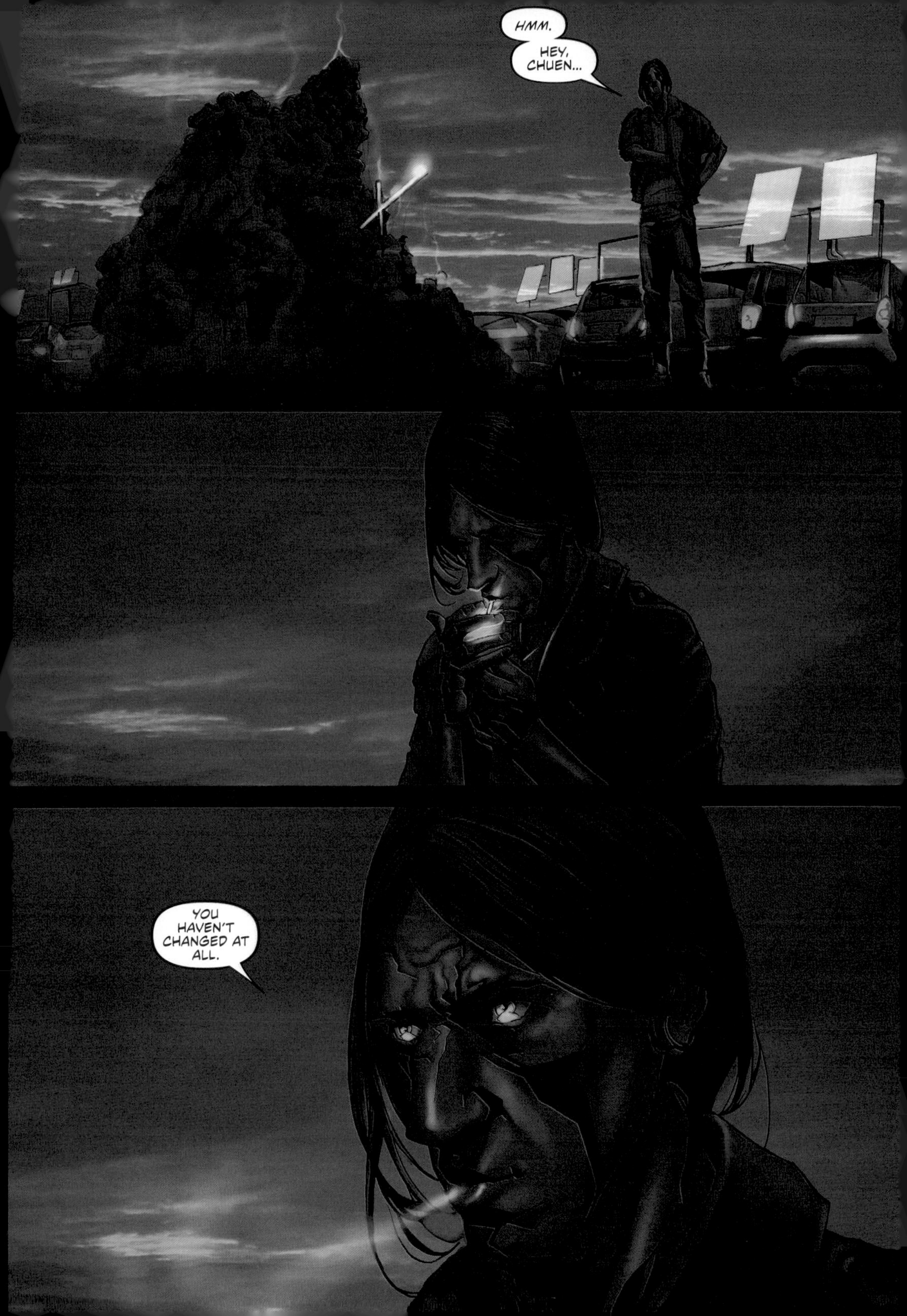
HMM.
HEY, CHUEN...
YOU HAVEN'T CHANGED AT ALL.

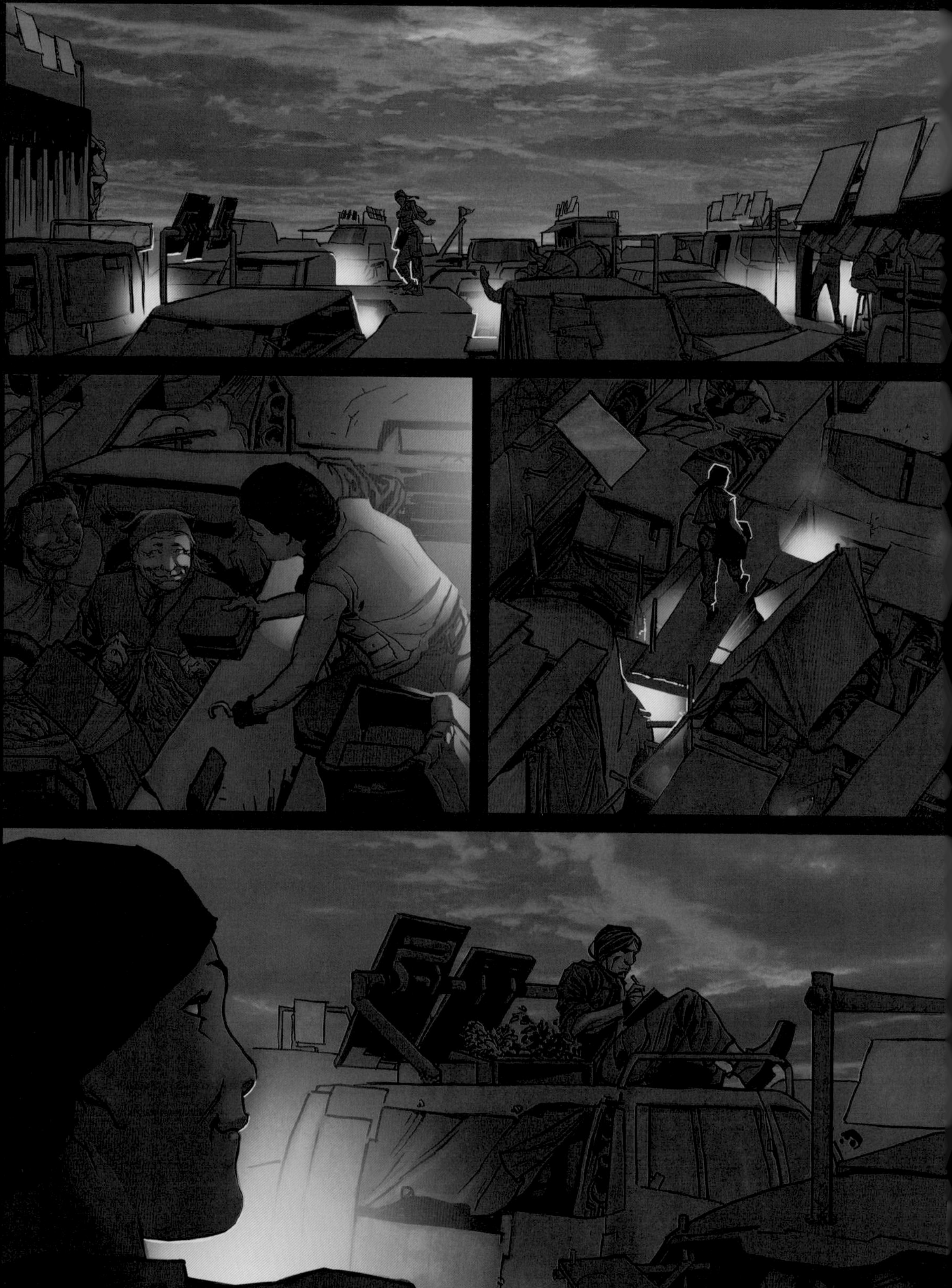

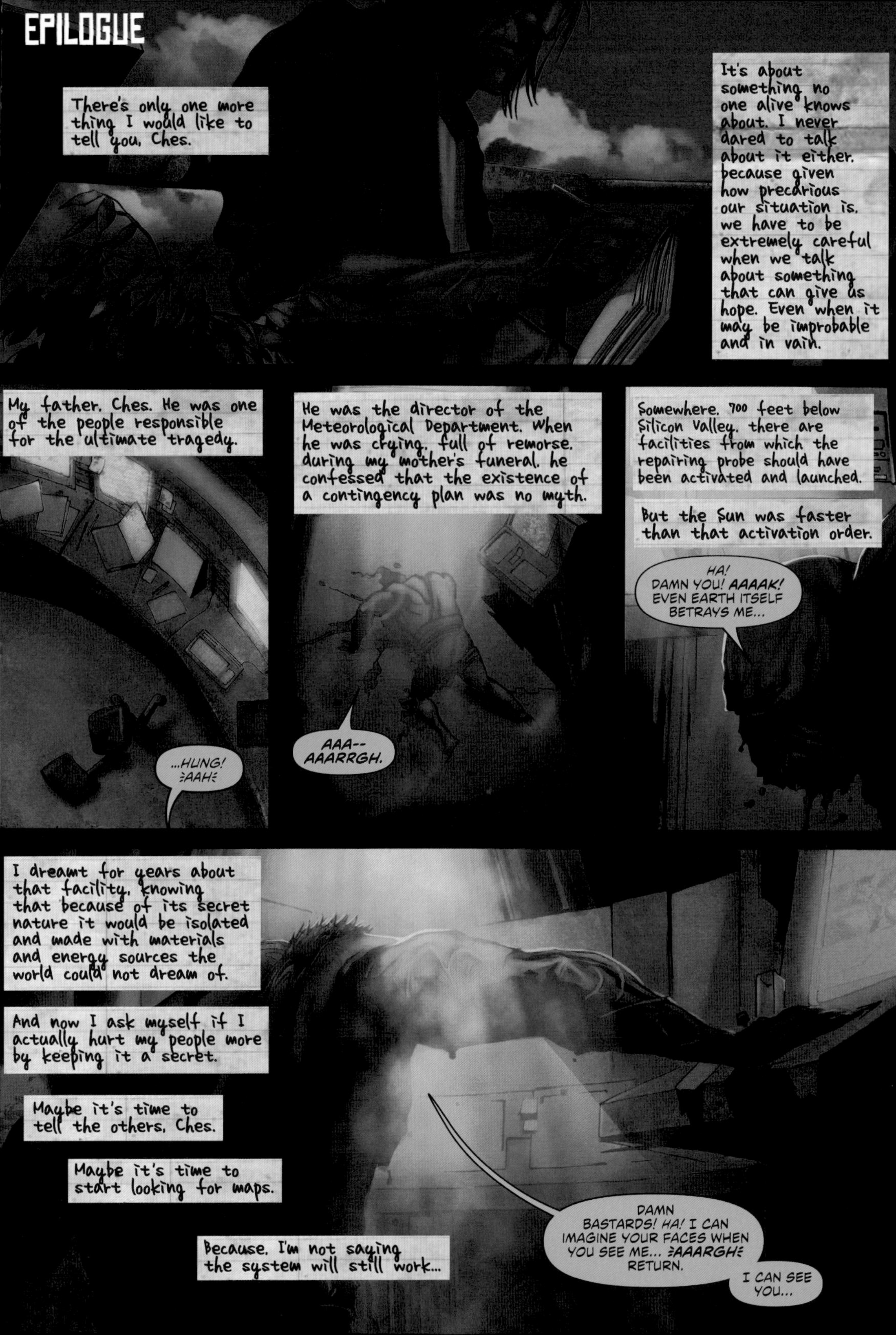
EPILOGUE
There's only one more thing I would like to tell you, Ches.
It's about something no one alive knows about. I never dared to talk about it either, because given how precarious our situation is, we have to be extremely careful when we talk about something that can give us hope. Even when it may be improbable and in vain.
My father, Ches. He was one of the people responsible for the ultimate tragedy.
...HUNG! AAH
He was the director of the Meteorological Department. When he was crying, full of remorse, during my mother's funeral, he confessed that the existence of a contingency plan was no myth.
AAA-- AAARRGH.
Somewhere, 700 feet below Silicon Valley, there are facilities from which the repairing probe should have been activated and launched.
But the Sun was faster than that activation order.
HA! DAMN YOU! AAAAK! EVEN EARTH ITSELF BETRAYS ME...
I dreamt for years about that facility, knowing that because of its secret nature it would be isolated and made with materials and energy sources the world could not dream of.
And now I ask myself if I actually hurt my people more by keeping it a secret.
Maybe it's time to tell the others, Ches.
Maybe it's time to start looking for maps.
Because, I'm not saying the system will still work...
DAMN BASTARDS! HA! I CAN IMAGINE YOUR FACES WHEN YOU SEE ME... AAARGH RETURN.
I CAN SEE YOU...

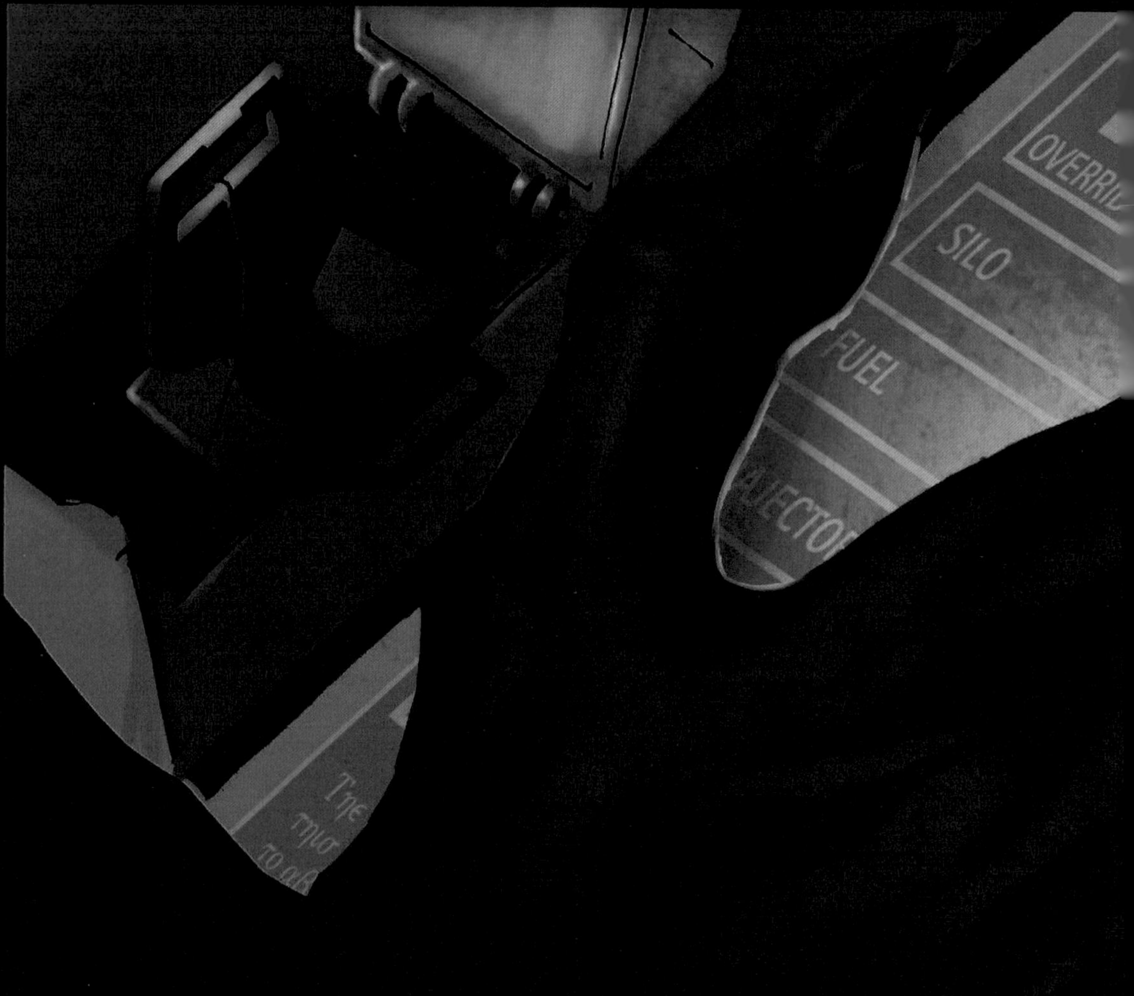
SILO
FUEL

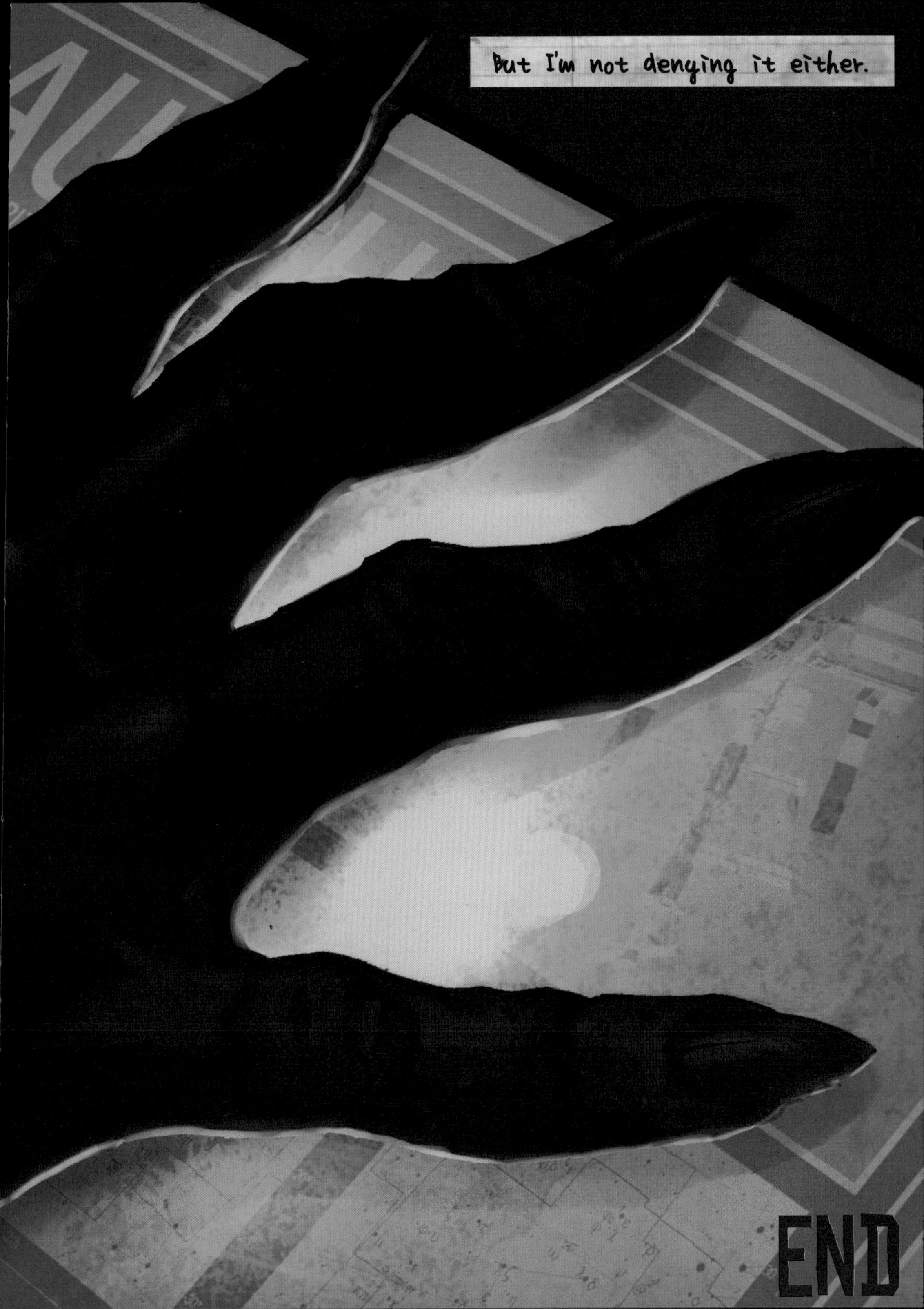
But I'm not denying it either.
END

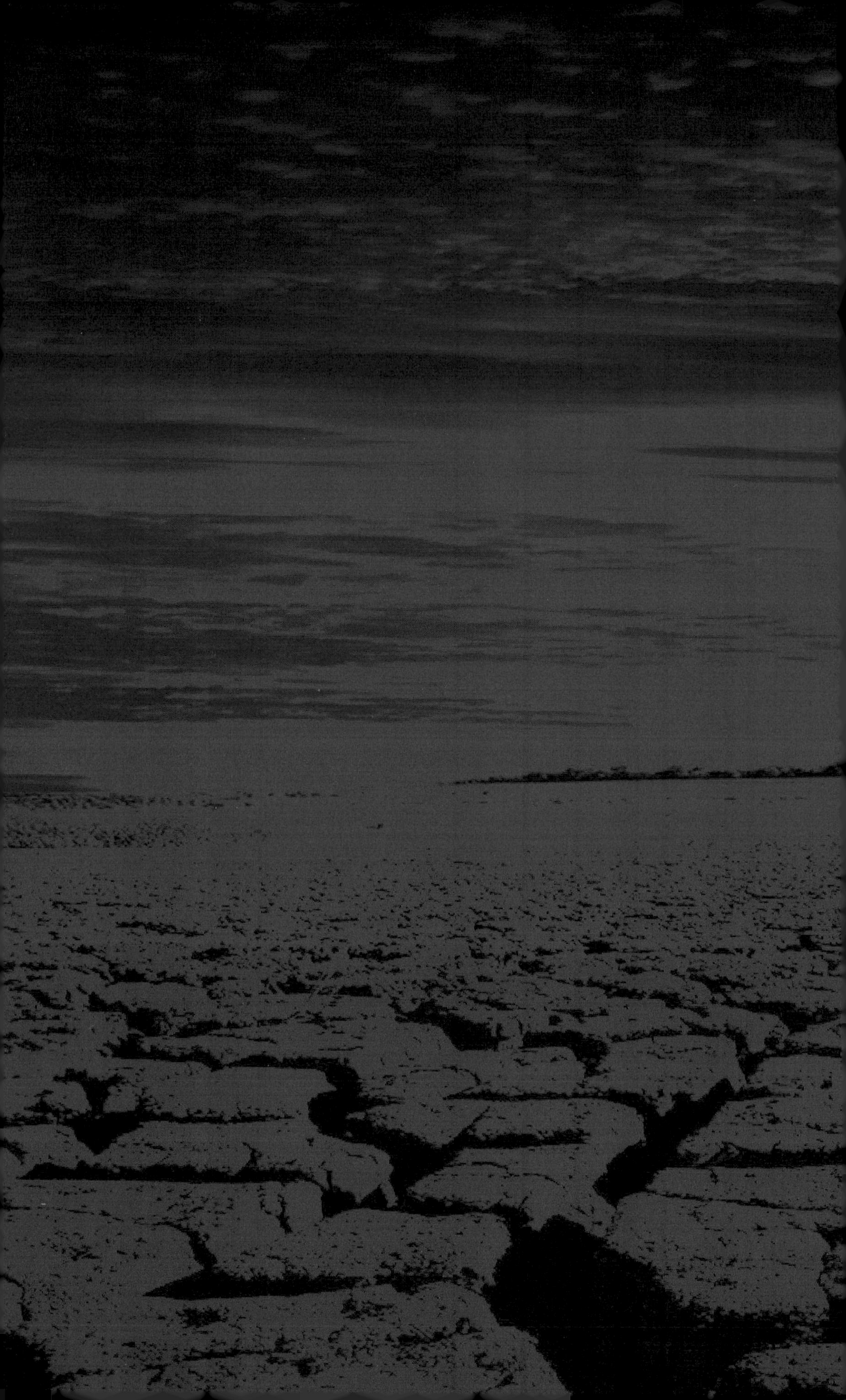

GALLERY

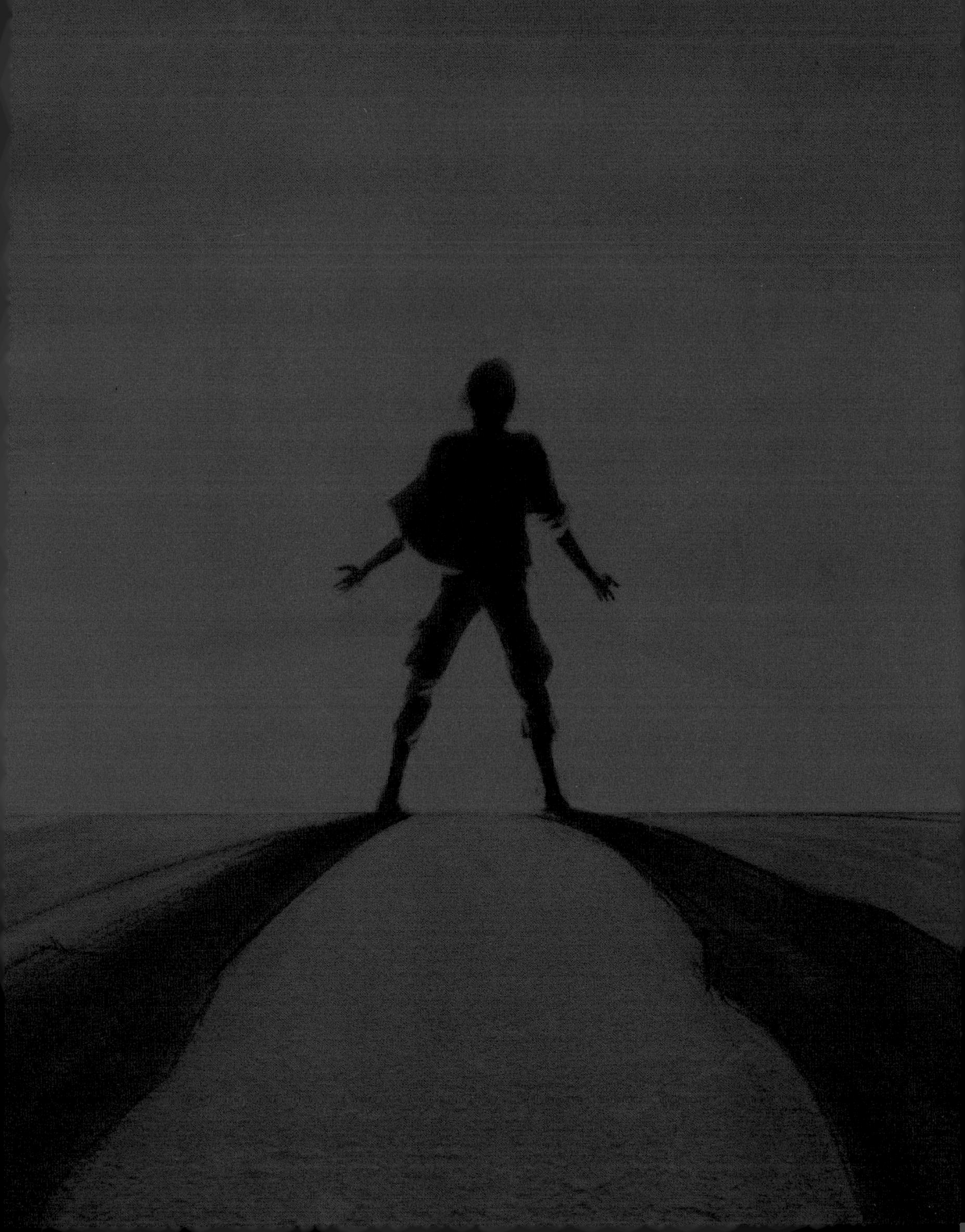

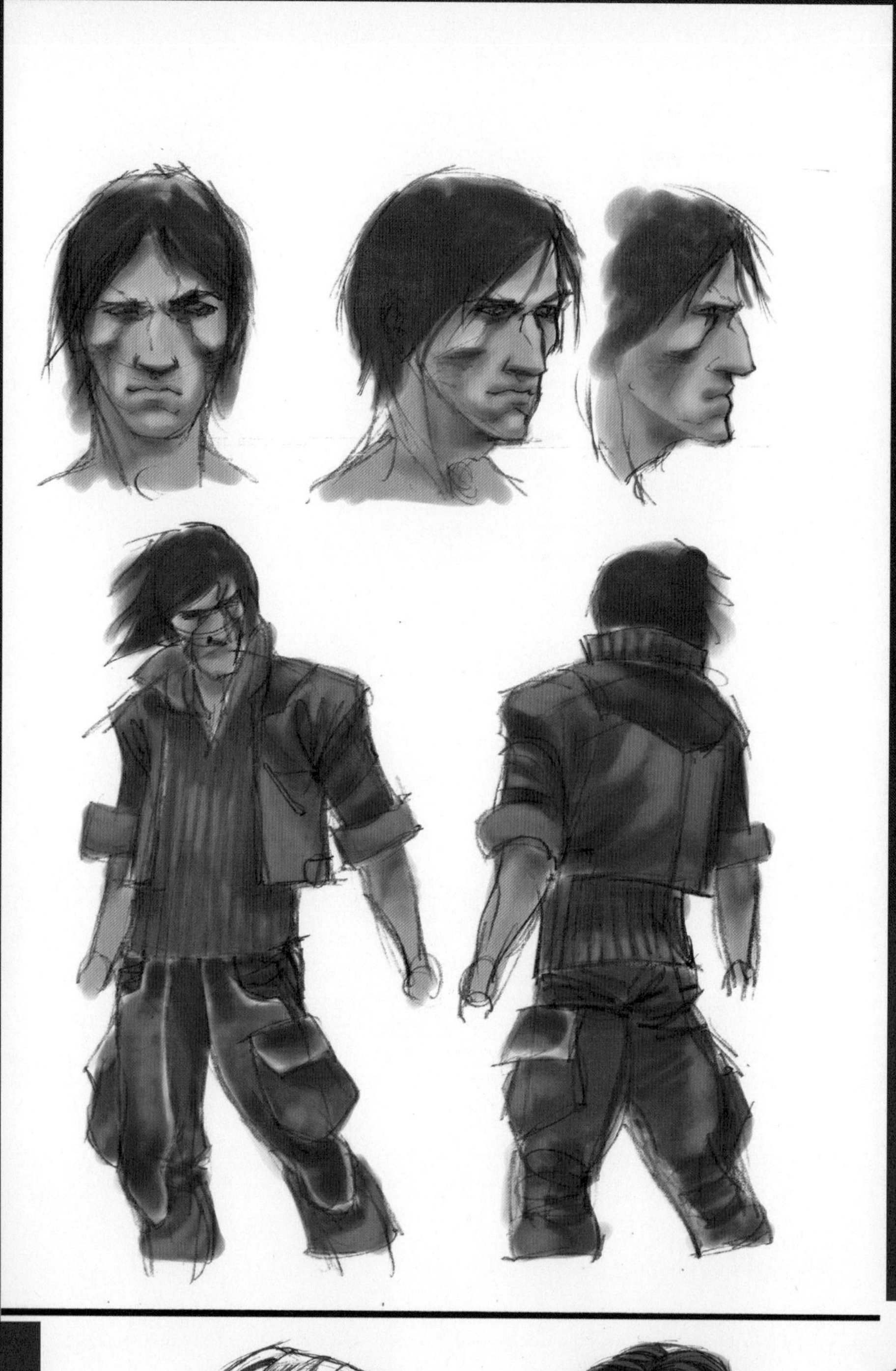

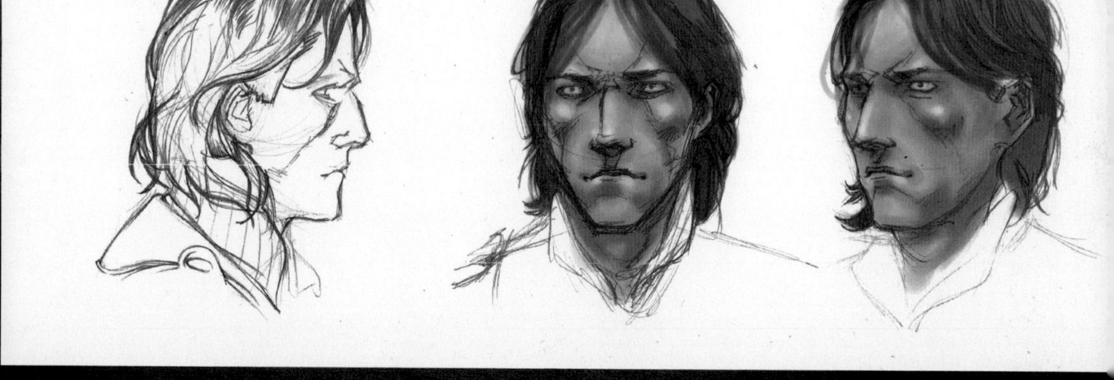

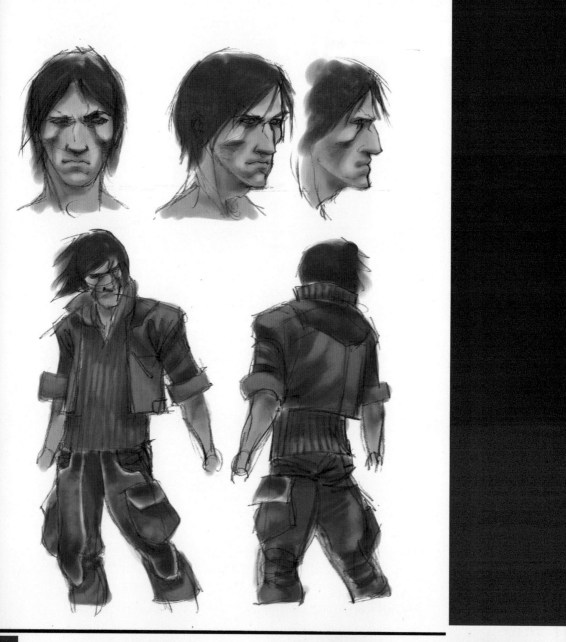

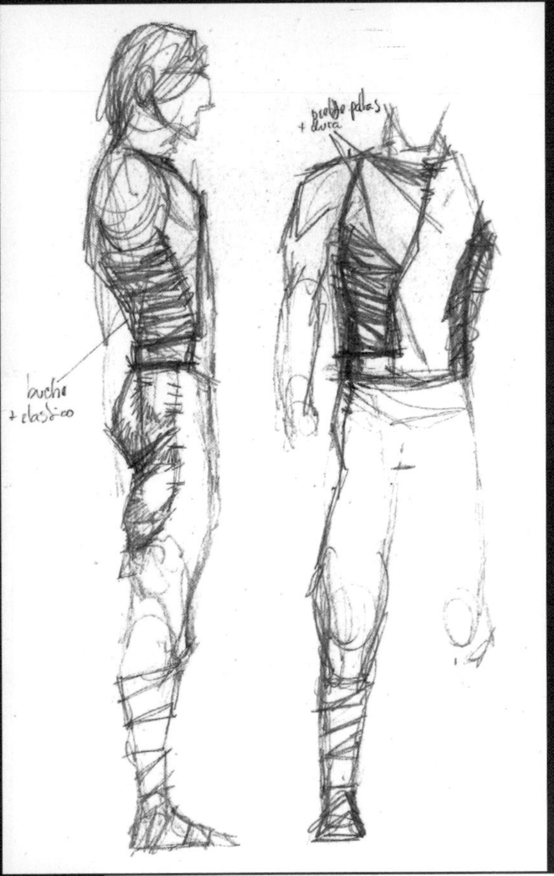
+ dura
bucho
+ elastico

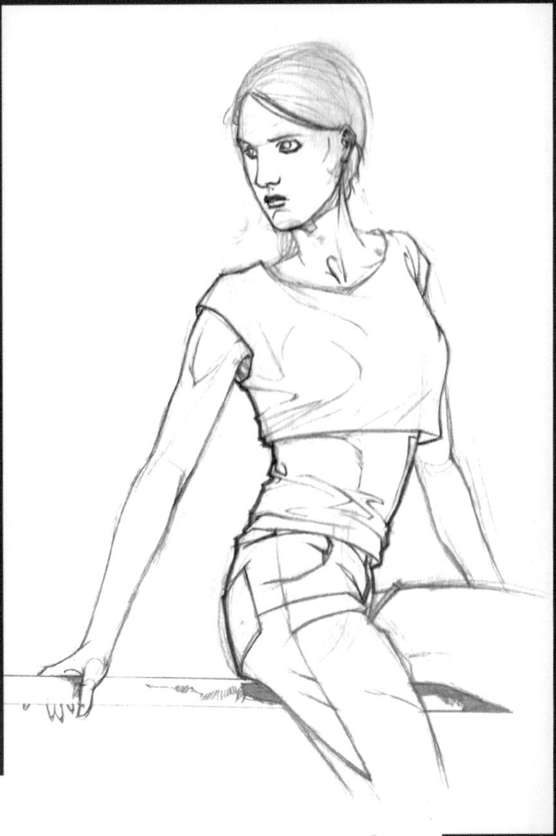

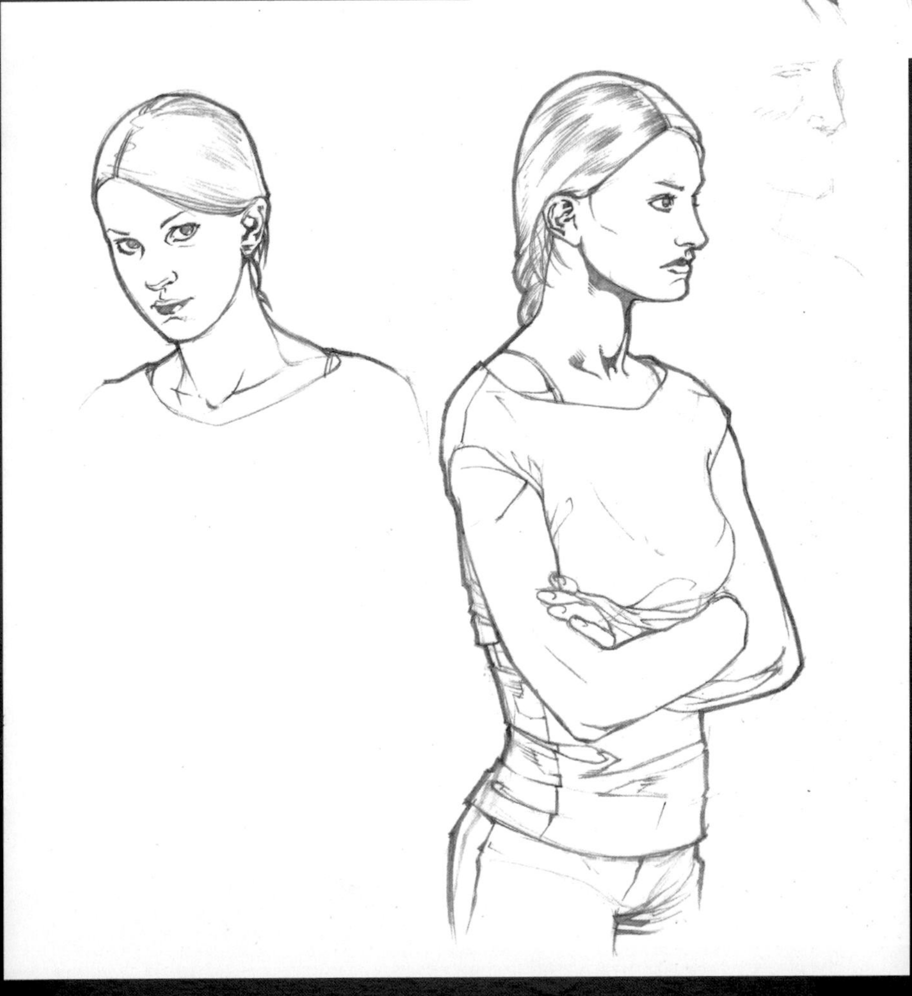

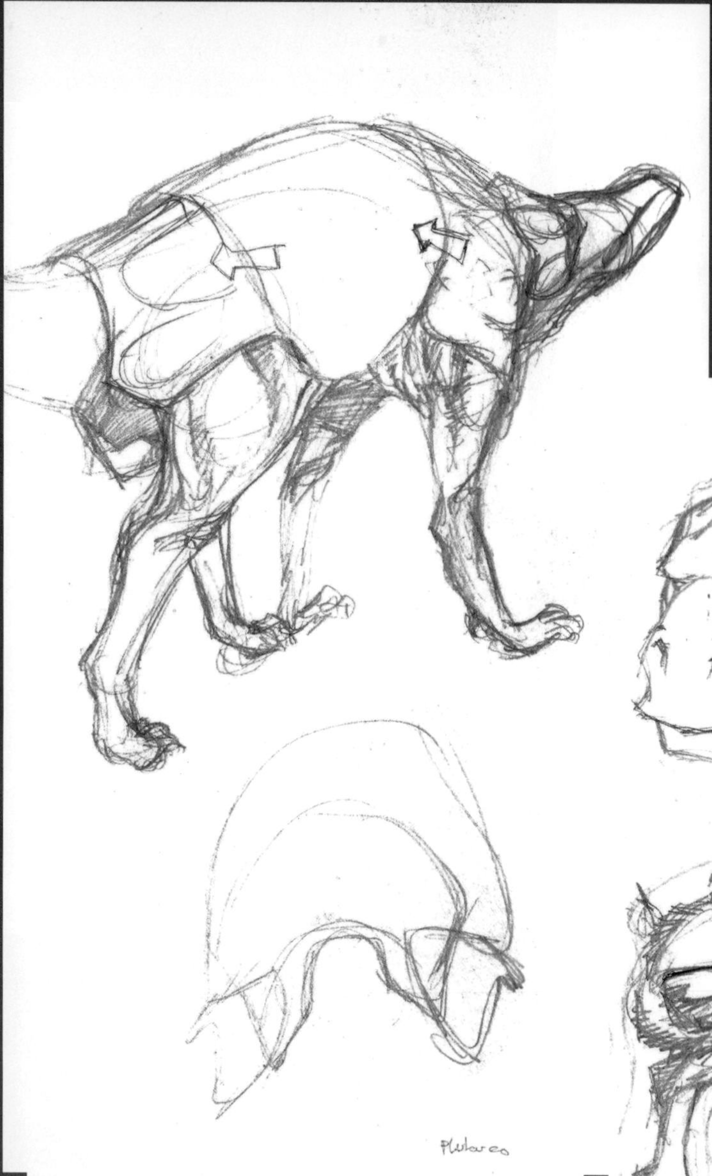
Plutarco

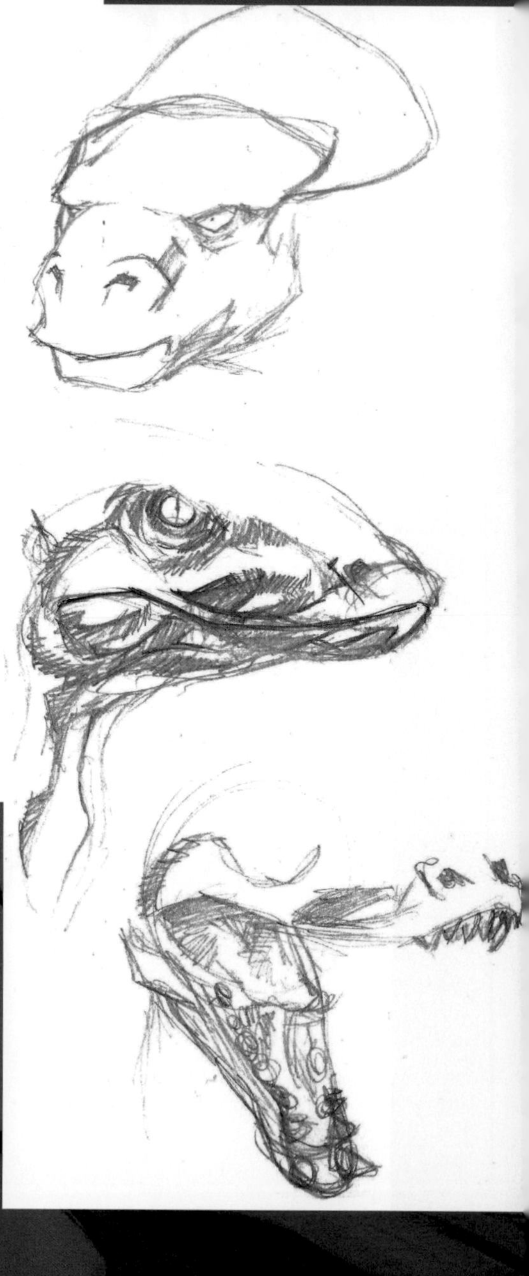

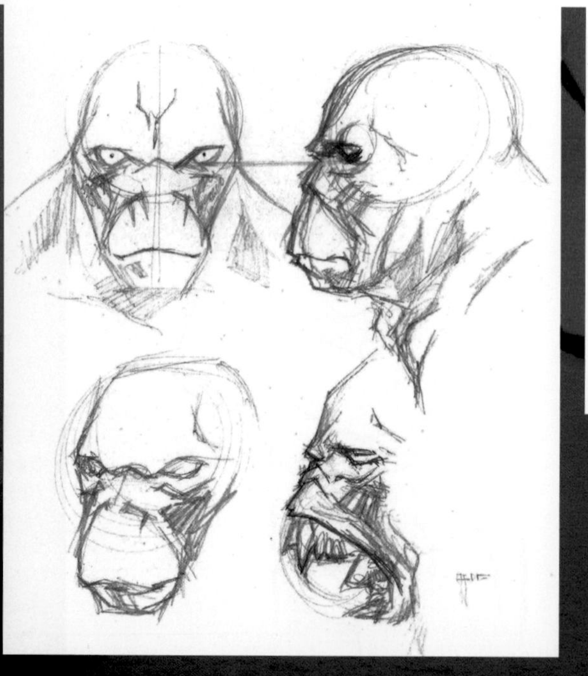

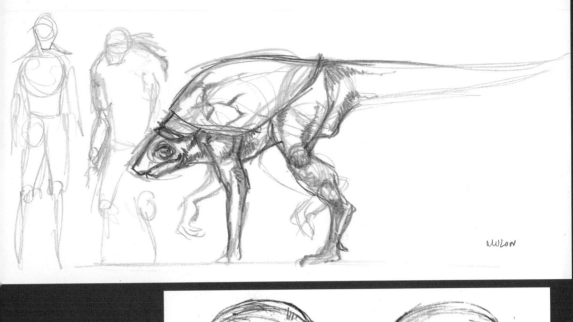

NULON

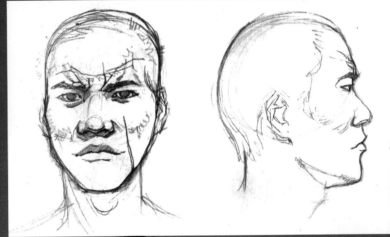

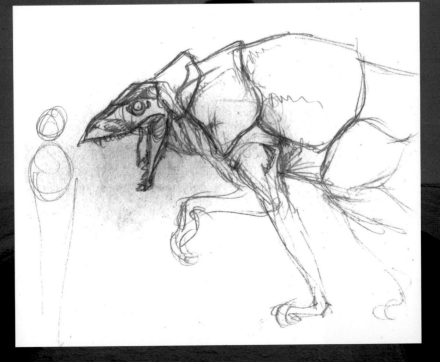

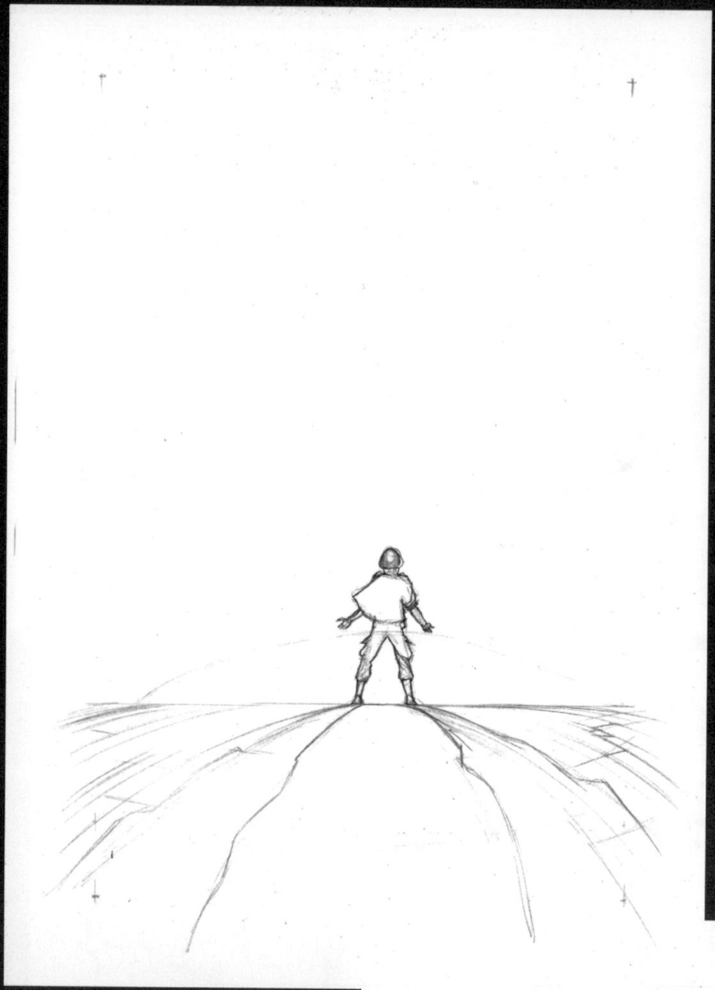

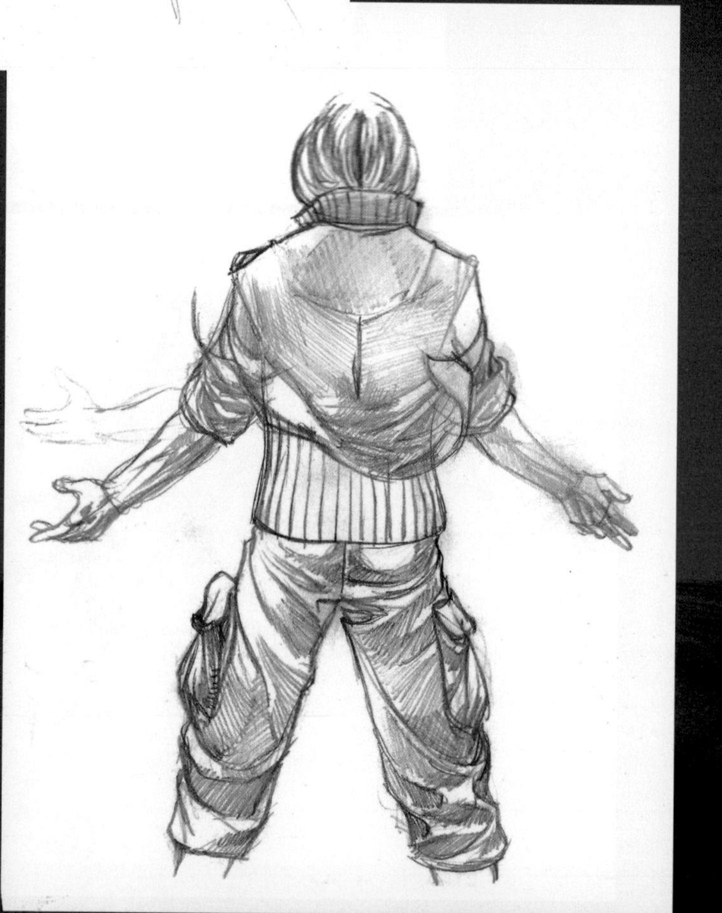

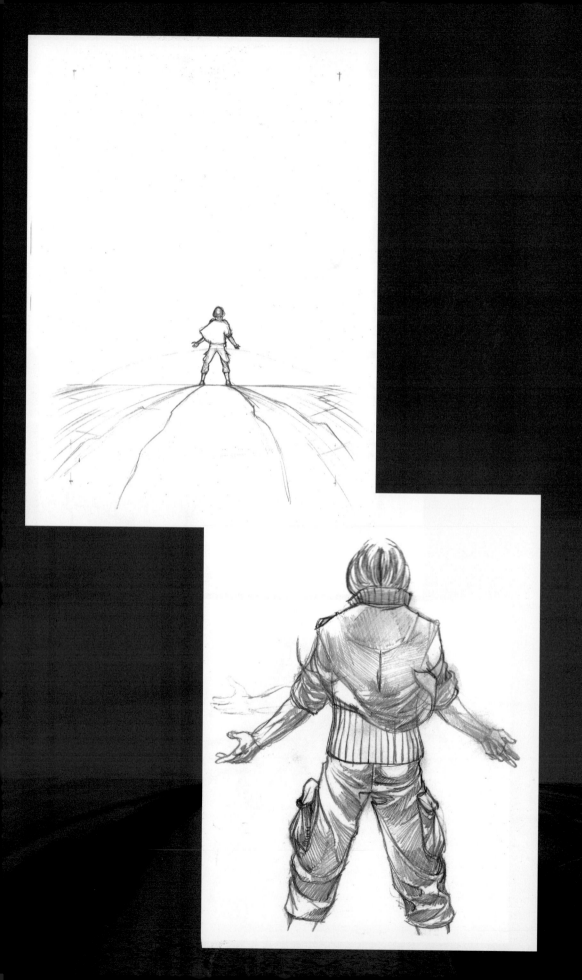

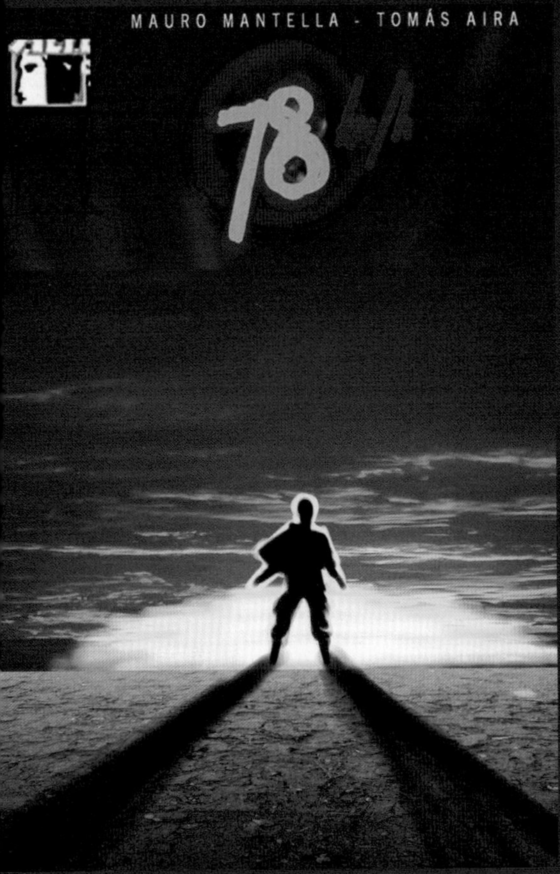
MAURO MANTELLA - TOMÁS AIRA

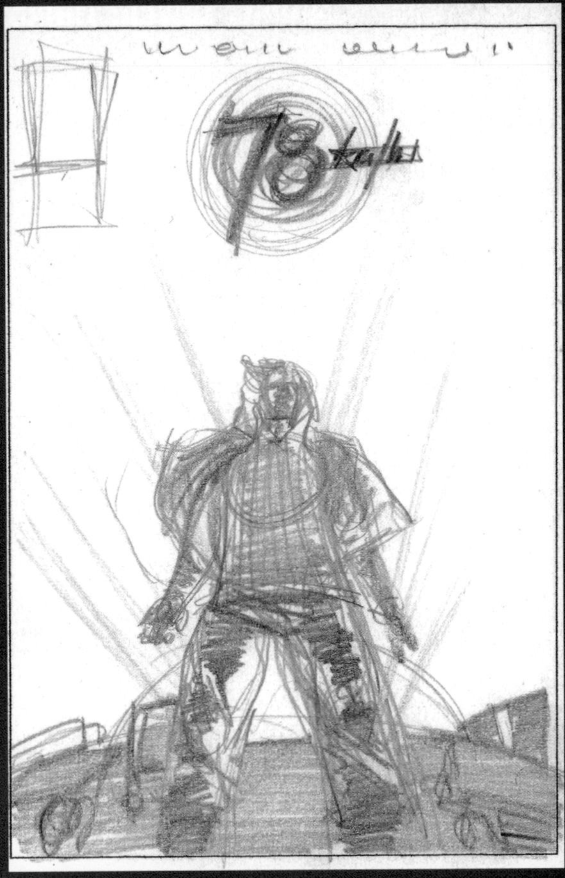

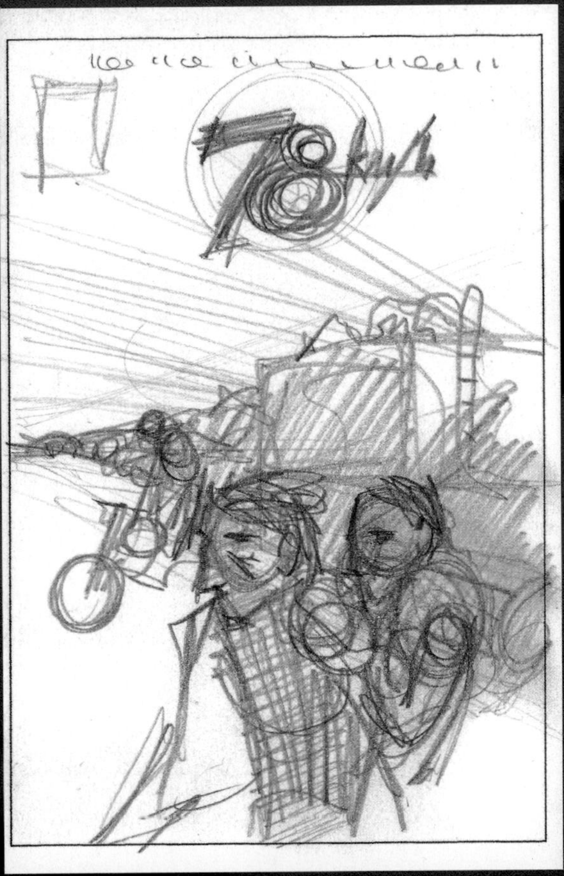

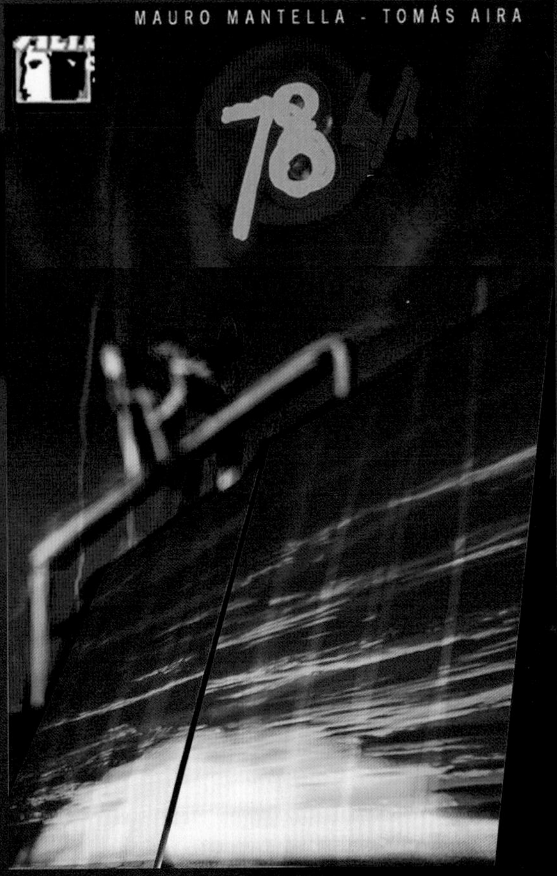
MAURO MANTELLA - TOMÁS AIRA

VARIANT COVER: TOMÁS AIRA AND GÉRMAN NOBILE

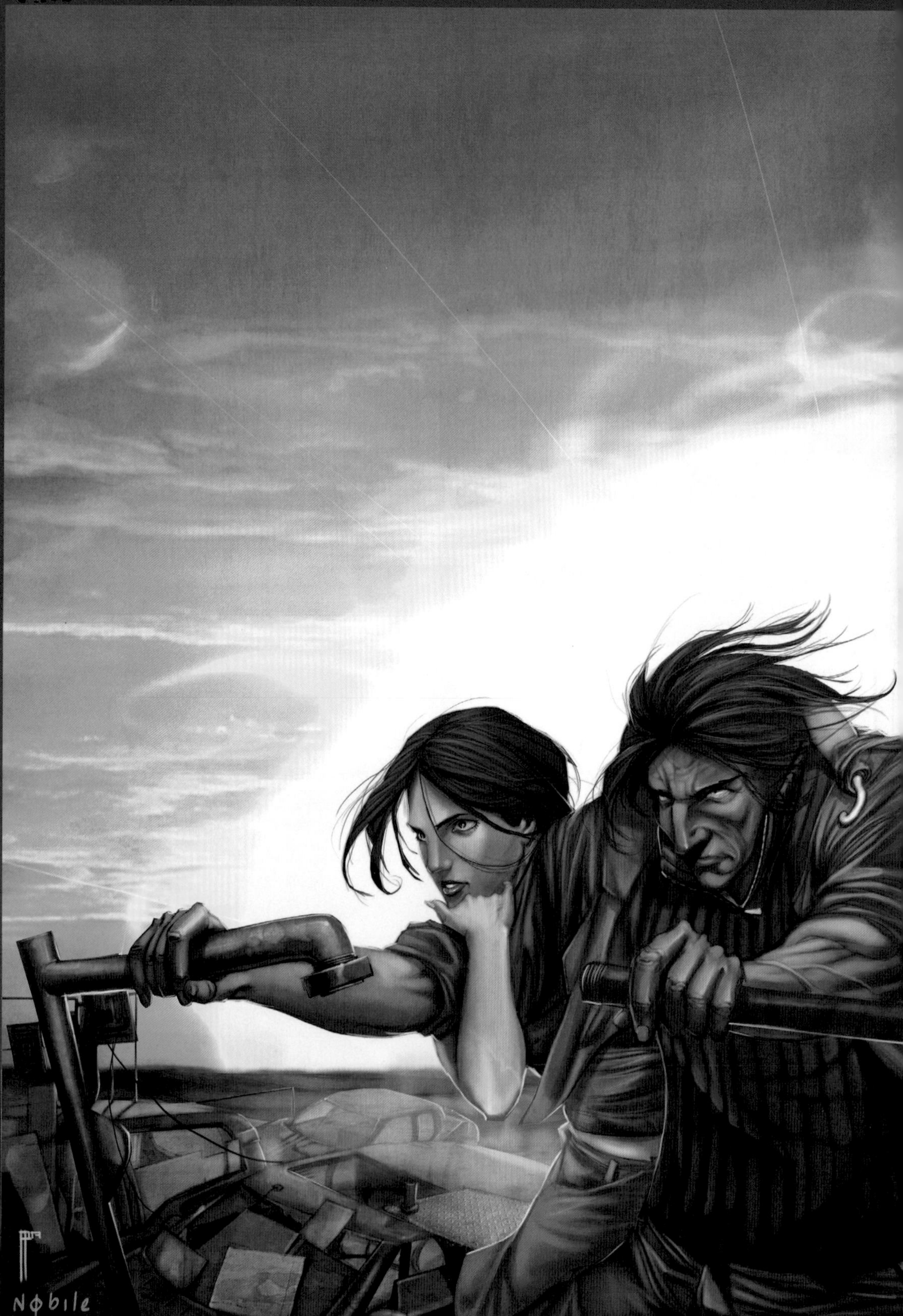
Nobile

COVER SKETCH: GÉRMAN PERALTA

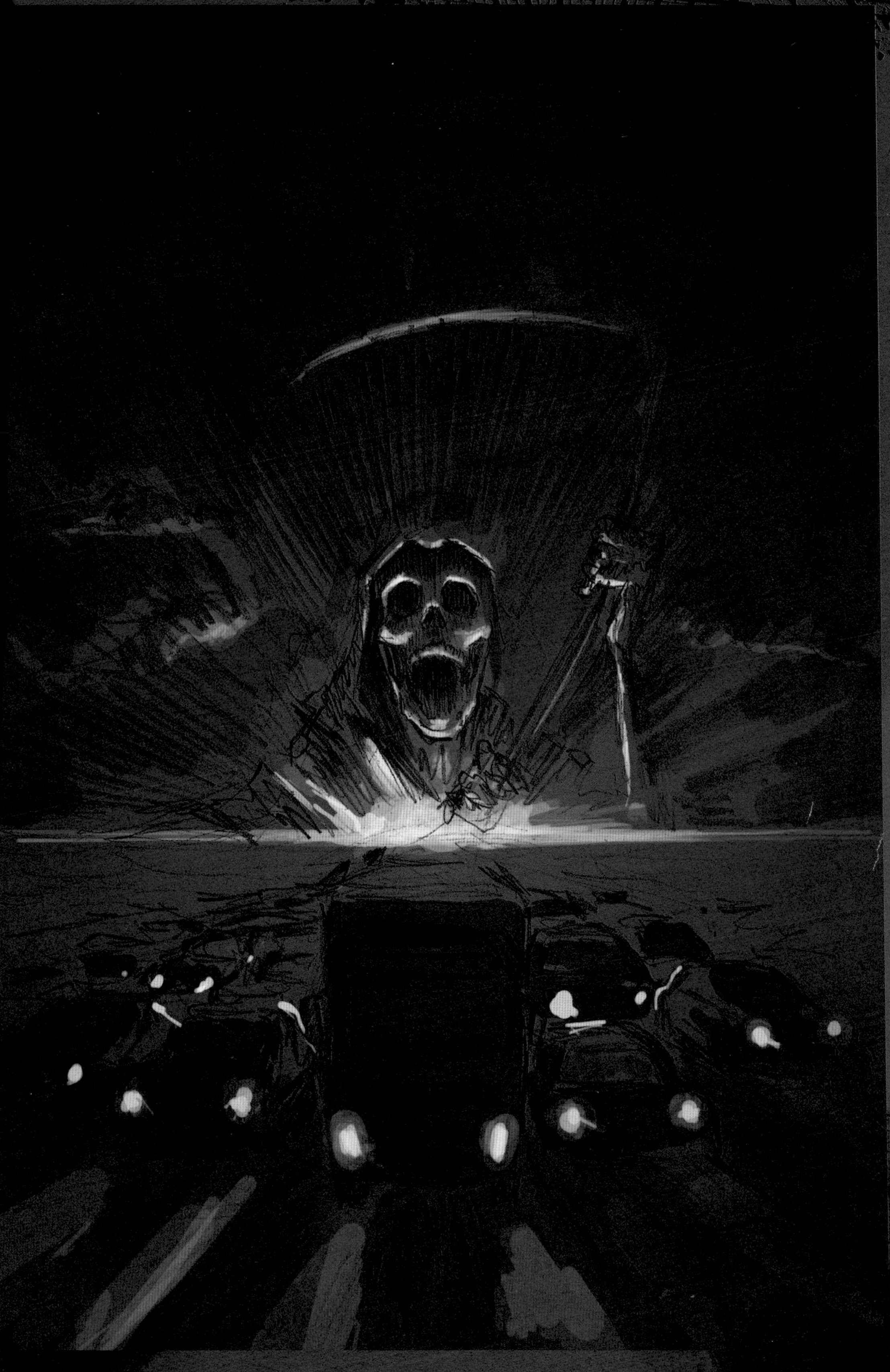

OTHER WORKS BY MANTELLA

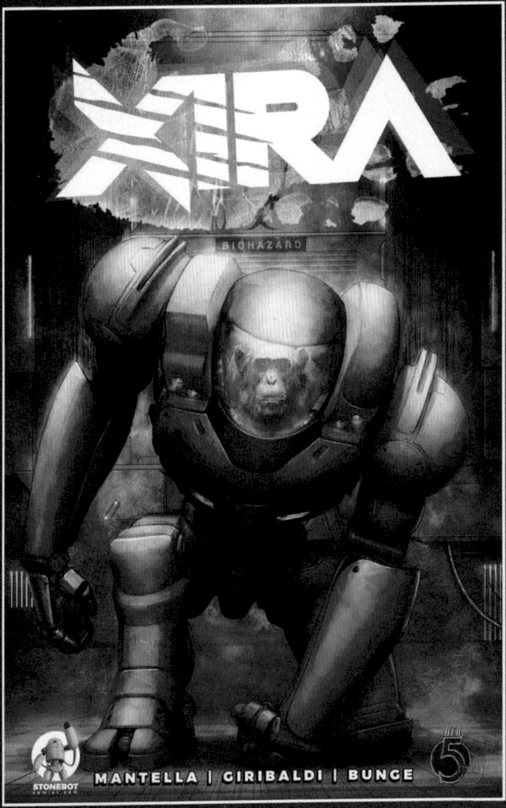
XIRA
BIOHAZARD
STONEBOT
MANTELLA | GIRIBALDI | BUNGE

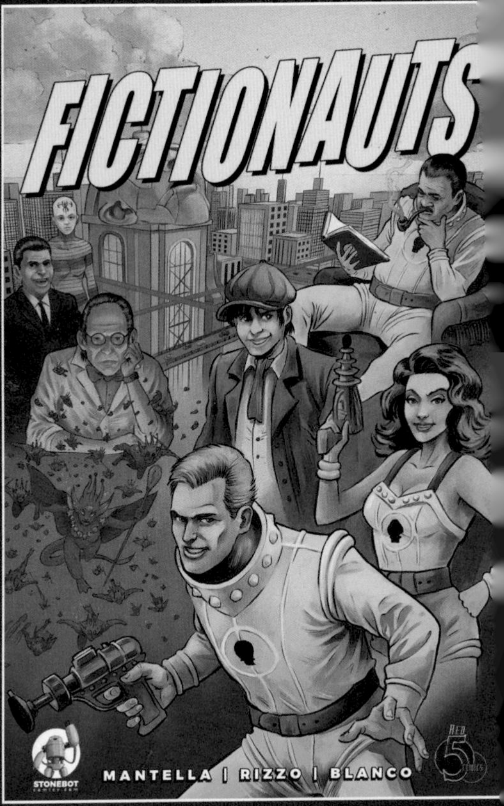
FICTIONAUTS
STONEBOT
MANTELLA | RIZZO | BLANCO

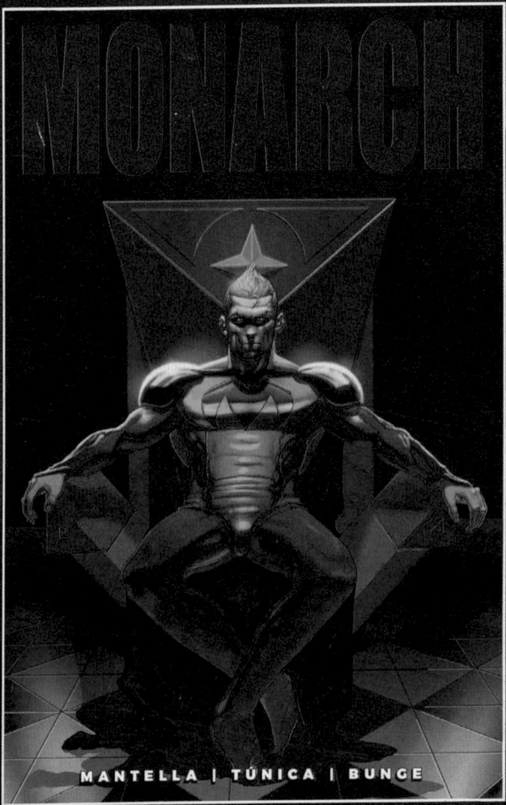
MONARCH
MANTELLA | TÚNICA | BUNGE

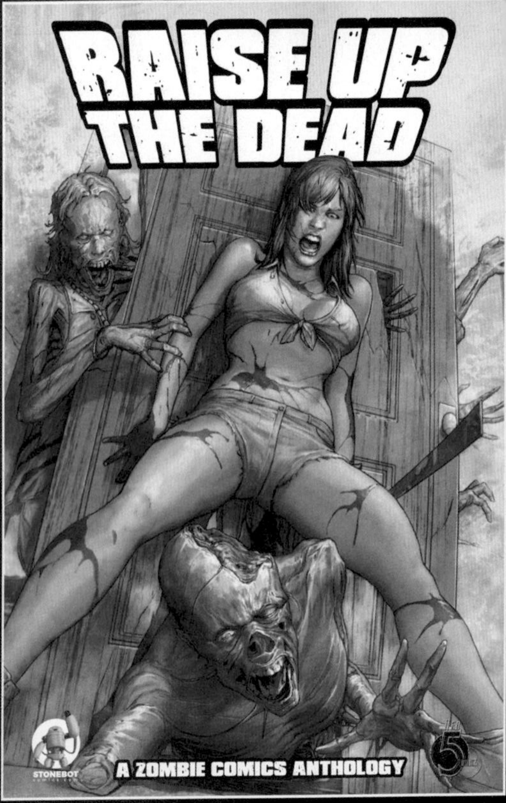
RAISE UP THE DEAD
STONEBOT
A ZOMBIE COMICS ANTHOLOGY